W9-BAG-079

DEAD RECKONING

DEAD RECKONING
Glenis Wilson

Severn House Large Print
London & New York

OS
LT
Wilson,
Glenis

This first large print edition published 2017
in Great Britain and the USA by
SEVERN HOUSE PUBLISHERS LTD of
Eardley House, 4 Uxbridge Street, London W8 7SY.
First world regular print edition published 2017 by
Severn House Publishers Ltd.

British Library Cataloguing in Publication Data
*A CIP catalogue record for this title is available from the British
Library.*

ISBN-13: 9780727893253

Severn House Publishers support the Forest Stewardship Council™
[FSC™], the leading international forest certification organisation. All
our titles that are printed on FSC certified paper carry the FSC logo.

Typeset by Palimpsest Book Production Ltd.,
Falkirk, Stirlingshire, Scotland.
Printed and bound in Great Britain by
T J International, Padstow, Cornwall.

Dedicated with love to my family and especially to the one where the honour lies.

Acknowledgements

'*The legacy of heroes is the memory of a great name and the inheritance of a great example.*'
Benjamin Disraeli

To the one who has gone before, the great master of horseracing novels, Dick Francis, thank you for all those wonderful reads. I offer my sincere gratitude and humbly follow in your footsteps.

Nick Sayers at Hodder & Stoughton. His belief in me and the manuscripts kept me going.

Everyone at Severn House Publishers.

David Meykell, former clerk of the course, Leicester Racecourse, for allowing me to 'do' a murder on his racecourse.

Roderick Duncan, clerk of the course, Southwell Racecourse.

Jean Hedley, clerk of the course, Nottingham Racecourse.

Mark McGrath and Bill Hutchinson, former managers, North Shore Hotel and Golf Course, Skegness.

Tom Hindle, present manager, and all the lovely staff, past and present, at the above hotel.

Wally Wharton, jockey, superb horseman and life-long friend.

David, Anne and Elaine Brown, printers and friends.

Sarah at Sarah's Flowershop.

All the library staff at Bingham, Radcliffe-on-Trent, West Bridgford and Nottingham Central.

The police at Skegness and the staff at Nottingham Prison for checking facts.

Management at The Dirty Duck at Woolsthorpe, near Belvoir Castle, Leics.

All the people who have helped me in whatever way during the course of writing the 'Harry' novels.

And of course, all my lovely readers, bless you for your wonderful comments and emails. To every one, may I say a very big thank you – have a great read.

Prologue

The dark street was deserted. The population of Newark had gone to ground. With the changing of the clocks, winter had come rushing in. It was freezing cold.

I pulled up and parked in the golden puddle of light beneath a street lamp. I hoped Alice would be in. A swift ten minutes to update her on the news, as promised, and I'd be on my way again, heading for home.

Nowhere like home – warm, comforting, safe. Everything that had been lacking in my life for the last few weeks I was going to appreciate and enjoy to the full. There was a fire laid ready for lighting, a whisky with my name on it and a cat, Leo, an enormous ginger tom that would jump on to my shoulder in greeting the moment I entered Harlequin Cottage. Couldn't wait.

I walked up to Alice's front door. It could have done with a good wash down but probably wouldn't stand it. The paintwork was cracked and peeling badly. No doubt all the knocking it had taken from her punters – Alice was a prostitute – hadn't helped.

I rang the bell. Nobody answered. I tried a knock, then knocked again, harder. The door swung inwards a little – it wasn't fully shut. Hesitating a moment, I called her name. Silence.

Feeling uneasy, I pushed the door open and stepped

inside. Calling out her name louder, I walked down the hall to the kitchen. The street lamp outside shone a glow through the window. The light wasn't bright but it was enough for me to see her.

Alice lay on the kitchen floor, face down. She was dead. Must have been dead for several days judging by the smell emanating from her body, the blood congealed and black. The back of her head had been smashed in.

In shocked horror, I stood and stared down at her. I'd liked Alice. Brash and common she might have been, but underneath she was good-hearted, had cared a lot about her friend, Jo-Jo, who was also a prostitute. I'd thought her a survivor in a harsh world. I was wrong.

And then it really hit me. I knew who'd killed her. I could hear again Jake's words as he'd sat opposite me in the pub a few days ago. Recently released from prison after serving time for GBH, he'd been talking about his late sister, Jo-Jo.

'If Jo-Jo hadn't met *him,* she'd still have been alive . . .'

It had been Alice who had introduced Jo-Jo to Louis Frame. Frame had set Jo-Jo up in a flat for his sole attentions – much to Jake's disgust – but they'd both been killed when their car crashed into the back of a horsebox.

Jake Smith had also said he'd spent the night with Alice.

What he hadn't said was he'd killed her.

Looking down at her lifeless body, I also knew I was the only person who could identify her killer.

I'd been here before.

What the hell did I do now?

One

The churchyard gates stood open. By four o'clock this afternoon they'd be closed and padlocked. The churchyard kept short hours during the winter.

But it was only two o'clock. Plenty of time to walk up the rise and over to the east side, by the hedge, under the branches of a rowan tree. The sacred spot where my closest family lay buried, immune from the indifference, the savagery of this world.

I looked down at the bunch of flowers in my hand. Earlier today, I'd been to see Janine at the flower shop. There was no need to tell her what I wanted – she knew.

'Your mother's favourite white roses?'

'Yes, please, Janine. But this time, I'd like you to add a further bunch.'

'Ha, yes, and these would be white freesias?'

Hiding the pain that knifed through me, I smiled and nodded. It wasn't only Annabel, my estranged wife, who loved the beautiful fragrance and purity of white freesias; they'd been Silvie's favourites, too – Silvie, my severely disabled half-sister.

Always on the fourth of November, Mother's birthday, I bought a bunch of white roses. Today was certainly the fourth, but today for the first time the blooms were a mix of roses and freesias.

I lifted the flowers, took a long, appreciative sniff of their fragrant sweetness. They were really beautiful. How long they'd remain so was unknown. Not long, I'd guess. With the night temperatures now dropping to freezing, it seemed like cruelty to place the delicate blooms in the integral vase within the headstone . . . leave them outside in the cold cemetery.

I revised my thought: not cruelty – murder. Seemed it was something I just couldn't get away from. I pushed the obnoxious thought away. This was not the time, nor the place. Today was for the placing of the flowers on Mother's grave; I was the only person left to do so. Despite Uncle George being my only living relative, it was more than his peace of mind was worth to bring flowers. Aunt Rachel, his wife, had her reasons to limit Uncle George's activities in this direction.

So, that just left me.

I walked on, up the rise, over to the east side. Then I stopped short in disbelief. Over by the side of the hedge was the grave, but it had fresh flowers *already* placed in the vase – they were white roses!

Who? The one word repeated in my mind as I stood and gaped. *Who?*

I'd had enough of surprises, most of them unpleasant. Another mystery I didn't want. Reaching the side of the grave, I bent over and nudged the flowers apart. Nestling down near the bottom of the stems was a small white card. I hunkered down and read the message.

Forgive me, Elizabeth. I should have had the courage to ask you long ago. Too late for us now – my loss. May you and Silvie comfort each other.
My sincere love to you both.

4

The card was unsigned.

I rocked back on my heels and blew out a gusty sigh. What on earth was *that* all about? The message told me nothing about the identity of the person, except that whoever had penned it must have known my mother a long time. Had known her preferred choice of flowers. Not only that, he knew about Silvie, too. And just what was it he'd wanted to ask my mother? I was assuming it was from a man but, if so, what connotations should I read into it?

I had enough problems right now; I didn't need any more. Tomorrow, I was supposed to put in an appearance at Newark Police Station. Finding a dead body wasn't something most people did. With myself, it seemed to be getting a habit.

Mentally, I'd drawn a red line under the last few weeks, had thought life was back in balance, the past truly dead and buried. What a joke. When I'd found Alice's dead body, I'd been pitched right back up to my eyebrows in the foul mess, and now I couldn't see any way out.

Two

'Me?' Mike's face was creased in bewilderment. 'Why would I put flowers on your mother's grave?' He dug a fork into a pile of cheesy scrambled egg and chewed enthusiastically. 'Not me, Harry.'

We were sitting in the kitchen at his racing stables having breakfast between first and second lots. As

5

a racehorse trainer, he was right up there with the best. We'd gone to school together as kids. He was still my best friend. And he was also my boss; I was his retained jockey.

'More scrambled egg?' Pen smiled and waved a wooden spoon at me. 'Plenty left.'

'No, thanks, but it was delicious.' I laid down knife and fork and stirred a spoonful of honey into my coffee. 'Any more and I'll never get on the next horse.'

'I don't have that problem, my sweet.' Mike beamed at her. 'Tip it out on my plate.'

She leaned over, dropped a kiss on the top of his head and scraped the last of the eggs from the saucepan. Since Pen had recently moved in with Mike, she'd seamlessly taken over the household organization including cooking the all-important breakfast, eaten after doing nearly three hours of stable graft, including riding out first lot. She was a big asset and I knew Mike still couldn't believe she'd reciprocated his love and was happy to share his tough lifestyle. His face was one permanent smile. Except on an odd occasion, like just now when I'd asked him if he was the unknown flower-giver.

'Got to be a simple explanation, mate,' he said, forking up the last of his breakfast. 'How about it being Victor?'

'Never thought about him,' I admitted. 'Suppose it might be.'

Victor Maudsley, Elspeth's ex-husband, a retired racehorse trainer, had a long-standing acquaintance with our family.

'The flowers came from Grantham. The name of the shop was printed on the reverse of the card.'

'Well, if it's bugging you that much, why not go over and ask at the shop who bought them?'

'Yeah, I'd thought I might. But it'll have to wait till I get out of the police station. Got to go there this afternoon.'

'Ha, yes,' he said and cleared his throat, 'Alice . . .'

I inclined my head. 'As you say . . . Alice.'

'You going to let on about Jake Smith?'

'Don't know, to be truthful.'

'Hmmm . . . might draw his fire in *your* direction if you do.'

'I'd thought about that.' I pulled a face. 'Not a man to trifle with.'

Pen placed a hand on my arm as I got up from the table to put my empty plate and mug in the sink.

'If he did kill that poor woman . . . well, I think it's your duty to tell the police, don't you? She deserves justice, even if she was a prostitute.'

'Exactly what I'd thought about poor Jo-Jo when she, along with Louis, were killed in that car crash.'

'You think that was Jake Smith's motive for killing Alice, because she introduced Jo-Jo to Louis Frame?'

'Jo-Jo was Jake's sister . . . her death hit him hard. Alice told me he was a man that didn't mess about.'

I recalled Jake's words, spoken to me in what should have been the sanctuary of my own bathroom.

'Somebody's going to pay the price for Jo-Jo's death. And if you don't find the killer, it's going to be you.' This from a man who'd just been released from prison for GBH. Jake was a man who carried out his threats.

Mike added his empty plate to mine. 'Work calls . . .'

We left Pen to it and walked back down the stable yard.

But the memory of finding Alice was strong in my mind and I couldn't shake it off. Whoever had smashed in her skull certainly hadn't been messing about. He'd meant to kill her.

Three

'For an amateur detective, you do seem to have been extremely successful, Mr Radcliffe.' The police officer facing me across the table shuffled papers in the open file.

'I'm not a detective, amateur or otherwise, I'm a jump jockey.'

'But you have been involved in attempted murder and murder cases, haven't you, sir?'

I pursed my lips, couldn't deny it. 'I would say coerced would be a better word. Involved seems to imply I was a willing party. And I wasn't.'

'Have you any idea who would have wanted to kill Alice Goode?'

There it was, the 'straight in the face' question I'd been dreading.

'She was a prostitute,' I hedged, 'trouble and danger would seem part of the territory.'

8

'That's your theory then, is it, sir? She was killed by one of her . . . clients?'

'Well, it seems likely, don't you think?'

'At this stage of our inquiry we are keeping a very open mind, sir.' He changed tactics. 'Have you heard anyone issue threats, or warnings, against Alice Goode?' The inspector smiled thinly. 'Think very carefully, sir. This *is* a murder investigation.'

Inside, my guts curled like a cobra that had been trodden on. It was definitely the 'meat in the sandwich' moment. And I'd no doubt the recording machine would be taking careful note of my reply. If I didn't come clean about Jake Smith, the long arm of the law – when it found out I'd withheld relevant information – would descend swiftly upon me.

And if or when I divulged Jake's oblique threat, they were going to come after me with the next question of why he'd issued the threat. To answer that would give them the clear motive of revenge. OK, it would certainly divert them away from me but it also set me up as the dolly for Jake's fire.

I didn't know which of them I was most afraid of right now.

'Let me put it another way.' Leaning forward, almost conspiratorially, he said, 'Did you have sex with Alice Goode that night? Before she died?'

'No. I have never had sex with her.'

'But you knew her, didn't you? You've been to her house before, haven't you?'

'Yes.'

'But you've never had sex with her, right?'

'I've told you, no, never.'

9

'Oh, come now, sir. We've known for years Alice was practicing as a prostitute on our patch. Let's say, she was a very persuasive woman.'

I thought back to the only time I'd visited Alice at her house. My preconceived, distasteful idea of a prostitute had been correct only in how she was dressed: in an extremely short, provocatively tight black skirt, buttocks bouncing, Alice had shimmied away down the hall in front of me. At her trade of getting men going, she was undoubtedly an expert.

For a wild moment, I wondered if the inspector had experienced that same, calculated turn-on, too. And if so, how had he reacted?

For myself, all I'd been interested in was how I could get Alice to tell me the name of the man who had just beaten me up.

But before leaving, I'd seen the other side of the hard image with which Alice surrounded herself. It had dissolved, literally, as she'd cried over the death of her close friend and I'd found myself warming to her, not as a prostitute but as a caring woman. The fact that just before I left she'd offered a short utopia for both of us – which I'd declined – I discounted.

If the man in front of me had followed Alice down that hall, had he been strong enough – or sufficiently scared of sullying his reputation – to decline? I looked at the handsome, chiselled planes of his face, the expensively cut hair. He met my gaze with sardonic raised eyebrows. If I was allowed to bet, I'd take six to four on that Alice's powers of persuasion hadn't failed her. Pity I couldn't prove it, couldn't use it as a lever against answering his question.

10

What it came down to was a long, slow burn in Nottingham prison for perjury versus a swift end at Jake's hands.

I told the inspector what he wanted to know.

'Much as I like dear old Leo, a ginger tom is no defence. What I suggest is you trade him in for a couple of German shepherds.' Mike took a long slurp of tea.

'Thank you for that little diamond.'

Pen giggled and thrust a steaming mug into my hand.

'Thanks. Look, what choice did I have?'

'You could always enter a monastery, Harry,' she said.

'Pen, my sweet, Jake would simply don a habit and walk straight in unchallenged.'

'What Mike's trying to say, Pen, is now I've snitched to the police there's no hiding place for me.'

'But what's the worst he could do?'

Mike and I raised an eyebrow to each other.

'Let's hope he's hauled in smartly – and kept in.'

I played down the probable scenario that, even if he was, Jake could still activate what Darren Goode, Alice's husband – currently serving time in Nottingham Prison – had called 'his long reach'. Apparently, even if you were already in jail, it was no safeguard. If you were on Jake's hit list you could confidently put a sizeable chunk of money on getting hit.

'Shouldn't think he'll find you at the races, though,' Pen said with satisfaction.

Again, our eyebrows were raised without her being aware.

It had been at Market Rasen racecourse that Jake had first contacted me. That contact had set off what I thought of as the 'second round', and he'd been in prison at the time.

What I desperately hoped was that there would be no 'third round'. I'd put my life in danger by being forced to answer the inspector's questions about Alice's death and felt it was now their baby – nothing to do with me. I was very sorry indeed about Alice; she didn't deserve her violent end. But having to sort out who was responsible and mete out punishment wasn't my problem.

I pushed back my chair. 'Better make tracks to the track.' I was due to ride in three races this afternoon at Towcester. My hunger to retain the champion jockey title was still as strong as ever but with the way my life had gone in the past few months, right now it seemed as likely as catching a hot air balloon to Mars.

'Good luck.' Pen smiled.

'Thanks. I think I'll need some.'

None of the horses were from Mike's stables and all three of them were pretty much no-hopers, would be extremely fortunate to come in the frame, but the bottom line was I needed rides. Needed the income. A jockey's cash flow came from the bread-and-butter fee from simply riding in a race. The jam, if there was any, came from a percentage of the winnings. At the moment there were quite a few no-jam days.

I'd parked up at Towcester, was making my way over to the weighing room when I heard my name called out.

12

'Harry, over here . . . glad to see you.' The racehorse trainer, Clive Unwin, stepped forward through the crowd of racegoers. 'How are you? Is that arm in working order?' He nodded towards my upper left arm.

'Yes, thanks, Clive. I'm a fast healer.'

I didn't add that I also enjoyed the additional plus factor of receiving spiritual healing courtesy of my estranged wife, Annabel. She was a fully qualified spiritual healer and I'd had cause to be extremely grateful to her in the past for her help. Her unselfishness in helping me to get fit for returning to racing was staggering. Especially so because it was my racing career that had driven her away in the first place.

Annabel couldn't stand seeing me suffering from injuries caused by all the falls a jump jockey inevitably sustains. For her to consistently give me healing so I could continue riding spoke loudly about her unselfish, caring nature. I was still hopelessly in love with her – and hopeless was the right word.

When she had finally left, she'd gone to live with Sir Jeffrey, the man in her life ever since. I'd still entertained the slim hope that one day she might return, but it was crushed when she found out she was carrying Sir Jeffrey's baby.

I had very ambivalent feelings towards him. As a man, I found myself liking his friendly personality and ethics but, conversely at the same time, I was wildly, insanely jealous that he was the baby's father, not me.

'Not like a broken bone, I suppose,' Clive continued.

'No. Once my body had made up the blood loss, I felt a whole lot better.'

No point in telling him that, in order to get to sleep, I took a couple of painkillers at night. Today was the first ride since I'd sustained the injury. No sense letting him know that either. The trainer, as well as all the punters, needed to have confidence in the jockey. It was up to me to project the correct positive image. Any niggling doubts I personally might have needed suppressing.

But a short while later, being carted down to the start by a complete yak that needed its head aimed at a crazy angle towards the rails to prevent a complete bolt, I felt the burn begin in my left arm. Race riding demanded its own level of fitness and it was hard luck that this first race looked like proving a bastard.

However, during the actual race, Milligrams had sweated up and used so much nervous energy already that, halfway round the course, he gave up fighting and trailed along as backmarker. There was no point in my trying to shake him up – his bolt was shot and I ended the race on a very tired horse. I just hoped Clive Unwin understood the animal's temperament. And, just as important, let the owner down gently, too. A disappointed owner was not something I needed. Walking back in, the stable lad took the reins.

'Not a surprising result, Harry,' Clive said as I dismounted.

'No,' I replied with some relief at his acceptance of the situation.

'See how you make out with Respirator.'

'Am I looking at a similar situation?'

He smiled. 'The owner is here but she just dotes on him. If you get round in one piece, she'll be ecstatic.'

I grinned. 'See what I can do.'

What Respirator and I did was not only get round in one piece, but at the second fence from home, when the leading horses came to grief in a horrible multiple fall, we took a beautifully clean jump. We landed safely, avoiding the melee of thrashing horses and colourful, rolling jockeys, and Respirator galloped away. He was one-paced but, finding himself out in front, gave his all.

Clearing the last fence, he kept on and just held the lead, taking first place by a short head. If I found it difficult to believe, it was nothing to what his lady owner thought. With tears streaming down her elderly, lined face, she clasped both hands together and kept repeating, 'I knew he could do it, I just knew he could do it . . .'

It was patently obvious to everyone that if the leading group of horses hadn't fallen at the second last, Respirator would have ended the race way back in the field, probably around eighth place, if he was lucky. But the fortunes in a race can and do change dramatically. Today was Respirator's day. For the first time in his life, he'd come first.

And I had gained my ten per cent of the prize money in addition to my riding fee.

But the joy his win had given to his owner was incalculable.

My third race of the day followed the example of the first and faded into obscurity. But I'd expected three also-rans this afternoon and Respirator's win had lifted the day. I was delighted for his lady owner and, as I walked back through the car park after racing, I was well satisfied.

My left arm had stood up to the race riding and that was a big relief. Once again, I gave thanks to the man upstairs for allowing me to continue racing. I was very grateful. It was a ritual now. I'd spent so much time in a hospital bed earlier this year with a smashed patella, among other injuries, facing the bleak prospect of the likelihood my racing days were over, that to be back in the saddle again warranted gratitude.

The Mazda was cold when I unlocked it – definitely in need of the heater on the way home, the first time this winter. I switched on, waited a couple of minutes then drove out of the gates.

I was concentrating on driving, avoiding the crowds streaming out from the racecourse and the heavy traffic, plus the heater was belting out and making a row, so it wasn't until I was several miles north of Towcester that I became aware of the sound of soft laughter. So soft that at first I couldn't place what it was or where it was coming from. But as I drove on the sound grew louder.

Then, in stunned disbelief, I recognized the sound – and I knew who was laughing. I turned my head to look.

A voice from behind the driver's seat said, 'Keep your eyes on the road, Harry boy.'

And my worst nightmare became reality. He wasn't safely banged up in a cell in Newark Police Station; Jake Smith was sitting behind me on the back seat of my car.

Despite the chill inside the vehicle, my hands on the wheel were slippery with sweat.

Four

Fear ran all the way through my body. My stomach felt like it was filled with ice cubes. Instinctively, I clenched my buttocks. That kind of humiliation I could do without.

'Keep your right foot down and drive.'

The sharp prick of a knife blade dug into the back of my neck, emphasizing his command.

'Where are we going?' My voice was high and betrayed me. Jake would know I was scared stiff.

'Back to yours, Harry boy.'

'To mine?'

'That's right. All you have to do is drive home.'

'You're coming back with me, all the way?'

'Too right I am. Now I'm getting my head down for some kip. But don't get any fancy ideas. You *will* regret it; I'm a *very* light sleeper.'

With that, the point of the knife was removed from my neck and reflected in the mirror. I saw him slide down and make himself comfortable on the back seat, pulling the travelling rug over him. He'd probably hidden underneath it before I got into the car at the races. My heartbeat gradually started to slow. I needed to calm down, think what to do.

It was a clever move on his part to go to the races. A classic 'hide a tree in a forest' job. With the crowds of racegoers milling about there, Jake could be fairly certain of remaining anonymous.

17

But what did he intend to do when we got back to Nottinghamshire? I had maybe an hour and a half to dwell on it. What were my options right now? There weren't many. If I flashed another vehicle down and tried getting out, I'd be placing the driver in extreme danger. That was if I could even get a car to stop. I could pretend we were out of petrol. But as a professional jockey dependent upon four wheels turning, it wasn't going to wash. Or I could try a controlled crash. Might get away with it, might not . . . I didn't fancy risking it. Any more injuries I could do without.

Which just left me doing what I'd been told – driving back home. Whereas before, there had been soft laughter, now it had turned into low snores. I marvelled at the coolness of the man's nerve. In his position, to be able to switch off to the extent of going to sleep smacked of a level of supreme self-confidence that was staggering.

I concentrated on driving. As long as I could keep hearing those gentle snores I knew I wasn't going to feel a knife in my back. And I'd had enough of being on the receiving end of a knife blade just lately. That thought wasn't the brightest to have at the moment. It brought my attention back to my arm, in particular my left biceps. It was starting to hurt like hell.

His snores lasted all the way as I kicked on north up the M1, past Leicester Forest East and up the A46. However, the snores stopped as I swung off at Saxondale and turned for home down the A52. We were getting close now. The cottage was only three miles in front.

'Before you ask,' Jake said from the back seat,

'I don't want dropping off anywhere. I'm a man who goes all the way, Harry boy. And when we get there, you can get the kettle on.'

At that moment, I realized when he'd said 'drive home' he'd meant it literally. Jake Smith intended to come back to Harlequin Cottage with me. And, worse, there was nothing I could do to stop him. But I had to try.

'You do know the Newark police are looking for you?'

'Since you put them on my trail, yes. Why do you think I was miles away at the races?'

'But you can't come home with me. I'll get done for harbouring.'

'Why do you think I'm coming home with you? Because Harlequin Cottage is the last place in the land the police will come looking. And, as you say, if you grass me up you'll get done for harbouring. Perfect solution, don't you agree?' He began laughing softly.

The sound made cold water run down my back.

When we got back to the cottage, he went straight upstairs to use the bathroom. He didn't need to ask directions – he knew where it was. Once, some weeks ago, he'd broken in and come looking for me. I'd been in the bath, soaking an injury caused by a horse kicking my thigh. He'd given me no choice that day either: find his sister's killer or get killed. Oh, yes, Jake knew where the bathroom was all right.

I fed Leo, who was prowling round, eyes wide and wary. He didn't like strangers, they made him nervous.

'I'm with you there, big fella,' I told him and

19

placed his dish down on to the red quarries. Then, dutifully, as directed, I made some tea.

Jake appeared in the kitchen doorway. 'So, how many bedrooms do you have?'

'Three.'

'All upstairs, I take it?'

'Yes.'

'Hmmm, well, you can make me up a bed on the lounge settee. I'll kip there.'

If he was going to take up residence in the lounge, it meant I'd either have to sit in the office or go to bed.

'There's a perfectly good bed in the guest room . . .'

'Save it, Harry boy. I'm not a guest, right? I'm staying in the lounge. No way am I going to be trapped upstairs if we get any visitors wearing blue.'

'There's the conservatory, if that's any good.' I was getting desperate.

'Forget it. They're useless inventions, scorching hot in summer and bloody freezing in the winter. No, I'll take the lounge settee.'

I spread my hands in resignation. While he was staying here he'd be running the ship, not me. I didn't like it one bit, but I was stuck with it.

Leo finished his meal and disappeared swiftly through the cat flap, jammy sod. I wished I could follow him.

'How long are you going to be here?'

'As long as it takes.'

'To do what?'

'For you to find Alice's killer. And pass me that mug of tea, it's going cold.'

'*What?*'

'I've every faith in you.' He clicked his fingers. 'Tea?'

Thunderstruck, I passed it over.

'You're saying you *didn't* kill Alice?'

'Got it in one.'

'You told me you spent the night with her.'

'I did.'

'But you didn't kill her?'

'We were busy doing other things . . . I'd spent the last four years banged up, don't forget.'

'She was still alive when you left?'

'Yep.'

'Why don't you tell the police that?'

'You think they'll believe me? With my pre-cons? Don't be fucking stupid.'

'But surely you don't expect me to find out who did kill her?'

He shoved the mug at me. 'Look at *your* track record. No use denying it – you're good at sussing out killers.'

'Oh, no, I'm done with that.'

His face darkened. 'You dropped me in it with the police, told them I'd been with her, had the opportunity and the motive. So it's up to you to clear me. And, believe me, you're going to. Because, if you don't, it won't just be your neck for the chop. Oh, no, Harry boy, Annabel gets it first – you get to watch.'

'For God's sake! She's pregnant.'

'So, you get me off and she stays alive to drop the sprog.'

Leo didn't come back for breakfast. I didn't blame him. Jake's presence filled the cottage.

21

The night had passed without incident and Jake was sitting at the kitchen table, awaiting breakfast.

'Porridge, Harry boy,' he'd answered in response to my query if he wanted anything to eat. 'You'd think I'd have had my fill of it, done my share of stir.' He'd laughed; this time it actually did contain some humour. 'But I just like porridge.'

'Sorry, not something I keep in stock. There's toast, grapefruit or eggs.'

'Well, you may be keeping weight off but I'm not. I'll have the lot.'

I cracked three eggs into a basin and slid bread in the toaster.

'You planning on staying very long?'

'Why?'

'First, I've got work to do, I'm due at the stables. And second, I'll have to buy in more food.'

'You think of anywhere safer, I'll go.'

'You could hand yourself in, tell the police you're innocent.'

'They'll bang me up again – that would leave my old man on his own. He couldn't take any more right now.'

'I'll come with you; tell the inspector I believe you.' We stared at each other.

He narrowed his eyes. 'You do?'

'Yes.' I nodded slowly. 'I guess I do.'

'Nice to know. But it won't wash. Unless they get a lead on the real killer, I'm their prime suspect.' He shook his head emphatically. 'No, I'm not going near the nick.'

'But you can't expect me to find out who killed Alice. I've not a single thing to go on.'

'You can do it – you've done it before. You *have*

22

to, Harry boy. It's my neck on the line – *you put it there.*'

I poured scrambled eggs on to his toast.

'What I have to do is go and ride out.'

'I meant what I said last night.' Jake's voice dropped chillingly low. 'I've got the old man to think about. I don't make idle threats. This time it's my skin . . . *or your wife's.*'

'You're going to have to give me a lead, something to go on,' I said, fighting down rising desperation. 'Last time you put me over a barrel, you gave me a list of possibles . . . without that I couldn't have done it.'

He glowered at me. 'Get off – do your riding. I'll think about what Alice told me.'

Driving slowly, of necessity, down the ice-covered Leicestershire lanes, I was late getting to Mike's racing stables, didn't bother with the usual drink, just got stuck into the mucking-out routine. Champion jocks didn't usually, but he was a mate.

The stable yard was freezing but it was warm inside White Lace's stable. The sheer size of the big animal gave off a good deal of natural central heating. She swung her head round, gave me a good-natured nudge against my shoulder and blew a gusty blast of hot air down her nostrils. It was like standing in front of a fan heater. I pulled one of her ears gently and ran my hand down the powerful arched neck. Paul Wentworth, Pen's brother, had been right when he'd commented that horses asked for very little and gave back so much.

I began grooming her. The rhythmic swish of

23

the Dandy brush down her withers was soothing. It freed my mind to range over the godawful mess I was in, through no fault of my own.

Sir Jeffrey had jokingly asked what would I do if there was a third time?

I'd jokingly replied I couldn't stand another hellish situation like the previous two. Now, yet again, I was facing having to hunt down a killer.

Jake was an enigma, I didn't trust him at all, knew he was entirely ruthless if he was crossed. Yet at the same time, I recognized, like everyone else on earth, he wasn't all bad. We shared emotionally painful common ground. I'd seen my own pain reflected in his eyes. And, I reminded myself, he'd not lost one member of his family but two.

I could sympathize with his concern for his father's welfare. Fred Smith wasn't coping with the sudden violent deaths of his son, Carl, and daughter, Jo-Jo. His excessive smoking and drinking, coupled with not eating, was rendering him a pathetic skeletal wreck. I knew. I'd seen him. Jake's concern was justified.

And I still couldn't throw off the guilt hanging around my shoulders that I was in part responsible for Carl Smith's death. OK, the guilt I felt was irrational and totally unjustified but it didn't help.

I leaned in against the comforting, warm bulk of the mare and brushed the silvery gleaming flanks. White Lace belonged to Chloe, Samuel Simpson's daughter. Samuel had bought the mare as a present for her. Chloe was also suffering from the fall-out following Carl Smith's death. I'd been amazed at the sympathy Samuel and Chloe had shown towards me when, just as easily, they could have shown antagonism. Apart from sympathy, they'd also become friends and Samuel had instructed Mike, as trainer, to give me rides on his other horses in the stables.

I finished grooming the mare, holding out the long, thick tail and running the brush down the strands of the silvery flow. All the time I'd spent grooming, I'd been running over options regarding Jake Smith's last comment. 'If you find me somewhere safer, I'll go.' Having him staying in Harlequin Cottage wasn't going to work. Although unspoken, we both knew that for a fact.

My overriding concern was for Annabel's safety. Jake had laid out his terms: find Alice's killer and clear his name with the police or risk Annabel's life. Not just Annabel either – she was carrying a baby. Two lives then at risk.

And Jake knew there was no way I could refuse to do as he said.

I was back over the bloody barrel.

So where the hell *did* I hide a wanted man?

Five

Breakfast in Mike's kitchen, two hours later, was the usual mix of banter, laughter and good humour. Since Pen Wentworth had moved in, though, it was much enhanced. I'd never seen Mike so relaxed and happy. Only happy wasn't the best word – joyful was much better.

25

Pen had effectively stopped Mike's ongoing grieving for the loss of Monica, his first wife. The irony of it was that Mike hadn't displayed any signs of depression or, indeed, sadness following Monica's death. On the surface, I doubted if he realized he was grieving. He was fine, taking life as it came and rejoicing in his work, especially when the stable had a winner.

I was, perhaps, the only person who could see through the protective layers to the rawness inside. Maybe it was because I'd lost Annabel that the empathy between Mike and myself had strengthened in the last three years. The arrival of Pen in his life had effectively given him back his joy in living.

Deliberately, I swallowed a tiny, bitter bubble of jealousy. Never in my life had I ever felt the slightest bit jealous of someone else's success or happiness.

Until Annabel had told me, gently, she was expecting Sir Jeffrey's child.

It had bombed my world, killed the slender, fragile hope that maybe one day she'd return. The green devil of jealousy had descended, swamped me, enervating, stultifying, a hateful feeling to have. I was still doing battle. Any more jealousy I didn't need.

But I wasn't jealous of Pen. She was a warm, straightforward woman, exactly right for Mike. But I recognized that the situation between Mike and Pen, their personal relationship, the magic one-to-one exclusive closeness, was holding up a mirror in front of me. It showed me what I was missing out on.

'Harry, what's your poison?' Pen waved a wooden spoon back and forth.

'Beans, please, one slice.' I was riding Lytham at Leicester racecourse this afternoon. The horse belonged to Paul, her brother.

Previously, the horse had belonged to Benson McCavity, his cousin. Benson's wife, Helene, had lost her life in a car crash. Then the garage he ran near Grantham had hit financial trouble due to a road re-route and he'd been forced to sell Lytham, much against his wishes. The horse had been named after the place where Benson and Helene had first met. To help out, Pen and Paul had bought Lytham. 'To keep him in the family,' Paul had said.

We stood a good chance of a win today.

It was another reason why Jake's threat was not needed. If I was to have any chance of retaining the title of champion jockey, I needed scope to accept any, all, rides that were offered. Racing time was precious. I didn't need any other commitments eating into it.

Being late this morning had scuppered any chance of having a word with Mike on our own. And I needed to. For years he'd been my back-up in all sorts of ways. Without his help in the first murder case, I probably wouldn't be alive.

He'd once said, 'If ever you find your back up against a stable door, you can depend on me.' That phrase had proved shockingly prophetic.

I needed his help now. As a trainer with a lot of stable lads in his employ, he was responsible for providing accommodation. Their wages were low but one of the perks was free or heavily subsidised housing. I needed to ask him if he had any ideas where I could house Jake.

The big snag to this was I didn't want to implicate Mike. I was breaking the law right now by allowing Jake to live at the cottage without informing the police. But to involve Mike wasn't on. One way out would be to go to the police myself, come clean and point them straight towards Harlequin Cottage. If I did they would no doubt instigate charges against *me*.

They would certainly take Jake into custody. And however much I wanted him out of my home, out of my life, I couldn't do it. He was innocent of the crime. I had enough guilt hanging over me already – I didn't need any more. If I could, as he'd suggested, find somewhere safer, then it would give me a breathing space to negotiate.

If he came up with a viable lead on who the real killer was I could give it my best and, if it didn't secure the result he wanted, at least I'd have tried. He'd have to admit that. But the most pressing thing was to find some sort of safe shelter so he could move out of my cottage.

My chance to talk alone with Mike came later on in the morning. We had two horses loaded up and declared in two consecutive races at Leicester, which meant two lads were needed to go with them, plus the box driver. No more seats spare. Mike said he'd take his own vehicle; Leicester wasn't far away. I took the passenger seat and joined him.

I let three or four miles slide away beneath the tyres as we followed the horsebox south at a sedate pace. Without knowing how to broach the problem, I jumped straight in.

'I've got someone living at the cottage.'

'Have you now?' He gave a slow, knowing smile. 'Female?'

'No, and I need him out, like, before he arrived.'

'Don't tell me,' he said, laughing, 'it's not the dreaded Jake Smith?'

'I wish I could say it wasn't.'

His head whipped round. 'Dear God! Surely it's not?'

'Yes.'

'How do you do it, Harry?' He smacked the steering wheel hard. 'He's a wanted man. You've got to get him out.'

'Couldn't agree more, Mike, but he needs a billet. Any ideas?'

'Anybody giving him a bed will soon be joining him when they throw the man back in jail.'

'I know. But he didn't kill Alice. He's innocent.'

Mike snorted disparagingly. 'And you swallowed it?'

'I think it's the truth.'

'You think . . . with his record of violence?'

'Yes, Mike, I do.'

He drove in silence for a couple of minutes, absorbing my words. Having taken time to get my own head round it, I could appreciate his difficulty.

'I've always rated your judgement, Harry. Pretty sound, I'd have to say. So . . . if you're right, it begs the question: who did kill Alice?'

'Now you have the crux of this scenario. Jake's tossed the problem of finding out who it was into my lap. Says, quite rightly, I've dropped him in it with the police. He's parked in Harlequin

29

Cottage until I can come up with the killer's name.'

'That could take some time.'

'Hmm.' I nodded. 'But I need him out. I don't fancy risking jail. Equally, neither do I want to involve you in taking a risk. But it you've any ideas where Jake Smith could lie low, I'd really like to hear them.'

'Have to think about that. As you say, it's a risky number all round.'

'Let's shelve it for now. If lightning strikes, well, you can tell me after racing.'

Mike seemed relieved and we drove on to Leicester in an easy, companionable silence. Approaching the racecourse, the horsebox peeled off to the separate box park while we headed for the jockeys' car park. The familiar aroma of frying onions, hot dogs and fish and chips floated tantalizingly towards us as we walked towards the weighing room. The baked beans and single slice of toast had long since become a memory.

Mike must have seen my nostrils start to twitch. He grinned and lightly punched my right arm.

'We've got loads of time. Sign in and I'll see you in the bar, eh? Black coffee doesn't have any calories.'

I grinned back. 'Sure.'

Leaving Mike to amble along to the main bar, I walked on into the jockeys' inner sanctum to declare I'd arrived, and then went and deposited my racing saddle.

Shortly after, I wove an erratic path towards the bar through the good-natured racegoers. I'd always enjoyed my racing at our local course, despite the horrific murder that had been committed here. A happy, relaxed atmosphere permeated the whole complex. Everyone was here to have a good time and enjoy themselves – maybe get lucky with a judicious punt – and knew they would be able to fill their boots with whatever kind of food they preferred. I deliberately pushed the thought away. It was a good job the smell of food wasn't fattening.

I headed towards the glass doors and went into the bar, settling for a sugar-free black coffee. Mike was sprawled in a chair opposite a man wearing a striking daffodil-yellow waistcoat. Both looked up as I approached.

'Hello there, Harry.' The man in the eyeball-blasting waistcoat waved his glass at me. Nathaniel Willoughby, the famous artist, whose racing paintings were superb.

'Nathaniel.' I nodded. 'How's tricks?'

'Good, good. Even better now Mike's given me an unexpected commission.'

I cocked an eyebrow at Mike, hooked a chair towards me and joined them at the table.

'Not me,' he said. 'Well, not at the moment. It's for Samuel.'

'Don't tell me – a painting of White Lace so he can give it to Chloe.'

Mike gaped. 'You getting psychic?'

'No.' I laughed. 'But she does have a birthday coming up soon and what do you give a girl who already has most things?'

'Do you know,' he said, eyes narrowing, 'that

31

sounds like you got there with that idea before Samuel.' He looked across at Nathaniel, who innocently buried his face over his liquid lunch.

'I promise I won't breathe a word to Chloe or Samuel. Surprises don't need spoiling.'

'Well, that's a relief. Samuel had already sworn me to secrecy. I was hoping I might catch Nathaniel while you were in the weighing room.'

I shook my head. 'And there I was, thinking you were showing sympathy for my not having any lunch by suggesting I have a coffee when all the time you were being devious.'

'Give over.' Mike snorted. 'Just don't tell Chloe.'

I held up a placating palm. 'Promise.'

He pushed back his chair. 'Leave you with it then, Nathaniel. Things to do down the stables. See you in the parade ring, Harry.'

I nodded. They'd be saddling up soon. No doubt Samuel would be arriving before long. He owned one of the three horses I'd be riding this afternoon. No forelock tugging needed for the third horse's owner. He was away in Barbados with his missus, sunning himself. I smiled to myself at the thought. I didn't envy him one bit. Crazy, maybe, but I wouldn't swap my saddle for his sun-lounger. I'd get more satisfaction coming in first, possibly, than deepening a tan.

'So, Harry,' Nathaniel said, placing his empty glass on the table. 'Any ideas yet on the ETA?'

Nathaniel Willoughby, horseracing artist, in a class of his own, already commissioned by me to paint a portrait of Annabel's forthcoming baby, twinkled across at me.

32

'Sorry, I've no idea. Annabel hasn't mentioned a date.'

'Never mind, old chap.' He nodded sagely, screwing up his eyes, 'Let's just be thankful the baby's still on his way, eh?'

'You heard about that?'

'With all the media coverage, you couldn't very well not. But I suspect your part in the drama wasn't given the accolade due. You ended up on the receiving end, didn't you?' His eyebrows rose questioningly.

I flipped a hand dismissively. I'd deliberately played down my own involvement. Neither Annabel nor myself wanted that sort of notoriety. The quicker it faded from the public's memory the better. But I'd no doubt the old ashes would be raked again when Annabel gave birth.

At the thought, my guts gave a sudden clutch. Jake Smith. I'd forgotten about him for the last couple of hours – now he was back in the forefront of my mind. And the problem of where the hell did I hide him? All hell would break loose when the police traced him to my home. Without doubt, they would do.

'Thought it best to keep schtum just now, you know,' Nathaniel was saying, 'when Mike was on about work . . .'

I dragged my thoughts back to the moment. 'Yes . . . eh, yes, thanks. Not that it would matter really, Mike knowing.'

'Best to keep the ladies' surprise a secret. Be a shame to have it leak out and spoil their pleasure.'

'Absolutely, yes.'

'Mind, I told Mike I can't start work straight away on the one he wants. I'm going away on holiday for three weeks.'

'Somewhere nice?'

'Very nice. Visiting my sister in Switzerland . . . and my niece. Don't see enough of them.'

'Sounds good.'

And suddenly it sounded good to me, too.

'Where do you live, Nathaniel?'

'Out in the sticks, backside of Melton Mowbray. I've an old cottage, nothing grand, don't do grand. But it has got a studio in the garden. It suits me.'

I leaned forward. 'You could help me out here because, you see, I've a bloody awful problem . . .'

I didn't tell him the problem. No way was I going to shaft him, but I asked if I could have the keys to his place while he went to see his family.

'I can't tell you the reason why, or who the person is – for your own safety – but I desperately need secure accommodation, safe above all else. It will save my bacon and, if you are in complete ignorance, you won't have any flak flying in your direction. What do you say?'

He looked at me steadily. 'The answer's no, Harry.'

I felt the jolt of disappointment. I'd really thought this might have worked. However, I didn't blame him at all. It was entirely up to him.

'No, you can't have my keys, nor use my cottage. But . . .' he looked woefully at his empty glass, lifted it and upended it, '. . . you can buy me another drink and I'll let you have the keys to the studio. It's got electric and water laid on, a bog, a shower and a sink. Bring your own microwave. But it has got a kettle, so you can make tea.' He

34

slowly lowered the glass until it was sitting rim down on top of the table. Then he gave me a long, lazy smile. I returned it. I put my hand out and picked up the glass.

'Name your tipple.'

He covered my hand briefly with his. 'Let's say, it's the accolade you didn't get. I'm wiping the slate clean for Annabel's baby.'

'No slate to clean.'

He inclined his head. 'Just don't tell me who will be dossing in my studio. *And* make damn sure they're gone, long gone, before I get back from Switzerland, OK?'

'Deal.'

Six

Mike wanted in.

'I've never seen inside an artist's studio. Intriguing, don't you think, the creative force at work?'

On the way home from the racecourse I'd updated him about Nathaniel's generosity and said I was due to meet him for a handover of the keys at nine o'clock at Burton Lazars, the village where he lived.

'I think the man's generosity is amazing.'

I hadn't told Mike the underlying reason why Nathaniel had decided to loan me the studio. It hadn't been brave or heroic of me; I'd simply done what any husband would have. The fact that Annabel and I lived apart didn't enter into it. Notwithstanding

Sir Jeffrey was the man in her life, I still felt protective towards her – always would.

We'd returned to Mike's yard earlier in the evening with the partial success of my having ridden all three horses into third place in three races.

'Can't say you're not consistent, Harry.' Pen smiled as she ladled out dinner – in my case, carb-free chicken curry.

'Better if they'd all been first, though.'

'Men,' she said and shook her head, 'they're never satisfied.' Then turned pink as Mike, chewing a mouthful of dinner, guffawed and nearly choked himself.

Nudging the jug of water towards him, Pen said innocently, 'Want to stay over tonight, Harry?'

Mike gave a massive, gulping cough, cleared his airways and gave me a narrow-eyed look.

'No, no. Thanks for the invite but, when we're back from Nathaniel's, I'll get off to the cottage.'

'Sure?'

Then I remembered Jake Smith, still in residence, and my heart dropped. Not a tempting choice.

I looked at Mike who, no doubt seeing my momentary waver, narrowed his gaze some more.

'Oh, yes, I've a feline to feed.'

'I'd love to meet this Leo. He sounds like some cat.'

'Anytime, Pen.'

'Not tomorrow, sweet,' Mike chipped in, 'I'm taking you out to dinner, remember?' He met my eye, meaningfully this time, and I realized he, too, had just remembered about Jake's presence in Harlequin Cottage. He certainly wouldn't want her to run into potential danger.

36

'How about I have a totally informal drinks and nibbles evening . . . say . . . Friday?'

'Oooh, lovely. Yes, please.'

'Suits me, Harry. Nothing on Friday, should be clear by then.'

Taking the hint, I said, 'Absolutely clear. Eight o'clock then?'

They both nodded.

Now, just approaching nine o'clock, Mike was driving me along a narrow country lane that was forever narrowing the further we went. The sat nav spoke up. 'Turn left and pull up. You have arrived at your destination.'

Obediently Mike hauled on the wheel, swung into a short gravel drive and cut the engine. On either side a tall holly hedge hemmed in the car, effectively preventing us seeing what building lay behind the prickly greenery. I felt an involuntary grin curving my lips. Even before I saw Nathaniel's pad it was ticking a good few boxes regarding isolation and privacy.

We left the car and walked on a few yards, following the drive round a bend and came upon a rambling, very old building. A twisting pathway led on down to the far end of an overgrown garden to a single-storey outbuilding.

I inclined my head. 'D'you reckon that's the studio?'

'Could well be.'

'Better speak to Nathaniel first.' I put a thumb on the doorbell.

When Nathaniel opened the door, we could see a suitcase was already waiting in the hall. He'd told me he was booked on an early morning flight to Switzerland.

Picking up a bunch of keys from the hall table, he took us down the garden path to the studio. Unlocking the door, he switched on the light.

'Come on in, see what you think.'

The first pungent impression we received was an overwhelming smell of paint and linseed oil.

All along the far wall, completed canvases were leaned up facing the wall. The side wall was fitted out with partitioned, open-fronted shelves. They were filled with pots and containers of paint and white spirit, plus jars filled with sticks of charcoal, palette knives and innumerable paintbrushes.

Only one door led off the main room.

'Toilet, sink, shower in there.' Nathaniel waved a hand towards it.

An old but comfortable-looking settee was placed beneath the west window. I deduced that was to double as a seat and bed. It would have to do. No doubt Jake had slept in much worse places.

Mike was looking round with great interest. 'Mind if I take a look at your easel?'

The easel was, traditionally, facing a very large, north-facing window. Nathaniel took the cover from it. 'Help yourself. I'm not precious about my W.I.P. but don't ask me who commissioned it. I won't tell you.'

'Wouldn't do.' Mike spread his hands. 'It's a privilege to see where you work.'

'Are you quite sure, Nathaniel, that you *want* to let me move someone in?' I asked.

Now that we were standing inside the studio, it struck me as a private place, not one that ought to be violated by any negative vibes. And whichever way you viewed it, Jake Smith *did* give off an aura of threatening menace.

He smiled gently at me. 'It's not a holy of holies . . . but I take it your "visitor" isn't going to trash everything?'

'I'll spell it out to him.'

'Not a clandestine lady, then?' He raised a mocking eyebrow.

'No. But how about we all move your paintings out of here so we know they'll be safe?' I knew I'd sleep easier if they weren't left in the studio to take their chances.

'Good idea, Harry.' Mike was gingerly inspecting the paintings facing the wall. 'These are damn good. Be a tragedy if they came to harm.'

'OK.' Nathaniel gave in to common sense. 'If you chaps can give me a hand, we can store them up at the cottage.'

Between the three of us, carrying a painting in each hand, we got the job done in about seven or eight trips. We took them into the music room, which proved to be a small extension along the back of the cottage, and left the paintings propped up against the inside wall. I breathed a genuine sigh of relief. They were obviously worth a great deal of money. If they had come to any harm because of Jake's presence, I'd have felt honour-bound to refund the cost.

'You play this Steinway?' Mike's voice held a note of respect. He nodded towards the piano.

'Not as often as I'd like, but yes, I do play.'

Nathaniel sat down on the swivel stool and trickled his fingers along the keys. Note by note, the second movement of Mozart's twenty-first escaped from the piano and filled the room with haunting sweetness. The music caught Nathaniel in its web. He played on and it was exquisite.

It meant a great deal to me. My half-sister, Silvie, had loved it. I glanced at Mike. His face wore a strange expression, a combination of hurt and wistfulness. Too late, I realized Monica, his late wife, had loved playing the piano. Before her death she'd often entertained us, running through her wide repertoire, usually after I'd gone round for dinner at the stables. They'd been enjoyable occasions, happy times. The lid of the piano had remained closed ever since her death. That particular Mozart piano concerto had been her favourite. Mike had instructed it to be played at her funeral.

The jolt of synchronicity took me by surprise. Monica had died on the ski slopes in Switzerland. And Nathaniel was flying to Zurich in a few hours' time. I wondered, briefly, exactly where he would be staying.

He played the last few notes and allowed the final vibrations to die away into silence before dropping his shoulders, sighing with satisfaction.

'A magnificent composer, don't you think?'

Mike pulled himself together with admirable speed. 'A great one.'

'My daughter, Coralie, usually twists my arm to play when I go over to visit. Her husband farms near Lucerne, has a massive dairy herd. The milk is bulk-bought for making chocolate. They have a good life together. And little Ellie-Anne, my granddaughter, she's a cutie, always playing tricks on me whenever I'm there.'

Nathaniel laughed and slapped Mike on the

shoulder. 'Talking of which, if I don't get started I'm going to miss my plane.'

'Flying from Nottingham East Midlands?' I asked.

'I wish. No, got to drive down to Birmingham Airport. A right pain but there're no flights from East Midlands. Still, it's quick, only about three hours. I'll be having lunch with my family.' His face lit up with pleasure at the thought.

I experienced a lurch in my solar plexus. He was a lucky man. I'd no close family now to share lunch with. 'Have a great time.'

He turned, grinned and tossed me a set of keys. 'Yours for three weeks.'

'Thanks a lot. See you when you get home.'

The cottage was in darkness when I arrived back. Jake Smith had got his head down on the settee in the lounge. He was sprawled out, oblivious, when I opened the door. But before I'd turned to shut it, he'd uncurled faster than a compressed spring and had a grip on my neck.

'Hey,' I spluttered, 'it's the homeowner, not the police.'

He glowered then dropped his hand. 'Don't creep up on me. Not if you want to go on breathing.'

'I live here, right?'

'So do I, *right*?'

'Not for much longer.' I ignored his aggressive tone and dropped Nathaniel's keys into his hand. 'There you go, a safe, private billet.' His fingers closed around the keys; his eyes never left my face.

'Where?'

* * *

Well before dawn the next morning, I padded blearily downstairs into the kitchen. I turned on the tap and filled the kettle. Then stuck my head under the jet of cold water. I needed to sharpen up. Shoving the kettle on to the Rayburn hotplate, I grabbed the kitchen towel and scrubbed away my drips. Leo's basket was empty; he'd not shown up since Jake had descended upon us. Very sensible was Leo. A pity I couldn't emulate him.

I walked through to the lounge. Jake, cocooned under a duvet, was asleep on the settee. I shook him. 'Time to move.'

'Eh?' Reluctantly, he sat up. 'What's the time?'

'Nearly four thirty.'

'Bloody hell!'

'We agreed the time last night.' He grunted in disgust, running a hand through his hair. 'Tea's brewing in the kitchen.' I left him to it and returned to the bubbling kettle.

With a mug of strong tea inside, I felt the will to live returning. Last night, before seeking our beds, we'd stuffed the Mazda's boot with the various necessities of life: pillow, sleeping bag, spare kettle, mug, a couple of saucepans, decrepit toaster, cutlery, etc., plus toilet rolls, teabags, bread. I'd known there wouldn't be time this morning to mess about. The whole purpose of the early departure was to get Jake into Nathaniel's studio before dawn broke and any possible neighbours got curious.

'Ready when you are.' I reached for the car keys hanging on a hook behind the back door.

'Not so fast . . .' Jake opened the fridge door.

There was one unopened bottle of milk inside. He lifted it out. 'This is going with me.'

I shrugged. You didn't argue with Jake. If Leo came back today, I'd have to get the car out and go down to the Co-op in the village.

It was a trek to Nathaniel's but, at that time in the morning, traffic was practically non-existent on the winding country lanes.

'Looks like you've cracked it, Harry boy,' Jake said.

I turned off the narrow lane and pulled on to the drive, totally obscured by the holly hedges either side.

'Reckon this will do you?'

'A bog and a bed, and it'll do.'

I walked him down the garden path and turned the key in the studio door.

'As the owner said, it's not grand, but it's as safe as you're going to get.'

We unloaded the car and dumped the stuff in the middle of the floor.

'Leave you to it. I'll take the keys.'

'Like hell you will.'

'Sorry, but they're coming with me. Can't risk anybody walking in on you.'

'What about my grub? I'll need some before dark.'

'Don't count on it. I'm going racing at Wetherby. You've got bread for toast.'

He completely lost it, launching himself at me. Grabbing my dodgy left arm, he forced it up behind my back then twisted it savagely. The bastard knew the injury from the knife wound was still healing; he'd targeted it on purpose. I

43

felt the flesh and muscle tearing where the surgeon had stitched it back together after the stabbing. Agony roared through my body.

'You'd fucking better get back! If you don't, I'll break the window and burn the fucking place down.'

It was the worst of all scenarios, Jake threatening to torch the studio. Through a mist of agony and clenched teeth, I thought of the precious paintings. Thank God, Nathaniel had agreed to them being taken up to the cottage. They, at least, were intact and safe.

It remained to be seen whether I was.

Seven

'Did the delivery drop go OK?' Mike inquired at breakfast, after I'd arrived – late – for morning stables.

'Well, he's installed. How long for . . .' I shook my head. 'I'll take him some fish and chips when I get back from Wetherby.'

'Hmmm, feed the beast, eh?'

'His temper could do with sweetening. Still, I wouldn't like to be first choice for a murder rap.'

'Don't forget, Harry, right now you're definitely *first* choice for harbouring a wanted criminal. Whatever the verdict is on Jake, your charge stands.'

'You don't need to remind me. If I could ever get the chance of a full night's sleep, I wouldn't be able to drop off. I once visited a man in

Nottingham prison and once was enough. Chilling didn't come into it. And that was only in the waiting room, not in the cells.'

It gave me the quakes every time I thought about ending up in there.

That man had been Darren Goode, Alice's husband. I'd gone because I needed to pump him about a murder. I'd thought afterwards the only reason he agreed to see me on a visitor's pass was because he wanted to pump me about Alice's state of health. Had he known of a threat against her? It was something I'd not considered before. But now Alice had been murdered . . . How was he taking the news? I didn't need to speculate. Like an enraged – and caged – bull elephant. God help the warders at Nottingham prison.

'Expect you could do with a catnap.' Mike peered at me. 'Come to the races in my car – I'll drive. You can have a bit of a kip on the way.'

'Sounds good.' Without warning, I gave an enormous yawn. The late night followed by an extremely early morning had left me too lethargic to be comfortable. A jockey needed to be mentally on it. The dousing with the kitchen cold water tap in the pre-dawn obviously hadn't cut the mustard.

I'd missed first lot this morning but pulled in a ride second lot on Jellybean. I needed the exercise. I felt stiff and uncoordinated. The tension of treading eggshells around Jake had tightened my muscles and tendons. That coupled with the icy cold on the exposed high ground above the stables exacerbated the tightness.

Jellybean was a massive seventeen hands and

45

a puller. They could have used him in the Middle Ages and dispensed with the rack. However, pounding the cold gallops as I sought to try and hold him while he used his superior horsepower in effortless opposition to my puny strength, practically pulling my arms from their sockets, had me warmed up and breathing heavily before we were even halfway finished. But the tension had not only tightened up my body, it had an energy-guzzling effect and, I admitted to myself, I was bloody tired. I could use a safe powernap.

And, in Mike's car, it would certainly be safe. Unless the blues and twos decided to pull us over.

I was riding two of Mike's horses in the first consecutive races at Wetherby. Two, even if I managed to win on both, were not going to gain me any titles, but there was always the chance of an odd ride should any of the jockeys have an awkward fall, God forbid. Not only that, other trainers were likely to approach with an offer of possible future rides. But in the state I was in just now, two rides were probably all I could manage.

Mike's altruistic offer of chauffeured transport was in keeping with his generous nature but also rang a warning chime in my head that he wanted me fit for the job. His owners expected nothing less. An hour or two of undisturbed sleep would set me up for a couple of races. With Jake out of the cottage when I got home tonight, I could guiltlessly have an unashamed really early night.

Then I remembered: after racing I'd have to motor over to Nathaniel's place, picking up fish

46

and chips on the way and, as Mike had phrased it, 'feed the beast'. So, no early night after all. And tomorrow I had five rides booked. Sleep deprivation, I could do without.

Even as I thought about it, the groan-inducing realization dawned: today was Friday. I was supposed to be hosting a drinks and nibbles do at the cottage. I had to cry off. Nursemaiding Jake didn't allow for such social indulgences.

I turned to Pen across the breakfast table. 'Have to take a rain check on tonight's bun fight – just realized I'm double-booked. Sorry, Pen. Could we set another date?'

'No worries.' Pen poured herself more coffee. 'I know you and Mike are both busy boys.'

Mike snorted disparagingly. 'Boys? Pen, my sweet, I think you should toddle off to the opticians for a sight check. Us two haven't been boys for getting on for . . . thirty years?'

'Ignore him, Pen. I'm still in my first childhood, even if he isn't.' I downed a Bovril drink.

'If you've got a bit more time to plan, how about you invite Annabel for drinks? She sounds an interesting lady.'

'Could do. Depends if Sir Jeffrey is home, though.'

'Isn't he usually?'

'Doesn't seem to be.'

'That's a shame. Perhaps he will be when the baby arrives.'

I smiled and nodded and managed to hide the emerald-green stab of jealousy that her words engendered.

'You having another drink?'

47

'No, thanks.'

Mike drained the last of his massive mug of tea. 'I'm done. Think we'd better make tracks. The travel forecast warns there are roadworks on the A1, so we ought to allow a bit of extra time, given you're riding in the first race.'

'Have fun, my darling.' Pen lifted her face to receive the kiss Mike gave her.

'Fun, woman? It's hard labour.'

'Well, it probably is for Harry.' She was laughing as she looked up into his face, her gaze warm, loving. Their happiness was almost tangible. Mike was a lucky man. But he'd waited years for this type of happiness and he deserved every precious second.

We arrived at Wetherby with little time in hand. Mike had been right about the roadworks.

I went straight into the jockeys' weighing room to dump my racing gear before joining Mike in the bar for a bracing black coffee. I was ready for one. Having let down the passenger seat as far as it would go, left Mike to concentrate on getting us to the racecourse, and with no possibility of being ambushed, I'd enjoyed a deep, refreshing sleep. I couldn't wait now to swing up into the saddle, try for a winner.

Black Tartan, my first ride, belonged to Samuel Simpson. He was a good chap; Mike and I played golf with him. We often played a foursome with the three of us plus Victor Maudsley, the retired racehorse trainer, usually down at North Shore golf course near Skegness, a great venue. Victor lived, literally, a few yards from the course. It would be nice if I could come in first. It was probable Samuel

48

would be here today. Whether his lovely daughter, Chloe, would come with him was an unknown. We all shared dramatic history. The fact we were actually here now, still friends, said a lot for Samuel and Chloe's generosity of spirit.

Thinking of Victor Maudsley reminded me I'd meant to motor over to the flower shop in Grantham, check if it might have been Victor who had placed the white roses on my mother's grave. It was a loose end that needed tying. When I found out who had bought the flowers, I would need to follow that by inquiring about the meaning of the message written on the card.

But for now, I needed to back-burner all other thoughts and concentrate on the first race. The nine fences were stiff but Black Tartan had the advantage of running well on a left-handed track. I'd always liked racing at Wetherby – it was an easy and comparatively short drive up and had a great atmosphere.

Rejoining the rest of the jockeys inside the changing room, I stripped off my normal clothes, zipped the body protector around my chest and pulled on the purple and green racing silks, Samuel's colours. On the point of putting on my paper-thin racing boots, Henry Vale, apprentice jockey to one of the up-north trainers, dropped down on the bench beside me. Raising his voice a little to overcome the usual racket of good-natured ribbing and ribaldry, he passed on a message.

'Mousey Brown's looking for you, Harry. Knows you're racing today. Said would I tell you to meet him after your second outside the winners' enclosure.'

'What for?'

'Dunno. He was half-pissed, as per, but he dropped me a tenner to make sure.'

'I need to get back straight after racing.'

'Aw, come on, if you don't show he's not going to believe I told you.'

I took pity on him. It wasn't so far back I couldn't remember a tenner was, on occasion, a lifesaver for a lowly racing employee drawing a meagre pay packet. I'd been there. Ten pounds would feed him for a couple of days.

'OK, I'll be there. But only briefly, right?'

He grinned, gave the stable lad's habitual sniff – that could be read any number of ways – and said, 'I'll tell him.'

Henry was riding in the same race, the first one. I'd done my homework earlier, knew his horse was a no-hoper, but at least he'd get paid the standard riding fee. Thinking about it, he wasn't that desperate to keep Mousey's tenner. Still, I'd said I'd meet the man. Why he wanted to see me, I couldn't imagine. Right now, with jockeys beginning to stream out to the parade ring ready to mount up, I pushed it from my mind, pulled on my second boot and followed them.

Black Tartan was an odds-on favourite and, barring a disaster, was expected to win. Samuel had arrived while I'd been in the changing room and was now standing with Mike in the parade ring, eagerly anticipating the race. He pumped my hand.

'Bring him in, Harry.'

'Do my best, Samuel.'

'Never known you not to.' He chuckled. 'Even on an out-and-out yak.'

I grinned back. That was the one safe bet in racing: you couldn't *guarantee* any horse and even yaks had been known to have their day.

'No Chloe?'

He shook his head. 'No, she's got an appointment with the solicitor this afternoon.' He worked his lips sideways in grave distaste, 'The divorce . . . you know . . .'

I knew. 'Give her my best regards anyway.'

'I certainly will.'

The order to mount interrupted any further conversation and Mike flipped me up into Black Tartan's saddle. He was on his toes, primed and perfect for the race.

I had a job holding him on the canter down to the starting tape. The confidence he had in himself, coupled with mine in expecting to win, worked like a charm. It was a copybook race, if there was such a thing, and we saw off the pack and galloped up the couple of hundred yards' run-in about seven lengths clear.

I rode him into the winners' enclosure to the deafening cheers from all the happy people who knew a good thing when they saw it and, after watching him in the parade ring, had had a good punt. They wouldn't clear much profit at the odds but most likely they'd used him as a banker in accumulators. Whatever, Black Tartan appreciated the fuss being made of him and, with ears pricked, tossed his head up and down enthusiastically.

Samuel, of course, was delighted and busily slapping Mike on the shoulder. Black Tartan was

51

a fairly newly acquired addition to his string. The win validated his choice of horseflesh and he was wearing a wide grin. He was also the owner of Floribunda, the horse I was due to ride in the next.

I left them enjoying the high and went to weigh-in.

I'd ridden Floribunda before. He was an out-and-out stayer, although his jumping was less than reliable. But today my luck was holding. Floribunda gave me a great ride over the first five fences. I was in a good place, only four in front and the rest strung out behind. A gap appeared on the stands side and I squeezed the horse forward as we approached fence number six.

He took off too soon. I knew immediately he wasn't going to clear the jump. As Floribunda struggled over, he dropped his back legs and that was it. The drag of the brushwood fetched him down, pitching him forward on the landing side. And I sailed up and over his neck. To be honest, I can't remember much else after that.

Mike told me afterwards, I hit the ground head first, rolled and one of the following horses struck my head with a hoof shod with a metal racing plate. The impact of the blow had split my crash cap like an eggshell.

When I came to, I was lying in a hospital bed attached to a drip and the racecourse was a million miles away. Immediately, a wave of nausea swamped me and I was violently sick. The pretty little nurse, who had been detailed to take care of me, was totally unfazed. She dealt with the cleaning up in a calm, efficient manner and mopped me clean. She explained I had sustained a concussion, only that, miraculously, no bones were broken. My whole body was one big bruise but that would heal itself.

The good news was that somehow I'd escaped a fracture to my skull. With no further bumps to my head over the next two or three days, the concussion would sort itself out. I knew that – I'd had concussion before. But for the moment I was grounded. That was non-negotiable. Apparently the hospital wasn't taking any chances on further complications that might show up later. But I felt too groggy to even think of arguing. I was not exactly seeing double – two visions of the pretty nurse wouldn't be too bad, but the crack on my head had definitely affected my sight. I felt I was not so much lying in bed as in a boat. Closing my eyes against the undulations that were making me feel so sick helped, a little. Losing my stomach contents wasn't dignified, it was bloody embarrassing. So, I sank back into the seductive darkness that relentlessly drew me down.

The next time I awoke, Mike was sitting beside my bed. However, the bed had stopped swinging up and down now and my eyesight had steadied. I could see his face was wearing a grim expression.

'You can forget the coffin ordering,' I mumbled. 'I'm still in the game.'

'And thank God for that.' His face cleared. 'You gave us a bloody scare this time. Have you seen the state of your crash cap?' Without waiting for my reply, he bent over and lifted it up for me to look at. It was practically hanging in two halves; only the inner webbing held it together.

'Can't see superglue sticking that. Looks like it's going to cost me. Have to buy a new one.'

'Buy it out of your percentage winnings from Black Tartan.'

'Ha . . .' His words prompted my next ones. 'Tell me, Floribunda . . .?'

'Fine. Bit stiff the next day, naturally. I got the vet to give him the once-over. He passed him A OK.'

I felt the relief lift a potential weight from me. But the relief was fleeting.

'How long have I been here? What day is it?'

'Monday. You've been under quite a bit. Well, I think they've given you a bit of dope to help you heal.'

'Monday!' I struggled to sit up. 'What about Leo? He'll need feeding—'

'Whoa.' Mike held up a hand. 'Just you settle yourself. I've been over, checked out the cottage *and* fed the cat. Leo didn't need it, the crafty bugger. He'd been pigging out on pilchards.'

'One of his favourites. Who gave them to him?'

He grinned. 'Use your head. Oh, sorry . . . slipped out. It was Annabel, of course. She rang me later to see how you were.'

'She's a gem.'

''Course she is. I thanked her on your behalf.'

'Good.'

'So, no problems. You just get over the head injury, get some rest, nothing's spoiling.'

I flopped back gratefully. Right now, Leo probably had more strength in one of his ginger paws than I had in the whole of my body. But then a horrible uneasiness crept into my battered brain. It wasn't only Leo who needed feeding.

If today was Monday, Jake Smith had been locked in Nathaniel's studio for three days – without food!

Eight

I felt the sweat stand out on my face, run down my neck.

'Harry?' Mike was staring at me in concern. 'What is it? You in pain?'

'Nothing spoiling?' I grimaced, and not just from pain. 'Try Jake Smith starving.' I watched the horrified realization dawn on his face.

'Good God, Harry . . . I forgot all about him! The poor sod . . .'

He scraped back the plastic visitor's chair.

'I'll get there straight away.'

'Keys, Mike.'

'Where are they?'

'Last seen in the dash of my Mazda.'

'Which is now parked up at the stables?'

I tried to nod – tried.

Mike dropped a sympathetic hand on my shoulder. 'Stick with it. I'll be back tomorrow.'

I closed my eyes. 'Watch your back. Jake might try taking a bite out of you.'

'After three days without food, you could be right.'

* * *

I spent the next two days getting my act together before the hospital relented and shipped me off back home.

'But in view of the nature of your . . . work,' the doctor said with heavy disapproval, 'it would be wise – indeed, *sensible* – to take a few days off.'

Yes, no doubt it would, but since when has a jump jockey ever done anything *sensible*? Riding half a ton of straining horseflesh over massive jumps and pushing out for a finish at upwards of thirty-odd miles an hour wasn't in the least sensible. And the odds on falling off was something best not dwelt on. But I thanked him sincerely for patching up my head and returned home to the cottage with great relief.

Within five minutes, Leo's sixth sense had alerted him to my presence and he slid sinuously through the cat flap. Well, as sinuously as eight kilos of huge ginger tom can do. He was very forgiving and didn't hold it against me that he'd been ditched to take his own chances. He leapt up on to my shoulder with a loud bellow of welcome and bashed his head into my right ear.

'And I'm glad to see you too, mate.' I stroked his furry body, feeling the reverberating purrs rising up through his ribcage like a road drill on piecework.

Being in hospital had one advantage: my weight had dropped. Partly due to the size of the helpings and partly to my throwing them back up again. In contrast, Leo had piled it on. Sitting on my shoulder, he weighed a ton. The jury was out on Jake Smith's weight.

I'd received a telephone call from Mike to let

me know the bird had flown. Presumably, through the smashed up north window. I was going to have to do something about that fairly smartly before the local thieving locusts could descend and strip the place, and in any case before Nathaniel returned from Lucerne.

However, right now, I cranked up the central heating, brewed a mug of scalding tea and put on a Mozart CD. He was supposed to be good for the brain patterns, wasn't he? Whatever, all I craved at the moment was to stretch out on the settee with an abundance of squashy cushions packed round my neck to support my aching head and delight in the healing peace of being back at the cottage. Far, far away from the nightmare of frenetic activity and constant racket that constituted the hospital environment. No doubt of it, you had to be strong to survive going in there.

Leo immediately settled himself on my solar plexus; his rhythmic purring had a soothing, stress-busting effect. Home was security, warmth and peace. I lay back, sipped my mug of tea and counted my blessings.

I wondered where Jake Smith was going to lay his head tonight. I'd broken my word to him that I would bring him food; forced him to break out and find sustenance himself. When Mike had told me he was no longer in the studio, I'd been very pleased. Starving wasn't pleasant. As a jockey, I understood this stark fact very well, was prepared to accept this on a day-to-day basis of short rations. But that was my choice because it was relevant to my work. Forcing someone to go without food for days was indefensible.

I hadn't expected to fall off and end up in hospital, but it wouldn't have assuaged my guilt at causing suffering if Jake had still been waiting inside the studio when Mike arrived.

Outside, it was down to freezing point and falling. Leo and I were cosy, comfortable, but it was very likely that Jake was acutely aware of the cold. In his position, he had little chance of finding a warm billet. But he was an adult, not my responsibility. Still, I hoped he had found a safe shelter for the night. I set down my empty mug and closed my eyes.

Mozart's twenty-first played movingly to its climax and my mobile, incongruously, stridently, struck up the theme tune from *The Great Escape*. It shattered the somnolent atmosphere and brought me sharply to full consciousness.

'Harry, darling? How are you? Where are you . . .?'

Just the sound of her voice brought a stupid grin to my face.

'Annabel, great to hear from you. I'm on the mend and back at the cottage.'

'Are you sure you're all right? Are you on your own?'

'Yes to the first, no to the second. Leo's right here, spread out across my solar plexus, weighing a ton and snoring.'

'Oh, the darling.'

'Hmmm . . .'

'He's de-stressing you, Harry. Animals know when you're ill.'

'Anyway, where are *you*? Back at the ranch with Jeffrey?'

'No, no, Jeffrey's down in London on business.'

'He usually is,' I growled. God, didn't the man know what a prize she was? Leaving her on her own was a bloody waste. Any man would have been delighted to take his chance and move in on her, especially me. Jeffrey was all kinds of an idiot. 'So, if you're not home, where are you?'

'Just about to make my way back from visiting Aunt Rachel and Uncle George.'

'How come?' I frowned. I knew, since Aunt Rachel had learned of Annabel's pregnancy, she'd been acting as though the baby was a forthcoming member of the family, conveniently forgetting that Jeffrey was the father, not myself.

'Well, since the early summer we've sort of drawn a lot closer. I suppose because they're the older generation, I look on them a bit like surrogate parents.' I knew Annabel's parents were both dead, as were Jeffrey's. Jeffrey was a lot older than Annabel.

'You've been visiting before then?'

'Oh, yes, a couple of times at least. The previous time I was there was just a few weeks ago. We went out to lunch, had a stroll round Lincoln.'

'Oh.'

It was a surprise to me but, thinking of Jeffrey's habitual absences, I could see Annabel was probably fairly lonely.

'I know you don't approve of Aunt Rachel's attitude towards the baby, Harry, but, well, I quite like the attention . . . if I'm being honest . . .' her voice dissolved away, '. . . you know, a bit of fuss?'

'Of course you do, and nobody deserves being

59

made a fuss of more than you. Take no notice of me. I understand you needing company right now, really. But there's always me, you know.'

'I know, darling, but it's hardly the same and I don't want Jeffrey to feel he's . . . well . . . sharing me.'

'He's not.'

And he wouldn't; the 'keep off the grass' sign was clearly in place.

Both of us knew Annabel's pregnancy had irretrievably placed her in the 'do not touch' category.

'But if you're only a handful of miles away, why not do a detour and call in? I'm sure Leo would be delighted. And, talking of the pampered puss, thanks for feeding him while I was stuck in hospital.' She laughed; her spirits were never down for long.

'No thanks needed. I suppose I could drop in for a coffee, just a quick one. I don't want to be too late getting back home. I don't think it's going to snow but it's certainly very icy on the roads.'

'I'll leave it up to you. But we'd love your company.'

'Bless you, Harry. I really don't know what I'd do without you being around. See you in a few minutes.' She rang off.

I stared down at the mobile. Did she really feel like that? She'd never said so before. To know I meant a lot to her warmed me inside. I lay back with a pillow cushioning my head and closed my eyes, savouring the feeling. Leo, disturbed by my movements, stirred, stretched and then resumed his purring. He didn't know it yet but he was in for a treat.

So was I.

Drowsy from the 'feel-good factor' Annabel's words had engendered, coupled with the seductive warmth, I'd slipped gently, without realizing it, into a non-drug induced, natural healing sleep. The fragmented stuff you got in hospital couldn't be compared in any way with sleep at home.

A spitting hiss from Leo, as he dug sharp claws into my belly, brought life back into focus fast. I wished it hadn't. A rough hand encircled my throat and Jake Smith thrust his face within an inch of my own.

'Told you before, Harry boy,' he rasped, 'you can starve if you want, I'm fucking well not.'

I struggled to loosen his grip and couldn't, tried to get a word out and couldn't. I couldn't even breathe.

His fingers tightened like a vice. I struggled ineffectually against the strength of the man. His fingers were buried in the flesh of my neck and it was as useless as trying to prise open the clamped jaws of a bull terrier. Mike's words about guard dogs came into my mind as I kicked out wildly, trying to loosen his grip. God, if only Leo *had* been a German shepherd.

My head started to swim. I began to thrash about. Whatever damage it was doing to my already battered brain was incidental now in trying to get breath into my lungs. If Jake Smith, believing I'd left him to starve, really was intent on finishing me off, this was looking like a one-way only game – and he was winning.

My lungs were filled with liquid fire, fighting for oxygen, my heart pounding madly, struggling to keep me alive. But the agonizing iron bands holding me tight, squeezing my chest, were merciless. My sight was just an in-and-out red haze now. With sharp fear, I knew I was losing it.

Jake had dragged me up from the settee, was tossing me around the lounge. We lurched from wall to wall but already my legs were going. Once I was down on the floor, that would be it.

Then I felt Jake stumble. There was a hideous screeching caterwaul and Leo leapt up between us; all four paws, with grappling irons, dug into Jake's chest. The cat's lacerating claws flashed up at the man's face. The vicious strikes were a blur as he ripped again and again into the skin and flesh, leaving tattered red ribbons hanging.

Jake, screaming with pain, let go of me and grabbed for the cat. But Leo was too quick for him and jumped to safety on the top of the bookcase.

Vaguely, I was aware of someone rushing into the lounge from the hall, but I was rolling around on the floor, coughing and retching, desperately trying to force oxygen back into my tortured lungs. Gasping some precious air, I managed to get to my knees and heard Annabel screaming at Jake.

'You bloody, stupid sod! If you've caused more damage to Harry's head I'll have you charged with attempted murder.'

'I wasn't trying to kill the fucker, you stupid cow, just give him a frightener,' Jake yelled, his face dripping blood. 'If I wanted to finish him he'd be dead now, believe it!'

And I certainly did. I'd really thought he'd been intent on killing me.

Meanwhile, Leo, seeing the door was open,

jumped down from the bookcase and fled. I didn't blame him. He'd saved me, and the cottage, once before; tonight was the second time. By God, I owed that cat.

Annabel whirled away from Jake to where I was on my knees, legs like jelly, hanging on to the furniture.

'Let's get you on to the settee.' Thrusting an arm under my shoulders, she helped me up. 'Come on, darling, lay your head back . . . on to the cushion . . . that's right.'

Now the real threat of dying was over, I shared her concern for what damage might have been done to my head.

'Sit quietly, Harry. I'll pour a glass of water.' She peered closely at my throat. 'You've bright red wheals all over – it must be really sore.' She disappeared briefly and returned with a drink.

Gingerly, I massaged my throat. She was quite right – bloody sore was an understatement. Drinking was absolute purgatory.

Unnoticed, Jake Smith had taken himself off to the kitchen and now returned with a blood-soaked wad of kitchen paper. The lacerations to his face were deep and still bleeding.

'I wasn't fucking well going to kill him . . .'

'No?' Her voice was high with shock and anxiety. 'You very nearly did, you maniac.'

'Lost my rag a bit. I'd have let go of him in a minute or two. But that bastard cat . . . tripped me up.' He glared round at the bookcase but Leo was long gone.

Annabel squared up to him, eyes blazing with anger. 'If that cat comes to any harm,' she spat

63

the words at him and emphasized them by jabbing a stiff forefinger into his chest, 'believe me, you will regret it.'

Just what she thought she could do against a convicted GBH criminal, I'd no idea, but both Jake and I could feel the blistering fury behind her words.

He backed away, raised a palm. 'OK, OK, keep your britches on.'

Her hands went instinctively, protectively, to her swelled belly.

'Come here, Annabel, it's over,' I croaked. 'Don't distress yourself; we don't want any harm coming to the baby.'

'No.' She sat down suddenly beside me, 'No, we don't.'

'Yours is it then, Harry?' Jake said slyly.

'Just *bugger* off,' Annabel flared.

'Oh, oh, touchy . . .'

'You know damn well the baby's not mine,' I said.

'Well, seems like you're concerned for its future. Bit odd that, another man's kid.'

'My baby, *my* baby, is not an "it".'

'But he,' Jake nodded in my direction and his voice now held a cold, threatening edge as he added, 'seems keen to see it born.'

There was a long pause. Annabel was unaware of his threat to her and the unborn child but he was reminding me nothing had changed. If I didn't come up with the killer's name and get him off the hook, they were both still targets.

'The baby will certainly be born – and safely.' I challenged Jake to deny it.

'Let's hope so.'

'I've had enough of this conversation.' Annabel stood up. She pointed her finger at Jake. 'Have you seen where Leo puts his claws? If I were you, I'd get some antiseptic on those scratches.'

'Huh, not fucking likely. That stuff hurts too bloody much.'

'I see.' She smiled nastily at him. 'You can hand it out but you can't take it.'

I lurched to my feet and came between them. 'I think you should head home, Annabel. Jeffrey will be sending out a search party if you don't.'

She looked directly into my eyes and I read the puzzlement. Jeffrey, far from being at home, was down in London. She knew that, so did I – she also knew I knew.

'Last thing we want right now,' I continued, 'is anyone turning up on the doorstep who might report Jake's whereabouts to the police when they're out looking for him as we speak.'

She cottoned on. 'Yes, better get off. Now, you're sure you're all right, Harry?'

'Dead sure. Off you go. And take it slowly with the icy roads.'

I showed her out to the car and kissed her goodbye. Under cover of the kiss I whispered in her ear, 'Not a word to anybody that he's here, OK?'

'OK,' she murmured, 'but I want the full story later.' Then, raising her voice, said, 'Bye, Harry. I'll give you a ring tomorrow – see how you're going on.'

And she drove out of the gate and away down the freezing lane.

Nine

I watched her car's red tail lights disappear, then I went back into the cottage.

'You can't stay here, Jake.' I was expecting a flat refusal but his reply totally threw me.

'Wasn't going to. Expect the police will be here in the next day or two – when it happens.'

'*What?*'

'You'll hear about it soon enough.'

'Look, I'm not getting done for harbouring you.'

'Calm down, Harry boy. They're not coming about that. Anyway, you're driving me – and a load of grub – back to that studio place tonight.'

I gaped at him. 'No way, I wouldn't trust myself driving.'

'Why the bloody hell not?' Jake scowled at me.

'Because I only got out of hospital a few hours ago. That's the reason I couldn't bring you any food. Came off, didn't I, at Wetherby. I've been stuck in hospital ever since.'

'What with?'

'Severe concussion. I've been completely out, like a blown light bulb.'

'That's why you never showed up with any dinner?'

'Yes.'

He gave a low chuckle. 'Don't knock it. Even if you don't need it, you've got yourself a great alibi.'

66

'An alibi for what?'

'I'm not telling you, but you'll find out.'

I stared at him. 'You said the police aren't coming because of you. So, what *are* they coming for then?'

'And I told you.' He thrust his face close to mine. 'I'm not saying. You'll find out.' He drew back, chuckling unpleasantly. 'But you won't like it, I guarantee that.'

I shook my head slowly. 'Aren't you in enough trouble?'

'Yeah, and who was it that dropped me in the shit, eh?'

'Did I have a choice?'

'Well, right now you don't have a choice. Knock me up some food.' He held up a hand. 'Don't say there isn't any. You've got eggs, OK?'

We both had double scrambled eggs.

We both then hit the sack.

And the next morning, I drove Jake back to Burton Lazars. Mike, the good mate that he was, had had the broken window repaired. When you needed someone to rely on, if you couldn't operate yourself, he was the best.

Predictably, when I got back to the cottage, Leo was sitting beside his empty food bowl. He knew the danger was past and he was hungry. I filled his dish then made a mug of scalding tea.

Taking it upstairs, I detoured to the bathroom for the painkillers. My head was drumming hard enough to summon the entire Apache tribes. Dragging off my clothes, I sat in bed, knocked back two tablets and gulped down the tea. Then I let the rest of the day take care of itself while

I caught up on quality sleep. I didn't bother getting up for dinner – there was no point. There wasn't any food in the cottage – it was all over at Nathaniel's studio.

At one point I was aware of Leo joining me under the duvet.

'I owe you, mate,' I murmured drowsily, smoothing his silky fur. 'When I get some food tomorrow, the first thing I'll buy will be the biggest tin of pilchards I can get my hands on.'

He purred contentedly and tucked himself in deeper.

The next morning was a vast improvement. The Indians had claimed their drums and hightailed out.

I padded downstairs, grabbed the morning papers – one broadsheet plus the *Racing Post* – made tea and toast and took everything through to the lounge. I slobbed on the settee and enjoyed the peace. Chewing the last slice of toast, I opened the newspaper.

The headline stood out. Jake was quite right. I didn't like it. Not one bit.

Two men, on remand, awaiting trial, had been found dead. They were the men involved in Carl Smith's murder at Leicester racecourse. And I was the man who had solved the murder, the man responsible for putting them away. Now they were dead. I felt very cold; my emotions went into overdrive. The ongoing ripples from their deaths were going to affect a lot of people: Samuel and Chloe; the horse-box driver, John Dunston, one of the deceased had been a member of his family. Victor and his family, Darren Goode, maybe . . . I was convinced these were link-ups to Alice's murder. And of course Annabel, Mike, myself, the list ran on . . . I found myself wondering what Matron at Silvie's nursing home was thinking. Jake's dad, Fred Smith – did he suspect Jake's involvement? The puzzle was like an octopus, tentacles spreading everywhere. Man was certainly not an island – these were connecting pieces of a jigsaw that all joined together.

I was beginning to catch a tantalizing glimpse of the picture but there was a long way to go before it became clear. Darren Goode, Alice's husband, when I'd visited him in Nottingham prison, had told me Jake Smith had a long reach and, whether in prison or out, it didn't make any difference. If Jake wanted you dead, it was a given. And although Jake Smith hadn't personally killed them, he had certainly given the orders. Carl had been his younger brother.

At that moment, I realized how lucky I was that he didn't want me dead. Understood why he thought the police might call. It was an odds-on certainty they would. What questions they might ask me was the unknown. And if they also asked if I'd seen Jake or knew where he was . . . well, since I couldn't shop him, it was also a certainty that I'd be digging myself in deeper by denying all knowledge.

Two choices: go to ground for a second day running or take off and stay away.

I was feeling much better and lying around in bed wasn't appealing; if I wasn't careful it could get to be a habit. But I couldn't go to the stables – work was out. So, where did I take myself off to?

I supposed I could go and check out the flower shop in Grantham that had supplied the white roses. But there must be something more important I could do. Time off from racing was precious. I needed to make the best use of it.

If I could progress forward in trying to find out the name of Alice's killer, it would placate Jake. I was well aware the only reason why he didn't finish the job the other night was because he needed me. But he was expecting a result. And the name wasn't going to come to me, I needed to get out and ask questions, try and link up any suspects. Jake was right. I had done it before, ergo, I could do it again – perhaps.

I leaned across the desk and retrieved the piece of paper Jake Smith had left me. I'd read it before downing the painkillers; it hadn't made any sense then. I reread it. It still didn't make sense. Basically, it was what he remembered from the pillow talk between Alice and himself. He felt it was important that she'd let slip a confidence imparted to her from a previous punter. Jake's theory was that it was blackmail material.

The cryptic message said: *I hope you're not going to reveal the follies of callow youth. Not after playing cat and mouse all these years.*

This was followed by what Alice had replied. *Cat and two mice – with a piece of cheese.*

Jake had no idea who she'd been speaking to. But he wasn't making it up, I was sure of that. The phrasing of the first quote immediately ruled him out. Flowery, definitely flowery, it singled out the man who had said it as being an educated man. Someone Alice had known for a very long time

70

by the sound of it. From as far back as schooldays, maybe. No, that didn't ring true; Alice would doubtless have been educated in a state school, secondary modern maybe, depending on how old she was. I thought back to the first time I met her. It had struck me then that she was a good deal older than she both dressed and acted. It was difficult with women to actually make a halfway decent guess. And in her 'profession', it was crucial to appear as young as possible for as long as possible; any hint of being beyond her 'sell-by date' and she'd be out of business.

The man, however, may have attended a grammar school or even gone to a private one. But their paths had met up, with a dodgy outcome by the sound of it.

I wondered if Alice had any children. She was married to Darren; they could have had offspring. It spawned the thought: had she any children apart from Darren's? It was the first and most obvious explanation of youthful follies. But it was a bit late to drop a paternity claim on the man's head. The child would be grown up by now.

I suppose it might have blackmail mileage if the man was happily married and didn't want it imploding. But if he was happily married, why should he go elsewhere looking for pleasure, and particularly with a prostitute?

I shook my head. It simply didn't gel. And the words Alice had replied lent themselves to almost any interpretation.

Leo jumped up on to the settee beside me. Absently, I stroked his head while I brooded on the problem. Leo was a tom but generally, when you thought of a cat, it was of a female, a queen. The

71

word cat in the quotation, I felt, was meant to be female, a woman. In fact, Alice, herself.

That presupposed the mouse, or as she'd put it, two mice, must be men. And it wasn't a long jump from there to assume they were probably both clients of hers. Which meant both men were long-standing acquaintances. Which could also mean they might know each other.

So, that left the piece of cheese. Both cats and mice loved cheese. Was this a reference to a fourth person? If so, what sex? It was logical to think this person was a female – it made for a cosy foursome. But if so, was this woman another prostitute? Somehow, I didn't think Alice would tolerate competition on her patch. Prostitutes were notoriously territorial.

So, if I'd been right so far in my deductions, in which direction did it point me? None came to mind except the obvious one. Darren Goode would be able to answer my query as to whether Alice had any children. But that was the one lead I couldn't follow. Apart from the practicalities of trying to obtain a visiting order – not viable because of the time delay involved – no way was I going inside that prison again. And his agreement to see me wasn't a certainty. Darren would be one hellishly angry man. His wife had been murdered while he was stuck, impotently, behind bars. He'd be lashing out at whoever came in striking range.

Now, on top of Alice's murder, there were two other deaths. I'd have bet Harlequin cottage on Darren knowing exactly what the SP was for both men's murders. His last remark before I left the visiting room at the prison had contained more than a hint that another death was on the cards. But I hadn't expected two, with both victims behind bars themselves.

However, from a purely selfish angle, the police couldn't connect me with the killings, nor would anybody be putting pressure on me to discover who the murderer was. There could even be more than one person involved. I didn't give the police very good odds in discovering the killer's identity. If any of the inmates knew, they wouldn't be singing. They'd be far too concerned about using their breath to keep on breathing. I had no doubt the shadow of Jake Smith ruled. The two deaths proved it.

Breaking into my dark thoughts, the telephone on my desk gave a shrill double ring. It startled me – and electrified Leo. He shot up into the air and streaked out of the room. I heard the cat flap in the kitchen snap closed behind him. He'd gone out into the jungle of a garden. It was safer out there. I shook my head in sympathy. Boy, were his nerves in a bad state.

I lifted the phone. 'Yes?'

'How's the head?'

I didn't immediately recognize the voice. 'Hello, who is this?'

'Forgotten what my voice sounds like, Harry? Probably that bang on the head. Mousey here.'

Mousey? Oh, Mousey Brown, of course. But mouse . . . as in one of the two mice? Could it be him? No, it was too much of a coincidence.

'We were supposed to meet outside the winner's enclosure at Wetherby but I'll let you off.'

'Yes, sorry about that, Mousey.'

'You ended up in hospital, eh?'

73

''Fraid so.'

'OK now?'

'Near enough.'

'Not back in the saddle, though?'

'No, the powers that be won't let me, you know.'

'Aye, I know. Anyway, I need to see you, Harry.'

'Can you tell me over the phone?'

'Rather not. Bit . . . er . . . *delicate.*'

'Fair enough, so when's your best time?'

'Seeing as you're free at the moment, how about today? Can you drive up to the stables?'

'Sure. About elevenish do?'

'Do nicely. Tell you what, come and have lunch in our local pub – does a very mean steak. On me, of course.'

'Guess you've twisted my arm, Mousey.'

He chuckled, 'See you, Harry.'

I leaned back in the chair. Going up to Malton would solve my location problem very nicely. The reason *why* he wanted to speak to me and wouldn't say over the phone could prove tricky. Delicate, was how he'd described it.

I mooched into the kitchen and made a mug of strong coffee.

If I was driving up north, I needed to stay awake.

Ten

The Old Rectory Stables was an L-shaped run of boxes facing a majestic, rambling old house. Its glory days as a residence for God's representatives were long over. However, it had metamorphosed into a gentleman's des res. Whether Mousey could be described as a gentleman was a bit questionable.

Apparently, in his youth he'd been a wild card, not noted for sobriety or observing convention, plus his driving was legendary. But that was before my time. Mousey had always treated me fairly and with respect. I treated him the same.

I drove in between the high pillars either side of the entrance, did a swing round at the end of the long drive and cut the engine. Mousey couldn't have driven down to see me – he was an alcoholic who'd had his licence withdrawn a long time ago. These days his eldest son, Patrick, himself an ex-jockey, held the business reins and Mousey was the figurehead. The reason for his sink into alcoholism had been because his wife, Clara, had sustained an appalling injury that had led, a couple of years later, to her death.

Racing, being the close family it has always been, had given its collective support in many different ways. Allowances were made for his excesses.

Owners, less forgiving, were on the point of withdrawing horses. But after seeing Patrick bring home much-needed winners, decided to leave their horses where they were. I'd ridden for Mousey a few years back but Patrick seemed to favour the younger jockeys.

That thought pulled me up. A jump jockey's working life was considerably shorter than riding on the flat. Perhaps it was time for me to give some thought to what my future might be. But what did I want to do? Most people didn't know – that included me.

I went up to the impressively studded oak door and rang the bell. Patrick's wife opened the door. A nanosecond later, recognition brought a smile to her lips.

'Harry. You've made it, then? I'm sorry you've been injured.'

'Thanks, Jackie.'

'Do come in. Stanley's expecting you.'

It took me a moment to realize she was talking about her father-in-law. He was in the study, ensconced in a huge burgundy leather armchair, buried behind a copy of today's *Racing Post*.

'Morning, Mousey.'

'Harry, my dear chap.' He heaved himself to his feet, letting the paper slide to the floor. 'Very good of you to make the effort, much appreciated. By God, I miss my own set of wheels. Damn fools took away my licence. I know when I'm safe to drive . . . or not.'

It was just short of eleven o'clock but a blast of whisky fumes engulfed me as he shook my hand vigorously. Damn fools? I didn't think so.

'Have a seat, do.' He gestured to a leather Chesterfield beneath the window. Then, raising his voice, shouted, 'Jackie, lass, coffee, please.'

But the summons wasn't needed. She appeared in the doorway bearing a tray. The smell was wonderful.

'Thanks, I could just do with this.' I took the mug she offered me.

Still facing me, she murmured, 'And Stanley certainly can.' Then she turned to smile, full-bore, at her father-in-law. It contained all the love and caring needed to take away any possible sting in her words.

She handed Mousey a mug with the words 'World's Best Dad' emblazoned on the side in red.

'Thanks, lass.' He took a quick slurp, saw I'd read the lettering and twinkled at me over the rim. 'Pat brought it back for me from a school outing. It's lasted a long time, like me.' A shadow passed across Jackie's face.

'And we all want you lasting a lot longer.'

'Do what I can.' He turned to me. 'How long are you grounded for?'

'Couple of days, thereabouts. The doctor's got to stamp my card first.'

'Aye, damn red tape. The world's tied up with red tape.'

Companionably, we drank coffee and I waited for him to broach the subject of why he wanted to see me.

But instead, Mousey said, 'How's your boss doing?'

'Mike?' His question had surprised me. 'He's fine, yes, doing fine.'

'Has she helped?'

'Who?'

'His new lady friend?'

You couldn't swap your socks in racing before the news was doing the rounds.

'Pen's been good for him, yes.'

'Aye, well, he's a young chap – needs a woman around. And what about you then, Harry? Got yourself a nice woman?'

'Not sure I want one.'

He snorted, ''Course you do. Going it on your own's no fun.'

'Sorry about Clara, Mousey.'

'Don't be, lad. The state she was in . . . wouldn't keep a dog like it. I just wish she'd gone straight off . . . y'know?'

I nodded. I did know. Clara had gone on a skiing holiday in Switzerland with Monica, Mike's wife. A freak snowstorm had blown up. There'd been an accident and both women had gone over the edge of a glacier. Rescue teams had battled to reach them and had finally airlifted them on stretchers into a helicopter.

It was too late for Monica – she was already dead. But Clara was still alive, just. However, apart from multiple fractures of ribs and limbs, she had suffered fractures to C2 and C3 of the spine. The injuries had meant she was permanently paralysed, reliant on a respirator and her life was measured in months as she suffered a succession of lowering lung infections.

Mousey had had to endure watching his wife dying for nearly two years, knowing there was nothing he could do to help except provide all the private medical care needed to keep her at home for as long as possible, which wasn't that long. The fact they had both endured emotional agony in the process was crystal clear.

Mike had avoided coming into contact with Mousey during the whole of the time Clara lay suffering.

'Can't face him,' he'd once told me. 'I've lost Monica, yes, but her end was quick and I thank God for that. But *poor* Clara . . . it's bloody terrible.'

I tried, gently, to steer Mousey's thoughts away from the pain and back to the reason why he wanted to see me at Wetherby racecourse.

'What can I do to help you, Mousey?'

Jackie jumped up and began collecting the coffee mugs.

'Leave you two to have a spot of man-talk in private. I'll be in the kitchen.' She turned to me. 'Stop and have lunch with us, Harry.'

Before I could answer, Mousey cut in, shaking his head, 'No, no, lass. I'm taking Harry to The Cat and Fiddle for a meal. My treat.'

'Well, if you're sure . . .'

'We've already arranged it.'

'OK, then, enjoy yourselves.' She disappeared with the tray.

'Rather speak to you over lunch, if that's OK? Wouldn't like our Jackie hearing what I've got to say.'

'Sure, that's fine with me.'

'Don't mean to be cloak and dagger, Harry, but I'm not proud of what I've done. And Jackie, well, she's a lass in a million, a trillion. I would hate her to think badly of me. She's been a wonderful help when Clara needed it. Patrick and me, we wouldn't have got through all this without Jackie being there for us.' His voice lowered. 'An' Patrick seems to be taking after his old dad.' He shook his head disapprovingly. 'Jackie doesn't deserve that. She worships our Patrick. Wouldn't like her to get hurt.'

'Look, Mousey, if you've changed your mind about discussing whatever it was, it doesn't matter. I can always shove off, leave you in peace.'

'God, Harry, no. Don't offer me a get-out. It's damn hard enough now. And I must tell you, I have to.'

He rose abruptly and motioned me through the door, grabbing his trilby from the hall peg as we walked through.

'We're going, Jackie. Not sure when we'll be back.'

'OK, enjoy the food.' Her voice trickled through from the kitchen. 'See you later.'

Mousey walked me out of the front door and we climbed into my car.

'Directions for the pub, Mousey?'

The Cat and Fiddle was a typical old Yorkshire pub. Little concession to modernization had taken place but from the welcoming open fire crackling away in the big fireplace to the smile on the land-lord's face, it gave off a reassuring cheerfulness. Before the smoking ban, it would no doubt have been filled with a fug of wreathing tobacco smoke but now, in the clean atmosphere, the many horse brasses adorning the walls were unsullied and gleamed brightly. There was a defin-ite 'coming home' feel to the place. Without doubt, you could easily get cast here. And it was already starting to fill up.

'Very popular, it is.' Mousey nodded to the landlord and made his way to a table in the far alcove. 'Started coming here centuries ago, when I was a young lad. It's changed but not that much. The food's first rate, though – basic beef but *real* food, if you follow me.'

I did. I'd scanned the 'Specials' board on the way to the table. The selection looked good to me.

'It's not fancy but neither are the prices. You want fancy, there're plenty of places selling that – and I dare bet half the tables are empty. Whereas, here . . .' He flipped a hand towards the door.

It was a good job we'd turned up early. The tables were filling rapidly.

I went to the bar and bought drinks while Mousey had a look through the menu. It wasn't a hard choice. We both had the same – T-bone steaks. And Mousey was right – it was damn good food. We finished with coffee and that, too, was excellent.

'Right then, Harry lad, the reason why I wanted to see you . . .' Mousey set down his cup with deliberation. I waited. 'Can I swear you to secrecy?'

'Is it legal?'

'You and I both know nothing's black or white in life. More like a mucky grey.' I waited some more. I realized why he'd suggested this venue. There was not a cat in hell's chance of being overheard above the hubbub in the crowded room.

His voice was so low I struggled to catch what he was saying.

'There's a lot of folk who would decry me for what I've done but that's their problem. All I want you to do is promise you won't spread it around nor say anything to Jackie – especially not to Jackie.'

'Whatever you tell me, Mousey, I guarantee I won't mention it to Jackie.'

'Good man.' He lifted his coffee and drained it before running a nervous hand through his short grey hair. 'It's about Alice . . . Alice Goode.' I stared at him in astonishment. 'Yes, I know, it was you who discovered her body.' A spasm of pain twisted his face. 'Was she in, y'know . . . a very bad state?' He hesitated. 'What I'm asking, Harry, is would she have suffered very much? Or could it have been a quick death?'

'You want the truth, Mousey?' He nodded. 'She wasn't in a pretty state. If I had to guess, I'd say hopefully she didn't live long enough to suffer. The first blow could have killed her but it looked like she'd been hit over the head several times. Sorry, but yes, she was in a terrible condition.'

He passed a hand across his forehead and made a low, animal sound of distress.

'Why do you want to know, Mousey? What was Alice to you?'

He took a handkerchief from his jacket pocket and blew his nose hard. 'Did you . . . were you . . . ever a client of Alice's?'

'The police asked me that question. And I'll tell you the same thing I told them – the truth. I never had sex with her.'

He sighed deeply. 'Somehow that makes it all right.'

'Makes what all right?'

'What I'm going to ask you to do.' He blew his nose again and struggled to get control of his emotions. And again I waited, but this time with a distinct shiver tracing itself down my back.

'Harry, you discovered the murderers of Carl Smith at Leicester races – the two that have just died in prison. Damn sure *that* wasn't an accident. 'Course, the police will never prove it, one way or the other. And then again, you found the killer of that golf course job.'

The shiver down my spine increased in intensity.

'Harry, I've plenty of money. I can pay you. I want you to find Alice's murderer for me. Make him pay for his crime.'

I'd known it was coming but his words still hit me like a bucket of cold water. We stared at each other and I shook my head uncomprehendingly.

'Why?'

He gave a brief, sad smile. 'Because, Harry, Alice was my mistress – for about thirty years.'

Eleven

My jaw must have hit the pub's flagstone floor.

'If you never slept with Alice,' Mousey continued, 'you wouldn't understand.'

'Try me,' I managed to croak.

'Clara, God bless her, was brought up strictly. She was a perfect wife in all ways. Except . . .' He stared at his empty cup. 'She did her duty, as she saw it, by producing my two sons. After that, well . . . there wasn't any "after that". You get my drift?' I did. 'Clara, she had the babies, was completely satisfied. But the babies weren't enough for me. You've been married, Harry, I don't need to say any more.'

'No, Mousey, leave it there.'

He sat back in his chair and sighed. 'Knew you'd understand. So, will you do the job?'

83

I played with a spare beer mat, buying some time.

'Come on, lad, what's to think about? Alice was lovely – in her own way, she was a lady.'

'Yes, I do know.'

'So you *did* sleep with her?'

'I didn't, not ever. But I know she was a caring person.'

'Oh, she was. She was that.'

I stopped fiddling with the mat and looked straight at him. The craggy, hard lines on his face seemed to have somehow softened, exposing an almost tender expression. I could see that, strange though it might appear, given her profession, if Alice had kept him going for thirty years, the man must, at the least, have held her in fond regard. I doubt it was love. His love had been reserved for Clara. But certainly Mousey had warm feelings for Alice. Or had done, until her murder.

The picture of her lying upon the kitchen floor came graphically into my mind. I could see the white, shattered skull bone, the darkness of the congealed blood, the bloated flies . . . Even the obscene smell, including the terror she must have felt at the last, came back and flooded my nostrils. I clenched my throat to prevent me starting to gag.

Alice had deserved a normal lifespan and a dignified end.

'Please.' Mousey reached for my hand and gripped it fiercely. 'It's the last thing I can do for her after all she's done for me. You will do it for me, Harry, won't you?'

I shook my head. 'No. No, I won't.'

He released his grip as though my skin had suddenly burnt him.

'But . . . I will do it, for Alice.'

A slow, satisfied smile spread across his face. 'Harry, lad, our Jackie is a lass out on her own but, by God, you're up there alongside her.' This time he grasped my hand and shook it vigorously.

'One thing, though . . .'

'Anything, Harry, just ask.'

'You don't pay me, right?'

'Nay, lad, I must.' He pulled me towards him. 'It's a matter of honour . . . I *must*.'

'Look, Mousey, it's the one condition. I'll do the job. I won't drop my hands. But whether I get the bastard who killed Alice or not, and I hope to God I do, you're not paying me.'

As a trainer, Mousey would know exactly what I meant when I said I won't drop my hands. It's a trainer's instructions to a jockey not to stop trying until he passes the winning post.

'I'm a Yorkshire man, lad, I pay my debts.'

We faced each other off across the table.

'Look at it this way, Mousey: any debts you owe, you've paid time and time again in the love you gave to Clara. Right?'

He sucked a breath in. 'Damn nigh killed me an' all, it did.'

'I know that, and so does everybody else. Some-times it isn't money that pays debts, and this is one of those times.'

'It'll cut into your racing time, lad.'

'Yes.'

'You'll lose money.'

'Yes.'

'An' you're not bothered?'

85

'Nobody likes to lose money but this is something different. Let me be honest with you: I'm damn sure there's more to Alice's murder than the police or anybody else is aware of. But the two prisoners on remand that got finished off, they're tied in to her death as well somehow, I think. And it goes back a very long way. Can I ask you, did you know if there was any other man, like yourself, who was a long-standing client of Alice's?'

'Well, obviously, it was her way of earning a living. Even though she is – was – married to Darren Goode, he's in and out of jug so much she hardly sees him.'

'Yes, I know about the casual clients but what I'm asking you is do you know of any other, shall we say, "special" client, from years back?'

'I don't know how to answer that. It wasn't something we talked about really. Well, you don't, not in those circumstances.' He pushed his empty coffee cup around in the saucer. I could see the embarrassment but I could also see he was holding something in reserve.

'Come on, Mousey, this is me, right? How do you expect me to nail the bastard if I don't have anything to go on?'

Fishing in my pocket, I pulled out the piece of paper that Jake Smith had written on.

'Here, have a look at this, then tell me what you know.'

He took his time, his face screwing up with the effort to understand what he was reading.

'It's a riddle, for sure. Can't make much of it, to be honest.'

I looked him squarely in the face. 'Was it you who said the first quotation?'

'Me?' His face was pure bewilderment. 'Nay, lad, it certainly wasn't me.' He reread the note. 'But I reckon you were right – looks like she had another long-term horse in her stable, doesn't it?'

'Yes.'

I believed him that he wasn't the man who had said the words. They were far too flowery for Mousey. But I was disappointed he didn't know the other man. However, looking at it positively, I had actually found out the identity of one of the two mice – Mousey himself. That meant two out of the four people were definitely identified. It was a start.

'Where did you get this from?' He flicked the note with a fingernail.

'I'm sorry, I can't tell you just now.'

'But it's referring to Alice, isn't it?'

'Yes, it is.'

'Oh, well, I'll leave it to you, Harry.'

'Just one more thing: did you know if Alice had any children?'

'Not with Darren, she didn't.'

It was the way Mousey said the words that made me hold my breath and wait for what came next.

'Not sure I should say anything, promised Alice I wouldn't.'

'Oh, come on, Mousey, it's for Alice's sake I'm doing this. I need a bit of help here.' There was a long, ongoing silence and I began to think he was stonewalling.

Then he said, 'I think she had a baby . . . something about it being adopted.'

'Do you know what sex it was?'

'Rumour going round it was a girl. But I don't *know.*'

'Thank you.'

'Shouldn't have said but . . . circumstances being as they are . . .'

'Do you know who the father was?'

'Not exactly, except he was in racing, an' he was probably married.'

We sat and stared at each other for a long moment, then I asked the big question.

'Were *you* the father, Mousey?'

He held my gaze. 'For my sins, I'm not sure. It kind of slipped out at a . . . delicate moment. Alice didn't really mean to tell me she'd got pregnant. She wouldn't say any more than that. I did ask her but . . .' He shook his head. 'I don't know whether she herself knew who the father was.'

'How long ago was it?'

'God, years.' He wiped a hand across his forehead. 'Years and years back. When I first knew her.'

'So, what are we talking, twenty-five years or so?'

'More like thirty, I reckon.'

'Do you know what happened to the baby, who adopted her?'

'No.'

'Was there anything different about Alice that last time you went to see her?'

'Now you mention it, there was. She was kind of nervous and excited. I asked if she'd won the lottery or something and she said, "Sort of." When I asked what she meant, she said something on the lines of how strange that the bloodstock was returning. Then she said she was expecting the

88

passport of the filly soon. Damned odd, if you ask me. I have no idea what she meant. Does it make any sense to you?'

'Hmmm . . .' I didn't want to say any more to Mousey but I was beginning to see the picture on the jigsaw. 'How long ago did you see her?'

'Couple of days or so before . . . before she died.'

As far as I knew, that meant Jake Smith was still the last person to have spoken with Alice. Apart from the killer himself, of course.

'That's all I can tell you, Harry. Don't know if any of it helps.'

'Oh, it does, Mousey. Thanks.'

'Best be getting back, lad. Our Jackie will start fretting soon about where I am.'

'Yes, of course.'

I stood up and together we left The Cat and Fiddle.

We drove back to his house and I dropped him off.

'Can't tell you what it means to me, knowing you'll be working on it. I feel I'm giving back to her. It's all I can do now. I wasn't like the other lads, after all the skirts. Alice was the only one, apart from Clara.'

'I'm sorry I can't level with you just now, Mousey. But if we can come up with the man's name and string him up in court, I'll tell you the whole tale. How's that?'

'Good enough for me, lad. Take care of yourself.' He raised a hand and walked on up to his front door.

I watched him safely inside, then gunned the Mazda back to Nottinghamshire.

Twelve

I didn't go back to Harlequin Cottage. If the police had my home under surveillance, they were going to be unlucky. Coming off the A1 at Ollerton roundabout, I took the road past Rufford.

In the days when Annabel still lived with me, we'd often gone to visit Rufford, walked round the old abbey with the original bath-house and orangery. We also, on some occasions, took my half-sister, Silvie, in her specially adapted wheelchair. She, like us, loved the walk through the bluebell-carpeted woods.

At the far end, the massive lake was home to an astonishing number of wild birds, including Canada Geese, Ruddy Ducks and Kingfishers. There was also a booth by the lakeside walkway that sold fabulous ice creams. Silvie had loved those, too.

The memories spooled through my head as I passed the impressive entrance gates leading to Rufford Park but I held down the emotion that accompanied them and drove on. If I could have foreseen how my life was going to pan out, I would have embraced and enjoyed each precious minute even more. But one certainty was life didn't stop, ever changing from one breath to the next, flowing on inexorably. Life was like a horse race – you couldn't ever go back.

Coming to Gunthorpe Bridge, spanning the

Trent, I swooped over and followed the road into Bingham.

It was barely evening but several eating places were already open and doing business. I dived into the fish-and-chip shop, queued and ordered two jacket potatoes with baked beans and salad – one I had doused liberally with mayonnaise and one, abstemiously, without. I would always be weight-watching while ever I wore jockey silks. Two bottles of Coke for Jake completed my order and I made my way back to the car park. The potatoes were covered in foil inside polystyrene containers with a double wrapping of paper. They wouldn't be piping hot by the time I reached Burton Lazars but they'd be hot enough to enjoy.

It was dark by the time I turned into the lane leading to Nathaniel's place but I wasn't taking any chances and had driven the last quarter mile with only the sidelights working. It was a reasonable bet that by now most commuters would be safely back behind their own front doors. But it only needed one person to spot us and the future was going to be very constrained.

Pushing away the thought of life behind bars, I pulled up between the now-familiar tall holly hedges either side of the drive, doused my sidelights and simply sat and waited. If someone eagle-eyed had noticed, it wasn't going to take long before they appeared. Nobody would stand around for long in the dark with the temperature plummeting.

On the other hand, two rapidly cooling dinners said there'd been enough hanging about.

I put a hand on the door handle then bit back

a startled yell as my heart went into overdrive. A face suddenly appeared on the other side of the glass and two eyes looked straight into mine.

Then the face smiled.

I flung myself out of the car and leaned against the wing. 'Bloody hell! You trying to send me to my grave?' I hissed.

The smile widened. 'Steady on, Harry boy, don't piss your pants. And if that's grub you've brought, hand it over. I'm fucking starving.'

I reached in, thrust the parcel of food into his hands and we proceeded down the garden path to the studio. Although I couldn't see his face in the darkness, his smile was almost tangible.

'You think that was funny, you bloody idiot?' Angrily, I rounded on him when we were safely inside with the studio door closed. 'I was waiting to see if anybody had seen me arrive.'

'And somebody had . . . me.'

'I should have locked you in.'

'I'd have smashed the window again.' He was still grinning as he ripped off the protective layers from the takeaway and the delicious smell of food seeped out and filled the room.

'Not all for me, then?' He'd seen the two portions.

'You reckon you could eat all that much?'

'Yeah, don't see why not.'

'Tough,' I swiped one from under his nose, 'this is mine.'

We shared the one knife for cutting up and I allowed him the fork while I made do with a spoon. He finished first and I chewed the last of mine while he glugged down a bottle of Coke.

'So,' I said and licked some bean juice from my finger. 'Two men dead . . .'

'Ah, you've seen a newspaper.'

'Yes.'

'Not worth a tear, either of the fuckers.'

'The law would have taken care of them. There was no need for you to order them killed.'

'And just who says it *was* me?'

'Now, come on, we both know it was.'

'And if . . . *if* . . . it was, it's saved the system the trouble, and forking out a packet, so I'd say that's a result.'

'You're not above the law, Jake.'

He shrugged and reached for the second bottle of Coke. 'Has the fuzz been round yet, then?'

'Haven't been home to find out.'

He chuckled softly. 'Can't fault you, Harry boy.'

'But I have been to someone else's . . .'

'Oh, yeah.' He eyed me. 'Like who?'

'Someone who knew Alice.'

'One of her punters?'

'A bit more than that, I'd say.'

'A mate, then?'

'Oh, yes, definitely a friend, a long-standing friend. As in about thirty years standing.' I screwed up the sticky wrapping paper. 'To be more accurate, though' – I pitched the balled paper into the waste bin – 'it was probably lying down.'

He gave a dirty laugh. 'OK, Harry boy, who was it?'

'Mousey, you know, Mousey Brown, trainer as was?'

'Boozy Brown . . . right.'

'Did you know about him and Alice?'

'No.'

'Hmmm . . . That piece of paper you gave me, with the quotes on it—'

'Yeah?'

'I've worked out some of the meaning.'

'Helped then, did it?'

'Yes.'

'So, have you found out who killed her?'

'No, but I'm working on it.'

Jake sighed. 'I'm fucking bored stiff stuck here, lost my bloody mobile . . .'

'What do you want me to do, Jake, pack it in?'

'What I want is for you to find the bastard, hand him in to the coppers on a spit and let them roast his balls.'

'Elegantly put.'

'Anyway, where's this Brown come into the frame?'

'Alice mentioned two mice . . . he's definitely one of them.'

'And the other?'

I shook my head. 'Not worked that out yet.'

'But you will, Harry boy, every confidence.' He drained the last of the Coke and, following my example, aimed it at the wastepaper bin.

'That last time you, er . . . visited Alice, did you happen to see a photograph lying around at all? It would have been one of a young woman.'

He gave me a wary, sideways glance. 'Why?'

'It's important.'

'Might have done.'

'Look,' I said, getting exasperated, 'I need some help here or I pack in trying. Did you or not?'

'It wasn't exactly "lying" around.' I waited. 'Alice went to the bogs, y'know, after—'

'Yes, I don't want the full SP.'

'Well, you're getting it. I was there all night, right? We had sex in her bed.'

'Jake—'

'Shurrup. You asked and I'm tellin' you. Like I said, after we had sex, Alice went to the bogs. While she was there, I put some money out for her. You know how it goes in her business – a raid's on the cards at any time. An' I wanted to make sure she got paid, like, not leave it till morning, you with me?' I nodded. 'But I didn't want her seeing the money just then. I mean,' he leered at mc, 'there was hours to go yet, before dawn, an' o' course I'd just got out of stir . . .'

'Yes,' I said hastily, 'you've made your point.'

'Anyway, she'd left her bag on the dressing table so—'

'You put the money in there?'

'S'right. An' that's when I saw the photo.'

My heart beat a little faster. This time we were getting somewhere.

'Nice bit of skirt, she was.' He pursed his lips and nodded. 'Could have done her somc damage.'

'Did you see a name at all? Maybe on the back?'

'The photo was sticking out a bit from an envelope addressed to Alice, postmarked three days before.'

'Go on,' I urged him.

'Well, I turned the photo over and it had 2016 printed at the top, followed by some handwriting.'

I felt familiar prickles down the back of my neck. 'What did it say?'

'It said, *Me, at Barbara's.*'

95

I stared at him. 'No name?'

He shook his head. 'No name.'

Disappointment obliterated my prick of excitement and I slumped in the chair. 'No help there, then.'

'Except . . .'

'What?'

'The photo had been taken in a stable yard.'

'*What?*' I jumped up. 'Did you recognize whose stables?'

''Course I fucking didn't. Not a jockey, am I?'

'No, sorry . . . wait a minute, though.' I ran through what he had just told me. 'The writing on the back of the photo said *at Barbara's*. There's only one trainer I know who's called Barbara.'

'Right, then, y'reckon it's her?'

'Can't be sure, I didn't see the stable yard in the photograph.'

'But I did, Harry boy.' We sat in silence, looking at each other. 'If you drive me to this Barbara's, I could tell you if it was the same stables.'

I nodded slowly. 'But it would be very tricky. Neither of us could risk being seen.'

'You said this photo was important. Do y'mean it could lead us to the killer?'

'Not directly, no, but if I find out who the woman in the photo is, I stand a fair chance of tracking down who her father was. Now that would certainly help.'

'Come on then, what you waiting for? Get your arse in gear and drive me over there.' He was up and at the door before he'd finished speaking.

I shook my head. 'It's too bloody dangerous. If we're seen we'll both be sharing a cell.'

He squared his shoulders and very slowly began walking back towards me, his eyes cold, emotionless. Gripping my shirt collar, he thrust his face to within an inch of mine. 'And if we don't, I'm still in deepest shit.' He shook me violently. 'How's this helping your concussion?'

He had effortlessly homed in on my weakness. I struggled to free his hands but he was locked on to me.

'So, get your car keys and get this show on the fucking road, now.' He shook me a couple more times to make sure the message had gone home before abruptly letting go. 'Got it?'

'Yes,' I mumbled, trying to reassemble my teeth, not daring to attempt a nod. What damage he'd done to my already bruised brain wasn't something to dwell on, but things were definitely spinning round. Staggering forwards towards the door, I was helped on by a solid shove in the middle of my back.

Thirteen

'Describe the yard, the actual layout. How many boxes were there?'

We were driving through Leicestershire, roughly retracing my earlier route. The lanes were narrow, unlit once we'd passed through the outskirts of Melton Mowbray, and yet again I was relying on sidelights.

'Boxes?' Jake snatched his head round to glare at me. 'What you on about?'

97

'OK, stables.'

'How the hell do you expect me to remember?'

'Your subconscious will have registered a lot more than you think. Just concentrate on the moment you found Alice's bag. Try to visualize the photo. How many stable doors do you reckon?'

'I don't fucking know.' Jake blew out a despairing sigh.

'A lot? Only four or five? More?'

'A lot more, yeah, there was a lot now I come to think about it. Seemed like the yard carried on an' all, like, round a corner, maybe.'

'Good. You're doing great – keep thinking about that photo. Tell me anything that comes into your mind.'

'Mostly I was looking at that bird. I could really fancy her, missen. A real bit of all right, she was.'

'OK, tell me what *she* looked like.'

'Phwaaar . . . a real cracking pair of Bristol's, she had. The rest of her figure was spot on, an' all.'

'What about her hair – what colour was that?'

'Dark, she was dark. Wore it long, down on her shoulders. An' she was tall.'

'How come you could tell that?'

'She was standing next to one of the stable doors. Her head was level with the top hinge.'

Before I could comment there was a tell-tale gleam of light beyond the next bend that lit up the hedgerow.

'Duck, I'm putting lights on.'

But he had spotted the approaching vehicle and was already sliding down almost out of sight into the passenger well. The car powered on without a glance in our direction.

'You can surface now.' I changed down and swung left. 'If she was as tall as the top hinge that would make her probably around five foot nine, I reckon.'

'Who cares? Like I say, she was a real looker.' He trumpeted out a noisy blast of air. 'I could do her some damage.'

I ignored him and concentrated on driving. For a man who claimed he couldn't remember he'd done amazingly well, albeit by employing his baser instincts. Two miles further on, I turned down an unmade track and carried on at barely crawling speed.

'This is a back way. I've used it before . . . safer than the main entrance. We'll have to risk if these lower stables are being used.'

'How likely is it?'

'Last time I was here, they were being used as storage. Let's hope they still are.'

The rough track eventually curved around a bend and, up ahead, outlined against the starlit sky, I could see the dark outline of buildings. Immediately it triggered with gut-churning clarity the memories of the night I received the knife wound in my left arm. I swallowed very hard, forced down the unwelcome remembrance and steered the car into the side.

'Now what?'

I cut the engine. 'Now we stay out of sight, walk up as far as the main yard and see if you recognize it.'

'And if I do?'

I shrugged. 'We'll know more than we do right now.'

Leaving the car, we walked towards the lower stable block, stooping uncomfortably, making sure we were below the level of the hedge on either side. Jake was taller than I was, much, much heavier and he cursed continuously under his breath as he followed me, his feet falling into unexpected potholes and stubbing up against loose stones.

'This had better be fucking worth it, Harry boy.'

I stopped abruptly, swung round. We were so close I could see the glint of his eyeballs in the starlight.

'Cut it out.'

'What?'

'You heard. Stop grousing. If anybody hears you, we're done for. And while we're at it, if you have a go at me again you can kiss goodbye to my help. I value my health. I get more than enough injuries racing.'

He gave a disparaging snort. 'And what about your lady friend's health, eh?'

'Leave her out of it.'

'Oh, I will, I will. If you come up with the killer.'

'If I don't, it won't be because I didn't try. But she's pregnant. And I don't think even you would stoop so low as to kill a baby.'

'But you can't be certain, can you, Harry boy?'

I gritted my teeth and, at that moment, I hated him. He was so sure of himself that maybe he *was* capable of such a sadistic act. I hoped to God he wasn't. The whole conversation seemed unreal. This was Annabel – and her baby – we were talking about. And because she still meant everything to me, despite being with another man, no way could I cop out from helping Jake. It was a complete bastard of a situation.

I think had it only been my own skin under threat, I'd have opted to drive over to Newark Police Station and turn him in. It would mean jail for me, but even that might prove preferable to being trapped like this. The whole situation was a bloody nightmare. But, as I desperately considered it even remotely viable, a picture of Annabel suffering horribly at his hands came into my mind and I knew I couldn't do it, couldn't risk her in any way.

'You're a grade A bastard. And when someone takes you out – because with your lifestyle, believe it, they will – you'll be burning in hell a long time.' I ground out the words. But I realized, even as I said them, he knew just how impotent and helpless I really felt.

He stood there silently in the dark lane – and then laughed in my face.

The sourness of humiliation came up like bile in the back of my throat. For no one other than Annabel would I submit to this emasculation.

Blazing rage surged up inside me with frightening force, threatening to sweep me away out of control. My nails were biting so deeply into the palms of my hands I could feel the stickiness where they'd pierced the skin, drawn blood. If I'd belonged on his level I would have killed him there and then.

Instead, I turned and raced away up the lane, burning up the negative energy, using it for fuel. I ran all the rest of the way, fetching up finally, gasping for breath, at the side of one of the buildings. I could hear Jake pounding after me but, without waiting, eased my way round the corner of the brick wall and came to the door. It opened to my push and I was again inside the stables where the violence I'd witnessed – and suffered – still seemed to hang menacingly in the air, an almost tangible energy. But that was all that was present – no horses, no people, empty.

They do say it is the sense of smell that evokes memory. Right then, I'd be forced to agree. There was an all-pervading odour of animal feed, horse nuts. It immediately threw me back to a hellish few hours spent in this place. When I thought of Annabel, as she had been that night, I felt rage and bile rise up at the back of my throat, threatening to choke me with its intensity. It was not a place I wanted to revisit.

Behind me, the door swung inwards as Jake Smith blundered his way in.

'Where the bloody hell are you? It's as dark as a nun's habit . . .'

'Keep it down. If anyone hears you, we've had it.'

'So, where's this stable yard I'm supposed to be sussing?'

'About a quarter mile further up. This is the overflow stables, apart from the main block. Follow me and for goodness' sake keep quiet. Barbara keeps a couple of German shepherds and a mastiff for protection. And believe me, if they're loose you wouldn't want to meet them. They're very good at their job.'

'Christ! I'm for off.'

'This was your idea, right? Let's finish the job.'

Without waiting for his reply, I headed off for

the occupied stables and he fell into step. We walked in silence and I kept my eyes and ears open and tuned out the usual night-time sounds. The hedgerow was alive with rustles and flutters from roosting birds alarmed by our presence. At one point a rat appeared almost at our feet before hastily sliding back into the dense herbage.

'Fucking things give me the creeps,' Jake growled.

'Yeah, enough germs in one nip to see off a regiment.'

But apart from the wildlife, nothing else stirred – no dogs, no people – and we cautiously ended up hugging the wall of one of the top stables. Following the line of the wall until it brought us into the main yard, I held up a hand.

'Wait,' I hissed. 'This is where we are most likely to come across someone. Now, can you see if this was the place in the photograph?'

'I don't know about see anything, but this place fucking stinks to high heaven.'

'Does it?' I said in surprise. I was so used to the, to me, magical smell of horses, including horse feed, tack cleaning materials and the inevitable muck heap, that I'd never considered anybody could dislike the smell of a stable yard.

He continued cursing while he peered around trying to identify the layout. Since it was merely starlight aiding our vision, it was tricky. Evening stables had long been and gone and it wasn't time for the final last check for the night so no lights were switched on.

'Was there anything significant you could identify?' I tried to help him out, mindful that, at any

103

moment, Barbara's canine troops could be sent out on manoeuvres – man being the operative bit. Or bite.

'That door,' he whispered, 'where she was stood. Well, at the side was a stretch of wall, right?' He pointed from below waist height for safety. 'I reckon it could be over there, before the stables turn away at the corner. Might see better if we get closer.'

I grimaced. It was going to take us well into bandit country to go in much further. But without waiting for my agreement, he flattened against the bricks and walked himself along sideways in the deeper strip of shadow. With no choice but to follow, I did the same.

'Yes . . .!'

I heard the barely contained exclamation of triumph and practically bumped into him as he abruptly halted.

'There . . . do y'see . . . that plaque thing, high up on the wall? It was on the photo, broke up the line of brickwork, y'know? I noticed that. Do you see it?'

I did see. It wasn't a plaque, it was a dated brick stating the stables had been built nearly seventy years ago. With an unpleasant lurch in my stomach, I realized if Jake was correct, this was the stable yard in the photograph. And my friend, Barbara, was the owner.

The name Barbara had been written on the rear of the photograph. This in turn raised questions about the girl. Just who was she? What was the connection between them? Did I actually already know her?

'Are you *sure* this is the place?'

Jake nodded vigorously. 'I reckon it is . . . so . . . what do we do now, Harry boy?'

'Get the hell out of here, back the way we came. I've met Barbara's dogs so they know me, but I certainly don't want to meet them again just now, not down here, in the dark.'

Harlequin Cottage was a still, black outline when I drove in through the gateway. There'd been no other vehicles parked up in the country lane on my approach, none parked up on my gravel in front of the cottage. And, since leaving Jake at the studio, I'd made very sure no one had tailed me.

I opened up, switched on some lights and breathed in the peace of being home. However many times I returned, the feeling of security and 'rightness' never diminished. This place was where I needed to be, a positive antidote to the crazy mayhem going on in the world beyond the gate. Since Annabel had left, Leo had deflected, to a certain extent, the feeling of coming home to an empty house. It manifested in a feeling of wrap-around welcome.

I made tea, took a mug through to my office and started typing up some notes on the computer. I found it by far best to immediately get my thoughts and feelings down, fixing them in place where I could reread them. I needed to try to remember the words that were said, the nuances of them, words that were left unsaid and, most importantly, the facial expressions of the person saying them. All too often, if I hadn't written them down until the following day, I struggled

105

to remember. Very often, rereading them at some future time, I'd pick up a pointer – an inconsistency maybe – which set me off on another stream of thought, often with astonishing results.

I supped tea and typed, corrected and typed some more. I'd reached the printing off followed by making more tea stage when Leo came through the cat flap. How he knew I was back was a mystery. A certain neighbour from the village, a good half-mile away down the country lane, had once told me she'd been out in her garden calling her cat in, had spotted Leo at 7.15. I knew he'd come home just after eight that night, five minutes after I'd arrived. His radar was superb.

'Hello, you,' I said in answer to his welcoming bellow. 'Dinner, is it?'

He'd joined me a few minutes later in the lounge where I was now stretched out on the settee. Hastily rescuing my printed pages from where they were strewn across my person, I made room for him. With a sigh of pleasure, he dropped his considerable weight across my solar plexus and purred with the subtlety of a road-maker's drill.

'Duty all done then with the ladies?'

He squinted up at me with vivid green eyes and purred louder.

'Take that as a yes, then.'

I returned my attention to reading over my notes.

Mousey had taken me into his confidence, exposed his less-than-virtuous past, but had trusted me. I wasn't about to betray him, but something in our exchange that I'd committed to paper was setting up a tingle of disbelief. I'd noted down some of his mannerisms – those I could recall –

and his answer to one of the questions I'd put to him had resulted in an evasive shuffling of his beer mat. Could be nothing, could be something.

I looked at the question again. The gut feeling persisted, grew. There had been occasions in the recent past when I'd been tracking a killer and paying heed to my instincts had been essential. I paid heed to them now. I liked Mousey, felt very sorry for him, but was forced to acknowledge the wisdom being shown to me.

When he'd answered that particular question, Mousey had lied.

Fourteen

'Face it, Harry, the situation's bizarre. Just where do you stand on this?'

We were in the bar at The Horseshoes having a lunchtime drink after morning stables – along with half the stable lads from the nearby racing stables. I'd just filled Mike in on the events of my nocturnal jaunt with Jake to Barbara's stables.

'I don't stand at all, Mike, I'm spreadeagled, over a bloody barrel.'

He shook his head. 'Couldn't you go to the police? Tell them everything from the beginning? It's what they get paid to do – sort out the messes of this world.'

'And then what? Go round to Sir Jeffrey, tell him he has to place a twenty-four-hour guard on Annabel?'

'One thing you could do.' He looked sideways at me, pursing his lips.

I knew I didn't want to hear. 'OK, what?'

'Start divorce proceedings.'

'*What?*'

Even above the noise in the crowded bar that would have easily qualified for noise pollution, my voice carried. Several heads turned.

'Calm down, Harry.' Mike flashed a quick, reassuring smile at the inquiring faces.

'I don't believe you said that.' I took a savage snatch at my beer.

'Think about it, mate. You go in for a divorce, Annabel's nothing to do with you any more and Jake the snake slithers away back into his hole. You'll be taking away his bargaining ace.' Mike nodded, pleased with himself for coming up with the idea.

'If that's the best you can offer, don't bother.' I glowered at him. 'It might help the cause if you could put a name to the woman in the photo instead of coming up with damn fool suggestions.'

He supped his pint thoughtfully. 'OK, well, how about I throw an impromptu party, invite some of the people that might be in the know – Barbara for one? I would suggest they feel free to bring a friend . . .' adding quickly, '. . . plus a couple of bottles, of course. You could get chatting – never know what might turn up. People get very loose-tongued after a few drinks. And if they're in what they consider a "safe" environment, they might let slip a gem or two they wouldn't normally have done.'

'That idea's just made up for the lousy one. I

reckon you could be right. Do you remember I told you about the party Elspeth Maudsley held at her house?'

'Just before she gave up as a trainer?'

'Yes. And what a gold nugget I found out at that bash.' I grinned at him. 'This is the sort of thing the police *can't* get through HOLMES or anywhere else. It's priceless hunting ground for gossip.'

He grinned back. 'I'll get on to it soon as we get back to the stables. Oh . . .' He hesitated.

'What?'

'I'll have to run it past Pen first, I mean.'

''Course you will.' I carried on grinning, 'You're not a carefree single man any more now.'

'And, by God, aren't I thankful for that. Now, another beer?'

'Better make it a mineral water,' I said regretfully, thinking of the weight I seemed to be packing on. 'I'll be back racing soon.' Even as I said it, my pulse quickened with pleasure. It seemed like weeks since I'd been racing. Then I found myself echoing his words. 'But, by God, aren't I thankful for that.'

'And so am I,' said a voice behind us.

'Samuel' – Mike swung round – 'good to see you. Have a seat. What are you drinking?'

'Not a lot since I'm driving today. But a pint would sit well.' Samuel turned to me as Mike motioned to the barman, tapped his glass and held up an index finger. 'Glad to hear you're on the mend, Harry. Best news I've heard since a couple of days ago.'

I cast a glance at Mike to see if he had caught

Samuel's drift. He obviously hadn't – bewilderment was spread across his face.

'It's the reason Chloe didn't come with me today,' Samuel went on. 'Had the police round to see us, asking if we knew anything. It upset her quite a bit. 'Course, we didn't know anything – nothing to help them at all. Reading between the lines, I don't think they've got a clue.'

'What are we talking about?' Mike's eyebrows had raised themselves to his hairline at the mention of police calling at the house.

'You must have seen it, I mean to say it was in all the papers, on television . . .'

'Samuel means the deaths of the two prisoners.'

'Oh, yes, the Leicester races murder. But I wouldn't say it was good news. I know the authorities are floundering, or seem to be; can't exactly make a case for murder but they can't seem to get to the bottom of it either. In any case, it's still basically two unexplained deaths.'

'Well, that's your personal opinion, Mike, and I respect that, I do, but from my perspective, and I'm sure Chloe's, it's a swift end to the whole dreadful matter.'

I'd not mentioned the deaths to Mike so his opinion was new to me. I suppose my own feelings fell somewhere in the middle. Yes, there was relief that, as Samuel had said, it had put a quick end to the horrible affair. And if anyone was going to be dancing on their graves because of what they'd done, I was the most likely candidate. However, I wasn't a vindictive man. Certainly didn't wish to be one. Hatred was a self-destructive emotion. But I could appreciate Samuel's strong

110

feelings. He was Chloe's father and suffering the fallout along with her. Just what Chloe thought about this latest shocking development was her own business.

What I had no intention of disclosing was Jake Smith's involvement. No way did I condone his behaviour. Frankly, he scared the hell out of me. The sooner I could free myself the sooner I'd sleep easy at night.

'Anyway,' Samuel continued, 'the police didn't stay long. Seemed satisfied we didn't know anything.'

And that, I decided, would be my own answer if they turned up at the cottage.

'Thinking of having a bit of a get-together at my place,' Mike said. 'Haven't decided what night – soon, though. When are you and your wife and Chloe free?'

'Nothing on at all this week, old man. Although next week's a bit trickier.'

'Not to worry, make it Wednesday, eh?'

'Sure, I'll clear it with them but I don't think there's anything booked in the diary.'

'Great. Oh, and feel free to bring a friend if you like.'

Samuel chuckled. 'Go on, say it. *And* a few bottles.'

'Right.' Mike laughed.

'Talking of friends, Victor Maudsley was asking if we'd like to make up a four at golf on Saturday. 'Course, if you're busy racing it would prove a bit difficult. What do you say?'

Mike looked at me. 'You're not booked to ride yet, are you, Harry?'

'No. I'm waiting on the doc's say so. Can't be long now, surely.'

'In that case, make the most of your enforced freedom. I'm sure eighteen holes at North Shore golf course would be just what he'd advise.'

'Go on, Harry,' Mike joined in. 'All rest without play's boring.'

I raised a placating palm. 'I'm outnumbered. Count me in.'

'Good, good. So, Mike, how did the new horse perform this morning?'

I sat back and let them discuss the merits of Samuel's horses. The mention of Victor's name had flashed up a reminder that I'd meant to ask him if he was the person responsible for leaving the white roses on my mother's grave. If we were spending the day in each other's company on Saturday, I could no doubt find a suitable opening to slip my question in.

However, it might be wiser to make the trip over to Grantham while I had spare time and ask at the flower shop first. It seemed the wisest course and could save me making a complete prat of myself.

And while I was over in that neck of the woods, maybe I could have words with Edward Frame. He lived near Grantham. I'd first met him while attending a golfing spree combined with attending his niece, Lucinda's wedding at North Shore Hotel. Edward had freely and happily informed me he'd been one of Alice's clients.

That was before the happiness of the occasion was completely obliterated by the horror of what happened later that evening. As I knew only too

112

well. It had been sod's law operating beautifully. I'd been the person who found the body.

I sipped some mineral water and thought about the quotes on the piece of paper that Jake had given me. There was the slimmest chance that Edward might be the second mouse, although I doubted it. But he *had* been one of Alice's clients. I'd completely forgotten about his revelations regarding the website, 'daddydating', which was where he'd met Alice. So, even if he wasn't the second mouse, it was possible he might know the man's identity.

I was shaken from my thoughts by *The Great Escape* theme playing tunefully in my jacket pocket. Excusing myself to Mike and Samuel, I answered the mobile on my way outside.

'Hi, Uncle George. You and Aunt Rachel OK?'

'Never better, son. And how's the head?'

'Good as ever.'

'Not back racing, though, eh?'

'No, unfortunately.'

'On the contrary. You've no excuse to avoid coming out for a meal with us.'

'Wouldn't dream of thinking up an excuse, Uncle George.'

'Take that as a yes, then. Rachel will be pleased.'

'Where and when?'

'We were thinking of the Dirty Duck at Woolsthorpe. The when, we'll leave to you. We're free any time.'

'Be good to have a catch up. How about on Sunday?'

'Sounds fine. Meet you there, say, at one o'clock?'

'I'll be there . . . regards to Aunt Rachel. Bye.'

It didn't occur to me until I'd put the mobile back into my pocket to ask if it was just the three of us eating. With a sinking feeling, I wondered if Aunt Rachel had it in mind to ask Annabel. Now, with the baby coming, my aunt seemed determined to bring me into situations where I couldn't avoid meeting my wife. I just hoped if Annabel received an invitation to join us, she would refuse.

Her pregnancy had killed any fragile hope that, maybe, our future might still be linked. It was a pity Aunt Rachel was taking the opposite view. She seemed to have blocked out Sir Jeffrey's part in the baby's conception. I felt my shoulders draw up at the thought, and it told me a lot. It wasn't fair criticizing Aunt Rachel for not letting go when I was still hopelessly enmeshed.

Mentally, I gave myself a shake. What I needed was work. But since my usual work was off limits right now, I decided to cut short my lunch with Mike and head off for Grantham. The personal approach was likely to produce more results than telephoning. I slipped back inside the pub.

'Something I have to do, Mike. I'll give you a bell tomorrow.'

'Fine.' He raised a hand.

'See you again, Harry.' Samuel smiled absently before continuing his conversation.

I nosed the Mazda cross-country through Harlaxton and found a spare parking space in Grantham. Since Margaret Thatcher's death, with the attendant reflected glory and publicity, the town seemed to have experienced a resurgence

114

of local pride and projected an almost tangible optimism. I hoped it would continue. The whole country needed a positive boost. People were sick to death of scraping by – they needed hope. Maybe it was the way forward for everyone in each individual town and village to be proud of where they lived. It certainly seemed to be working in Grantham. Frontages had been painted, shop-window displays were vibrant and eye-catching. As I walked along the High Street I felt my own spirits lift. I was glad I'd taken the decision to come in person, not simply phone.

The Trug Basket flower shop was awash with colour. Sturdy stemmed bronze Chrysanthemums in tall vases flanked the entrance, their perfume mingling with the other flowers ranked in multi-coloured tier upon tier, created a heady, intoxicating perfume.

'Can I be of help, sir?' A poised young woman, probably in her late twenties, appeared from a rear doorway.

'I certainly hope so.'

She smiled and waited.

I decided to dive in. 'Your shop supplies roses, I believe?'

'Oh, yes, people love roses, they're one of our bestselling flowers.'

'Do you sell white roses?'

'Of course, if it's what someone asks for. We try to give our customers a fully personalized service.' She began to blush. 'Forgive me, but are you . . . are you Harry Radcliffe, the jockey?'

'Yes, I'm afraid so.'

She smiled prettily, the blush staining her cheeks. 'It's a pleasure to have your custom.'

'I saw your card on a spray of white roses just a short while ago. Well, the fourth of November, to be exact. Can I ask, do you keep records of sales?'

Her smile wavered. 'Are you checking up on me?'

'No, please, don't worry. It's simply a personal thing. I need to contact the gentleman who placed the order. Can you tell me who it was?'

She shook her head regretfully. 'Even if I'd like to help, I can't. You know, of course, about data protection?'

I nodded. 'But could you give me any idea . . . you know, roughly where the man lived? Not the *full* address. I understand I can't ask you to do that, but some indication . . . anything?'

As I was speaking, she'd taken an order book from beneath the counter and was flipping through. Coming to the right page, she ran a pink-tipped nail down the list, then halted.

'Have you found the person that placed the order?'

She nodded slowly, biting on her lower lip. 'Don't tell anyone, will you? I could get into a lot of trouble . . .'

'Absolutely not.'

'Well, the person didn't live locally – not in Grantham.' She lifted her gaze from the page and stared at me. 'But it wasn't a man, it was a woman.'

116

Fifteen

I was mulling over what the flower-shop girl had said all the way to Wilsford. It was totally unexpected, a woman being responsible for writing those enigmatic words on the card. How on earth did that fit in? *I should have had the courage to ask you long ago. Too late for us now . . .?* I'd thought the obvious as I'd knelt beside my mother's grave. A former lover must have sent the flowers. But a woman . . . and even more unbelievable, a woman and *my mother*? OK, in today's anything goes world it wouldn't raise an eyebrow, but back then it was hidden, shocking and totally unmentioned.

Just the fact a woman had sent Mother's favourite flowers had left me shell-shocked. *If* the woman proved to have been a lover. What if the truth turned out to be something else? Could it possibly have been a secretary, sent by her boss? I felt myself clutching tight hold to this possible straw as a viable theory. It was possible. A damn sight more feasible than my mother having a female lover.

One thing was clear – the address hadn't been in Grantham. At least the florist had fed me that little crumb. Well, if it was a secretary, that seemed to discount Victor as prime suspect – face it, Radcliffe, the only suspect. Victor didn't have a secretary. He was retired. I groaned aloud. I was really floundering now. Just who the hell *could* it be?

One way of finding out occurred to me. I knew where the order book was kept that had the name written down in it. One quick glance would tell me all I needed to know. I even knew the page number. As the florist had run her finger down the column of names and addresses, I'd casually lent over the counter and just managed to read the number upside down. Mother's admirer was listed on page twenty-three. But to access the order book meant a spot of breaking and entering. Giving myself a mental shake, I quashed the thought. I'd been around Jake Smith too much. The criminal mentality was beginning to rub off. I was in enough trouble with the police now, albeit they hadn't sussed it yet. Any further illegal activities were a no-no. However, if a break-in was not on the cards a walk-in was legitimate. So, just how did I manage that?

How about I rang The Trug Basket, asked the florist out for a drink, say, straight after work? I remembered that blush spreading over her pretty face. She had fancied me. Sometimes being 'famous' had its plusses. Fame spelled power and the effect that had on females was well known. It was a fair bet she'd say yes. Really, Radcliffe, the depths you are sinking to, I chided myself. But it seemed like the only way to stand a chance of learning the unknown woman's name. And it wouldn't be any hardship, taking her out for a drink . . . she was a lovely-looking filly.

I wrestled with my conscience right up to the moment I saw the signpost reading Wilsford.

Then I pulled in off the A52 and cut the Mazda's engine. Fishing in my wallet, I took out the innocent business card and tapped the number of the flower shop into my mobile. It rang several times before a female voice answered. I recognized it instantly.

'Would that be the young lady who sells white roses?'

Her gasp of surprise, quickly smothered, was clearly audible. There was no doubt she knew who it was. I could already imagine that pretty, betraying blush pinking her cheeks.

'Oh, that's Mr Harry Radcliffe, isn't it?'

'It surely is.'

'What can I do for you, sir?'

'First, tell me your name.'

She hesitated. 'Why?'

'Well, you have the advantage, haven't you? It's a little unfair if I don't know who I'm speaking to.'

'Oh, I see . . . yes . . . my name's Georgia.'

'As in the song?'

She laughed, 'Yes.'

'It's a lovely name.'

'You said first . . . what comes second?' She was recovering fast.

I got in quickly. 'I think you're an attractive lady. Could I take you out for a drink when you finish work tonight?'

Another partially smothered gasp. 'I'm very flattered, Mr Radcliffe—'

'Harry, not sir or Radcliffe – just Harry.'

'I finish at about a quarter to six. Well, the shop actually closes at five thirty but I have to bring in all the display flowers and top up the water.'

'I'll be there at five thirty, give you a hand to carry in the heavy mob.'

She giggled. 'Wouldn't you rather pick me up later, when I've had chance to shower and change?'

I sighed. 'Can't do, sorry. I'm only free for the early part of the evening. And since I'm already in Grantham . . .' I let the sentence run out.

'Of course, I understand; you must be very busy.'

'Hmmm . . . .' I hoped excitement, curiosity, or whatever was taking her fancy wouldn't let her off the hook. She knew it was now or probably never.

'I'll see you at the shop, then,' she said.

'Great,' I said. And I meant to keep my side of the bargain by giving her an enjoyable hour or two. 'Have a think where you'd like to go – doesn't have to be in Grantham itself.'

'There's a very nice place in Woolsthorpe. Would that be too far out of your way? You did say you're only free for a short time.'

'Woolsthorpe would suit me just fine.'

'OK . . . and . . . thank you, Harry.'

'Nonsense. Look forward to it.'

I slid the card and mobile back into my pocket. Caution would be needed not to lead her on, give her any ongoing ideas. It wouldn't be fair. I already felt a bit of a heel for using her in this way. Still, as long as she enjoyed herself over the drinks, it was the best I could do. I started the car engine. It could prove tricky getting a look at page twenty-three. She would need to be distracted but I was determined to find out the name.

I drove straight on through Wilsford. There was only one main road, past The Crown pub, down a winding country lane and out into the countryside.

Edward Frame lived and operated from a converted barn, part of what used to be a working arable farm but which had now been sold off into several lots, the buildings all extensively renovated to top level and, no doubt, top price.

I parked the Mazda close to the stable door-type entrance, except your common or garden one usually wasn't made from solid English oak with a preponderance of iron studs and incredibly ornate locks and hinges. There was even a thick, black oxide-painted chain to tug upon if you wanted to gain access. I tugged. The distant peal of a bell would have done service for Westminster Abbey. The oak drawbridge opened and Edward appeared.

'Ha . . . yes . . . Harry.' I'd rung earlier to check he'd be at home and available. 'Come in.'

Obviously he didn't think I'd called on a business matter. Instead of leading me to an office, he opened a door that revealed a stupendous lounge. It seemed to spread forever and could have accommodated half of London's fleet of buses. 'You'd never guess it was used to store grain, would you?' His expression was one of happy, smug ownership.

'No,' I agreed, 'it's magnificent.'

'Alice loved to visit for the weekend. She called it Buckingham Palace . . .' His smile died away. 'I told you about Alice . . . you remember, Harry?'

'Yes.'

'Ghastly business.' He shook his head. 'Who

121

in God's name would wish her dead, eh? Do you think it was a maniac?'

'I don't know, Edward.'

'You found her, didn't you? It was on the news.'

'I'm afraid so.'

'Any ideas? I mean, you were the man who found the golf course killer. I don't think the police would have done.'

'It's likely they would. But their wheels turn slowly – have to when it comes down to checking DNA and gathering enough evidence for a definite conviction.'

'You're being very generous towards them, Harry. We both know it was your finding the murder weapon that enabled them to check for DNA. I don't think I've fully thanked you for bringing justice for the family. I just want to say how grateful I am, and also say a thank you as well from my brother. If Louis had still been with us I know he'd be clapping you on the back himself. 'Course, it won't bring them back but just think, Harry, if the murders had remained unsolved. There would have been no end to it. It would always be a case of looking at faces in crowds, wondering . . . y'know . . .'

'Really, there's no need to thank me. I'm just very glad the killer got put away.'

He nodded abruptly. 'Pity hanging has been abolished. Anyway,' he drew in a deep breath and added, 'have a seat. I'm just going through to the kitchen. Coffee's perking.'

I sat down in an engulfing armchair and took the opportunity to try and assess his reaction to Alice's death and work out what to say – or ask

– that could produce a possible lead. My first question was obvious. Maybe I should just allow the ball of wool to unravel from that.

Edward returned with a tray of coffee, the aroma alone demanding it be drunk with respect and appreciated. I was happy to oblige and it was that rare pleasure – a coffee that actually tasted as good as it smelled.

Edward was obviously a man who didn't stint himself. I wondered what he would do for sex or female favours now Alice was gone. He struck me as a man with a considerable appetite for life, in every sense.

'So, Harry.' Edward, cradling his coffee, leaned back and crossed his legs. 'What can I help you with?'

The identity of Alice's lover was the point I was leading up to so I started from that. 'You told me you found Alice through the website, daddydating.'

'Indeed I did.'

'Not that long back then, as in years?'

'Good Lord, no.'

'Hmmm . . . I thought not. Do you know anything about Alice's earlier life before you met her?'

'No, sorry.'

'Tell me, do you know of any other man that shared a history with Alice?'

'Phewww . . .' He blew his cheeks out. 'What sort of question is that? Why would I?'

Instead of answering him, I took the infamous piece of paper from my pocket and passed it over. 'What do you make of that?'

Edward replaced his drink on the coffee table beside him and put on his glasses. I didn't rush him. Under cover of taking a pull of my own coffee, I covertly, from the corner of my eye, watched the expression on his face. Interest, curiosity, bewilderment – the emotions flitted across but the one I was hoping for, understanding, did not. He shook his head decisively and gave the paper back.

'If you're looking for a result, Harry, I've got to disappoint you. Doesn't mean a damn thing to me.'

'To be honest, it was a long-odds job. But can I ask: did Alice ever mention a man who worked in racing?'

He pondered a few moments. 'Well it does seem to ring a bell, yes. One of the comments she did make was about jockeys . . .' He snorted with laughter at the memory. 'Something on the lines of being able to ride a good finish.'

I smiled with him. 'And you think one of her clients was a jockey?'

'Oh, not just one, Harry, no. She went on to say some won more easily than others.'

'And you think she *preferred* clients who were in racing?'

He thought some more. 'I remember her mentioning jump jockeys having to retire earlier than flat jockeys, but when they were riding for her that didn't apply.'

I nodded. Mousey Brown. But a thought struck me. 'Did Alice actually say "jockeys"? You know, meaning more than one who was, say, getting on a bit, no longer race riding?'

'Yes.'

124

'You've no idea who?'

'Afraid not. Although she did mention one of her clients was a dab hand at strokes even if his horses never ran.'

My breath caught and I tried desperately to keep poker-faced. I knew straight away who Alice had been obliquely referring to. It seemed that just as doctors respected patient confidentiality, Alice's own self-respect had been high enough to consider her clients should also be treated with respect. And although she had given out snippets of information, she had never named anyone outright. I'd just got to accept this facet of her character and stop chasing elusive names. What I needed to do was piece together all the tiny bits of information until the jigsaw revealed the right man.

My attention came back to Edward, who had started rolling a tentative finger around the rim of his coffee cup. He looked up and our gaze met.

'What?'

'There was one man, Harry. Happened to be a friend of mine – well, still is. But he really fancied Alice, you know, after I'd found her from that website.'

'And?'

'I warned him off. A case of I saw her first.'

'But she was a prostitute.'

'True, but Alice had her own rules. Could even call them ethics, I suppose. That was one of the nice things about her. He used to turn up here when Alice was visiting for the weekend.'

'And you weren't having any competition?'

'Damn right. My house, my woman so sod off,

friend or no friend. I was paying her – handsomely – and I wanted exclusive rights. Well, during the time she was here.'

'So where does this man fit in?'

Edward sighed. 'I'm pretty sure he became a client when Alice was back on her own patch. I did ask her but she wouldn't tell me.'

'Do you really think he would know any more than you do? It's doubtful when you'd known Alice a lot longer.'

'I just think you could make enquiries. There's no other man I can think of.'

'And his name and address?'

'Jim Matthews. Comes from Bingham.'

'Thanks, I'll go and have words. You never know when something interesting might surface. I've found it's usually the case when you've the least expectations.'

I drained the last of my delicious coffee. 'Have to go, but thanks again, Edward. And if you do happen to think of anything, perhaps you'd give me a ring?'

'Of course.'

I motored back the way I had come. It was knocking-off time in Grantham. I was spoilt for choice and easily found a parking spot close enough to keep the doorway of the shop in sight. It was barely ten past five.

I undid my seat belt and sat back to wait.

And while I waited, I ran through everything Edward had told me.

Sixteen

At five thirty I headed for the shop. Obviously no customers were taking up Georgia's time. She emerged on the pavement and began lugging in the heavy display tubs.

I quickened my pace. 'Can I help, miss?' As I spoke, I took the tub from her hands and hefted it over the step into the shop.

She flashed me a smile of amazed delight. 'You came back.'

I returned her smile. 'I said I would.'

'Wow, a man who actually keeps his word.'

'Yeah, I know, a seriously endangered species.'

Georgia collected the blooms and I brought in the containers. After topping up the water levels, she consulted her watch.

'Five forty. I'm out.'

I inclined my head. 'The pub it is then.'

I made the tone of my voice light. However, inside I was hiding my urgency to find the name on page twenty-three of the order book. Just how the hell *was* I to do it?' The book was tucked away under the counter only inches from where I was standing. It might as well have been in the next county.

Then Georgia said, 'Just have to get my bag. It's in the back cloakroom.'

Elation surged within me. 'Sure, no hurry.'

The instant she disappeared, I reached over the

127

counter and found the book. With mounting excitement, I turned up page twenty-three and ran a finger down the column. In seconds I found the correct entry: one dozen white roses. The flowers had been bought by a Mrs Smith and the address given was listed simply as Nottingham. My excitement gave way to frustrated annoyance.

Replacing the book, I knew the person who had requested the white roses had deliberately used the name Smith, being virtually untraceable, and not only that but the one word, Nottingham, wasn't even a clue, merely a blind. Whoever it was didn't want to be found, had made sure they couldn't be. I'd set up the date with Georgia merely as a follow-on from discovering who the person was, a kind of payment in lieu. Now it was pointless. I was no further forward.

Georgia reappeared with a wide smile on her pretty face and the shop keys swinging from her fingers.

'Ready?' I swallowed the disappointment.

'Can't wait. But, not being funny or anything, Harry, I need to get home after we've been to the pub. Makes sense to have my car.'

I appreciated that. And it would also make it easier to take my leave of her.

We ended up driving our own cars – hers a sparky, bright red Mini – and I followed her to Woolsthorpe.

I knew as soon as she tooted and turned left off the lane leading to Belvoir Castle, she was heading for the Dirty Duck. She changed to third and drove carefully down the narrow track. The pub was a landmark around here for miles. It was where I'd met Uncle George again after he'd been eighteen years in the marital wilderness. Mike frequently suggested we meet up there for a meal – a good blowout for him, a much more modest although no less tasty one for me.

In addition, I knew it would be all round the local grapevine, as well as the Internet, I'd been seen with a new lady friend. And I also knew it would, without doubt, come to the ears of Annabel. If I tried to explain with the truth as to how it had come about, she would certainly disapprove. For goodness' sake, even I disapproved. Georgia didn't know I was simply making use of her and I'd no intention of letting her find out.

At the far end, where the track met the Grantham canal, it petered out and it was necessary to take a left into the car park that encircled the pub on three sides. On the fourth was the canal. It was a real crowd-puller, giving views of the Leicestershire countryside in both directions down the peaceful, duck-littered stretch of water.

We parked both cars and went through the entrance lobby into the main bar. Over to our extreme right, the barman smiled a welcome.

'Georgia, good to see you. Harry.'

I nodded back and Georgia wiggled her fingers.

'Any preference, tables and drinks?' I asked her. It was still early and we had the choice. Later, it would be heaving.

'I'm going to take advantage of the fire, and a white wine would be nice.'

The barman was already fixing her drink as I saw her to the table nearest to the roaring fire.

I opted for a lager and took both drinks over to join her.

'Cheers.' She smiled prettily and we chinked glasses. Sipping the chilled wine, she looked at me over the rim. 'I know why you invited me out . . .'

I inclined my head and raised one eyebrow.

'But I can't give you what you want.'

'And what *do* I want?'

'You want me to tell you the name and address of my customer.'

I pursed my lips and nodded. 'Yeah, I admit I'd really like to know who it was.'

Her lips went down at the corners.

'But, now we're here . . .' I waved towards the cheerful blaze that flickered on the wonderful, gleaming array of brass pans decorating the walls, the cosy, subdued wall-lights, '. . . I can't think of anywhere I'd rather be right now. Shall we just enjoy our drinks and relax?'

She began to smile. 'Why not?'

'You said *my customer*. Does that mean you actually own the flower shop?'

'Hmmmm . . . I've always been interested in horticulture – well, more than just interested, it's a passion of mine.'

'You must have had training, I mean, all the different varieties . . .'

She was openly laughing at me now. 'Five years at college. I started at the bottom, literally, from the grass roots up – no, below that, all the different types of soil and what each plant grows best in, or doesn't.'

'Wow, five years. Commitment in capital letters.'

130

'I knew what I wanted and what it took to achieve it.'

'Hardly anyone does know. An awful lot of disheartened, unhappy people are still searching for that unknown.'

'Does that make me lucky?' She took a thoughtful sip of her wine. 'I guess it does.'

'It makes the two of us lucky. I'm doing the only job I want to do. Not many people can say that.'

'And some people never get the chance to follow their dream.'

'True enough. What college did you study at?'

'Riseholme, in Lincolnshire, near Gainsborough.'

'They do agriculture, animal husbandry, yeah?'

'Hmmm . . . and train jockeys.'

'Really, I didn't know that.'

'They also support Bransby Horses, the charity over at Bransby village.'

'Bransby rescue ill-treated horses and ponies. I've heard of them. Do a wealth of good work.'

'Hmmm.' She nodded. 'I've visited on an open day. You talk about my commitment – well, their level of care for those abused horses is just amazing. It's so good Riseholme is helping them. In my opinion, it definitely makes Riseholme one of the good guys.'

'I'd have to agree with you.'

'I certainly enjoyed my training there, thought it was a great place. You know, when you're doing something you're meant to do, even if it's work, it's pleasure. That's what tells you you're doing the right thing with your life.'

'Is it the only thing you've ever wanted to do?'

'Pretty much. Well, since I was about ten. You're a bit unformed when you're a child. Like, everything's in front and anything's possible.'

'With me it was always horses. Suppose you could say they're an obsession.'

'And you're extremely successful.'

I shrugged. 'You're only ever as good as your last ride. And if you take a fall, if it's a bad one, your career can come to a sudden full stop.'

'Then what?'

I grinned and drained my lager. 'You tell me.'

'Don't jockeys usually go into training?'

'A lot do, yes.'

'But training doesn't even come close to the buzz of riding winners, does it?'

'No,' I shook my head, smiling, 'not even on the same planet.'

'Then stick with it.'

'My wife wouldn't agree.' I could practically feel the sudden drop in temperature.

She stiffened. 'You're married?'

'Don't worry, we're not living together.'

'Oh?'

'Annabel lives near Melton, with her new man.'

'He's a jockey, too?'

'Good grief, no. He's in a safe office in London a good deal of the time.'

'Uh-huh. Do I take it the word we're looking at here is "safe"?'

'You're very perceptive.'

'And,' she gave me a quick, sideways look, 'that's the reason you're not together? Annabel couldn't take the harsh fact you were likely to get injured?'

'Not just likely, extremely likely – probable odds of one in eight rides actually.'

'She must love you very much.'

I gave my empty lager glass serious attention.

'Sorry, I didn't mean to . . .'

'No, no, it's OK. And, yes, you're absolutely right. The accident factor was the reason she left.'

'No stronger force in the world than love,' she murmured.

'What about you? Is there a man in your life?' It was time to divert her away from me. 'You sound like you're talking from personal experience.'

'Do I?' She dropped her gaze, turning the wine glass round in her hands.

'You don't have to answer. I've no right to quiz you . . .'

'Yes, yes, you do. We're here, together, just having a quiet drink. But we still need to explore *where* we are. If you see what I'm getting at.'

'Of course I do. But you don't have to tell me personal things.'

She lifted her chin and looked full into my face. I read a deep sadness in her eyes and it shocked me.

'You're quite right, I do know from personal experience. My boyfriend was a serving soldier, Afghanistan. He was killed in Helmand Province last year. To be factual, he was killed by an IED. I loved him – very much.' Her chin jutted some more. 'I still do.'

I reached across the table, took the wine glass from her then held her hands between both of mine. 'I'm a clueless prat. I'm so sorry.'

Tears began trickling down her face. I fished

into my pocket for a clean tissue and gently dabbed them dry.

'I'm fine, except when people are sympathetic.'

I nodded. I knew exactly what she meant. Personally, I could take any amount of pain or abuse but, given caring kindness, it did for me every time.

She withdrew her right hand and reached for the wine. 'I wonder, which is hardest, though?' She took a large gulp of the Chardonnay. 'To lose someone as I did and know that our love was ongoing or, in your own case, to have your partner still alive but not with you?'

I returned my stare to the last drop of lager in my glass. 'I was dead right, wasn't I? You are very perceptive.'

'I think most people would just call me Joe Blunt.' She smiled. 'Shall we move away from the past, give the present a chance, hmmm?'

'Let's do that.'

'Are we up for another drink? We *are* driving.'

I came to a quick decision. 'Are you in an almighty rush to get home, Georgia?'

'Not an almighty one, no. But I do have to do "water's up" and check over my two horses. The stables are on automatic lighting so that's not a problem.'

'You're a horsewoman, then? Do you ride? I suppose that's a daft question.'

'Only hacking, not jumps or hunting. My two old babes have had enough of that.'

'Don't tell me, you've taken in two horses from Bransby?'

'Hmm, yes, actually, I have. Pegs and Jacko.

134

They've been with me for about four years now so they're both clocking up the years.'

'I see. Can I treat you to a meal, then? Soak up some alcohol?'

She scrutinized me. 'I don't want you feeling sorry for me. I'm doing fine.'

'I'm sure you are. And I don't feel sorry for you – well, yes, perhaps, a little bit. I'd like to get to know you more.'

'What you mean is, because I've got two horses . . .'

I laughed. 'Do you *always* give a man this hard a time when he's asking you out?'

'I've never been asked out to dinner with a jockey before.'

I caught up the menu from the end of the table. 'Here you go; what would you like to eat?'

She took hold of the opposite corner. 'I still can't tell you the customer's name, Harry.'

'I know you can't. And I don't want you to, OK? As you say, we've moved on. This is just you and I right now.'

A beautiful smile spread across her face and she tugged the menu free. 'In that case . . .' she ran a quick glance down the list, '. . . I'll have a vegetable lasagne, thank you.'

It was a relaxed, happy meal and an hour later, still chatting, we returned across the car park to our respective cars. I saw her into the mini and straightened up, ready to go. She engaged first and, just as she was preparing to move off, another car came down the track to the Dirty Duck and swung in through the entrance. Georgia grinned and held back. I recognized the car and

135

the two occupants. I waved. They returned the wave and drove into the car park.

Turning back to say goodbye, I was too late. Georgia had gunned the mini forward through the gap and was gone.

But that was fine. I grinned. I'd already got her number.

Seventeen

I let the Mazda idle home down the back lane. No one was tailing me, I was sure of that. So I just needed to make sure there was no reception party waiting at home.

I slid quietly in through the open gateway and parked. You can tell an awful lot just by looking at a property. If it's empty, an almost tangible aura of stillness, waiting for a human presence, comes across. And I could pick this up straight away. My old cottage was giving off all the right vibes. I knew it so very well; I'd been born there, grew up there throughout my childhood.

After my father's death, I'd stayed on with my mother because her need was great. But an opportunity at the British Racing School in Newmarket had severed my roots and I'd gone away for the ten-week course feeling very honoured at being given the chance. Only one hundred youngsters per year were taken, ten to each course.

After that, of course, it was away again to a

racing stable and the start of my long, tough journey chasing the jockey's championship title.

However, marriage to Annabel and my mother's death had drawn me back to what I'd always called home. Although Annabel, herself, was no longer living here with me, Harlequin Cottage was my bastion through the tumultuous, raging seas of life. And I was so very glad to own it.

I slid out of the driver's seat and opened up the kitchen door. The so reliable old Rayburn gave off a welcoming cloak of warmth that wrapped itself around me. I shoved the kettle on to the hot-plate. Only one thing needed now to make coming home complete – a mug of tea.

A second later, a huge thud on my shoulder coupled with a bass bellow down my right ear announced I'd got that wrong – tea was the second thing. First, of course, was Leo, my enormous ginger tomcat who was now sitting on my shoulder butting his hard head against my cheek.

'Hiya, want some grub?' Stupid question.

Digging his claws in for balance, he leaned forward, watching me opening up a can of pilchards and scraping it out into his dish. But before the dish touched base on the old quarry tiles, he'd leapt down and was ready, waiting. Pilchards were most definitely his thing.

Usually his main supplier was Annabel; she was a complete sucker where Leo was concerned. But he wasn't picky. If I chose to indulge him with pilchards, he wasn't going to argue.

The kettle sang out and I took my tea through to the lounge, clicked on the wall lights and sprawled on the settee.

A few minutes later, Leo joined me, pumping my solar plexus with unsheathed claws and purring like a road drill.

'You pong!' I told him.

Leo was busy rolling his pink serrated tongue around his jaws and whiskers, extracting every last morsel and taste of the smelly fish.

His pumping claws met resistance. I dipped a hand into my trouser pocket and rescued my mobile. I'd switched it off before I went to interview Edward Frame and events, as they'd followed with Georgia, had made me forget to switch it back on. I'd have to think a bit deeper about that. It was somewhat disconcerting. Anyway, I switched it back on now and Leo and I slobbed some more.

We'd both reached the somnolent pre-nodding-off stage when the strident notes of *The Great Escape* jarred us back to full awareness.

It was Mike. 'Party's going ahead, Harry, Wednesday at eight p.m. I've just spoken with Barbara. Says she has to maintain her reputation as a merry widow now Sean's gone, is definitely up for it and will bring reinforcements, whatever that means.'

'Well done, Mike. What about Samuel? I left you two in The Horseshoes. Is he still coming?'

'Sure thing, says he'll ask his wife and Chloe.'

'I think we need to spread the net a bit wider, Mike. How about Victor and possibly Unwin from Leicester? Plus, maybe Mousey Brown and his son and Jackie, his daughter-in-law?'

'What's with all these trainers? Are they on the suspect list, then?'

'Well, no, to be honest, but they could well let slip information that would help.'

'I'll speak to them, give them the option, OK? If we're talking trainers, what about Tally and Jim?'

'Good thinking, yes, by all means. They're local so they might well come. I've still got to call Victor about golf tomorrow, so I can invite him for next Wednesday.'

'Right, and you, me and Samuel can all go to North Shore in my car in the morning. Seven o'clock suit?'

'Yes. I'll be going over to Burton Lazars in a short while – feed the beast, again! – and I can stock him up with food to last until Sunday. Give us the option of when we want to leave North Shore.'

'Oh, I don't want to leave early. We're making a full day of it, y'know. And that includes dinner.'

'I'll eat my ten per cent, Mike. Just now I seem to be making a habit of eating out.'

'Oh?'

I laughed. 'Tell you later.'

I'd barely finished the call when the phone rang again. It was Samuel this time.

'How're things, Harry?'

'Good, thanks, Samuel.'

'To let you know, both my wife and Chloe are intending to come to Mike's party.'

'Great.'

'Will there be many or just one or two friends?'

'I should think quite a few. When Mike gives a party, which isn't often, he doesn't hang back.'

'That lady trainer – you know who I mean,

don't you – does very well on the all-weather at Southwell. What's her name now?'

'You mean Barbara Maguire?'

'Yes, that's the one. She gives some pretty lavish dos. Have you been to any?'

I laughed. 'I certainly have, Samuel. You're quite right. Her parties are something else. They stay in the memory.'

'Is *she* coming to Mike's?'

'I believe she is, yes.'

'Knows how to enjoy herself, that one. Reckon it looks set for a right good night.'

'Hope so.'

'But we've a good day coming up tomorrow, first. A round at North Shore always hits the spot. By the way, Harry, can you contact Victor, check he's OK for making up a four?'

'Will do. Should be fine. He only lives a few yards away on St Andrew's drive and he's generally free to play. Except when he's doing his walking stick carvings. It's a fairly recent sideline. But he spends most of his time on the course, from what I can gather. He's always up for a round.'

'Shouldn't need much arm twisting, eh? OK, then, I'll be at Mike's about seven in the morning. See you, Harry.'

'Bye, Samuel.'

I eased Leo off my stomach to his great disgust and went to mash another mug of tea. One more call to make and I'd have to leave. The savage beast, not locked in any more – which was a dodgy prospect – was awaiting feeding time. Best not keep him waiting too long. Still, I took my time over the tea. It was not an enticing prospect making close contact with Jake Smith.

But when I could delay no further, I punched in Victor Maudsley's phone number. I'd ridden for him in my younger days when he was still working as a trainer. He and my Uncle George had been big golfing buddies years ago. Until the second biggest bang in history had occurred. However, recently discovering the truth about the situation, instead of going for an outraged score-settling with him I'd found myself actually feeling sorry for the man.

'Hi, Victor. Like a round at North Shore tomorrow?'

'Yes . . . I would . . .'

'But?'

'Struck down with the bloody gout again, aren't I?'

'Ouch, painful.'

'No kidding. I could light the way for Rudolph with my right toe. A beacon, it is, a right bloody beacon.'

'Sorry to hear it. Uncle George suffers from gout as well, says it's impossible to put any weight on it, the pain's excruciating.'

'I was speaking to him a short while ago and he's damned right.'

'You managing? Food-wise . . .? Can I do any shopping?'

'Thanks, Harry, but our Paula keeps coming over to fix my grub.'

Paula was Victor and Elspeth's daughter. She was married to Nigel, an up-and-definitely-coming Tory politician. It was all 'daddies and daughters' with

Victor, had been since she'd been born. If Paula asked for a star from the night sky he'd bust a gut trying to reach one.

'She's a good lass, Harry.'

'Yes, I'm sure.'

'Hmmm, especially since Elspeth's—'

'Good job you've got her,' I chipped in quickly, 'no sense in letting him get maudlin. If the pain was bad, and I didn't doubt that, he needed to keep on top to cope.'

'By, you're right there. 'Course, she doesn't see it as any hardship. Well, Nigel's away a lot y'know, down London. Has to be. Reckon she must get a bit lonely.'

'You could be right.'

Privately, with three kids to run around after, I suspected the loneliness was much more likely to be a projection of Victor's own need for company.

'Well, sorry about the golf. You be sure and let me know next time, eh? You can bank on me to make up numbers anytime.'

'Will do. Why not carry on with the carvings? Can you do those sitting down?'

'Yes. Don't feel like it, though.'

'No, suppose not. Anyway, don't let it grind you down, Victor. Be seeing you, cheerio.'

So it looked like a threesome for golf tomorrow. I upended my mug and swallowed the last cold dregs of tea.

But before then, I had the dubious pleasure of Jake Smith's company. It was a meeting I intended to cut as short as possible.

Jake was in a good humour at the sight of the

food, even helping me carry the goodies in. Then I upped his spirits some more.

'Something else for you – my cleaning lady found it when she moved the settee this morning.' I held out a small black object. 'Must be yours; it's not mine.'

'Yes!' he whooped and instantly relieved me of it. 'Well done, Harry boy.'

'So now you can stop grousing about losing it.'

He didn't answer; he was busy fiddling with the mobile phone. Poring over the screen, he gave a sudden exclamation. 'Well, fuck me senseless . . . forgot I took *that* . . . Come here, I want to show you something. Come on . . . take a look. Gets you going, don't it?' Leering, he held out the phone.

It was a photograph, obviously taken of Alice's original one, and showed Barbara's stable yard – and a stunningly beautiful girl.

'A looker,' I said.

And he gave a satisfied smirk.

I didn't want to spoil the moment by telling the truth. Actually, it had been Leo who had hooked an unsheathed claw around the mobile and drawn it out from under the furniture. He'd then patted it around the carpet for a bit of sport. Jake and Leo didn't get on – they were at daggers drawn. Or in Leo's case, claws. Still, a little subterfuge didn't come amiss in my own interests to keep Jake sweet.

The following morning I was not alone in feeling the familiar rise of spirits as our car turned off Roman Bank at Skegness and drove alongside

143

the sweep of golf course. Passing St Andrew's Drive, the tailgate of Victor's white Range Rover was just visible, parked, immobile, like its owner.

We'd left Mike's stables at seven and it was still well shy of nine o'clock. The storm in the night had brought down a lot of remaining leaves together with an assortment of twigs and small branches. But it had blown itself out towards dawn. The course was now a glittering emerald sward as the pale early sunshine played on the myriad raindrops clinging to the short grass stems.

'Makes you feel good just looking at it, doesn't it?' Samuel nodded his head in satisfaction.

'Yep, whoever invented golf was doing mankind a big favour,' Mike agreed, patting the steering wheel.

'What about womankind?' I ventured, flicking a finger towards a group of lady golfers, their vivid jackets and caps a bright statement in the pearly morning.

'Yes, but you have to agree, it's us men who need our tensions releasing.'

'I don't think I'd repeat that Samuel – well, not in hearing distance.'

'Oh, ho, I'm not daft enough to do that,' he chuckled.

'I'm looking forward to my bacon cob.' Mike smacked his lips and applied right-foot pressure. 'They surely take some beating. Got to line your stomach before you can swing your best.'

'Thank you, Mike,' I murmured, knowing one of the chef's massive offerings was, for me at any rate, a definite no-no.

'Sorry.' He grinned, unrepentant.

'Just think, Harry, when you finish race riding you'll be able to eat all you want.'

Even as Samuel said the words, I knew I'd rather forego any amount of big bacon butties to be able to ride. It was a bargain I'd made with myself years ago and not one I regretted in the slightest. Except, perhaps, when the capricious nostrils curled yearningly around the smell of grilling bacon inside North Shore's dining room. Thank God there were no calories in the smell.

Mike swung around to the rear of the hotel, crunching the gravel in the massive car park. We opened doors and the salt-laden air filled our lungs, welcoming us back. The golf course was quite literally brushing the edge of the wide beach. The breakers, soughing softly, reached towards us with creaming fingers. A perfect place to unwind and enjoy ourselves. Although, I suspected, a far cry from how it would have looked and sounded during the previous wild night.

I had also seen the golf course in its darkest hours – and it had been a very scary, dangerous place. Not an experience I hoped to relive.

I shook off the unwelcome memories. It did no good remembering, merely tainted the precious present. The horrific events could not be undone, never be put right. But today was about having pleasure, simply enjoying the course for what it was – a superb venue to play golf.

'Well, what are you waiting for?' Mike threw up his arms. 'It will still be here waiting when we've had breakfast. *Come on*, Harry.'

I nodded, took a last look at the wide, wide North Sea. Just looking shrank most problems, put them into perspective. I couldn't change the past, however much I might want to. I knew Mike had seen the dour look that had been on my face, knew he could make a good guess at what I was thinking. He was trying to lift my spirits. A better man to have on your side hadn't yet been born. Determinedly, I pushed the black thoughts away.

'I'm coming, might even indulge in a rasher!'

Eighteen

We went up the back steps into the hotel. However, Katie, on duty in reception, spotted us.

'Mr Radcliffe, so lovely to see you again.'

Mike chuckled. 'Celebrity status, eh?'

'And of course yourselves, Mr Grantley, Mr Simpson.'

'Good to be here, m'dear.' Samuel beamed.

'Likewise,' I said. I liked Katie; she had the same sunny temperament as Gavin, who had been on reception previously.

'Just go and refuel before we do the eighteen.'

'Of course, Mr Grantley. Breakfast is still being served. And John's on duty in the pro shop.'

We wandered through into the wood-panelled dining room that overlooked the sea. As ever, it was beautifully set out with a magnificent array of hams, cheeses, fresh and dried fruits, nuts, cereals and juices – all that before the full English. Tempting wasn't the word.

146

Most of the guests appeared to have already eaten and were no doubt out on the course so there was plenty of space. Mariusz, the breakfast waiter, came hurrying up.

'Good morning, gentlemen. Nice to see you.' He pointed out the tables suitable for three and took our orders.

The atmosphere today was one of relaxed indulgence, so very different from the last time we'd stayed overnight. Then, nobody could face any food other than possibly a slice of toast. I came down hard on the unpleasant memories. There'd be few occasions to visit North Shore once I had the all-clear to race from the doctor.

I determined to enjoy today and started with a dish of grapefruit segments with dried apricots, topped with flaked almonds and hazelnuts, followed by a poached egg and one grilled rasher of best back. The bacon lived up to its tantalizing aroma and tasted even better. It was rare that I indulged myself but remembering today would fortify me when I was back to the harsh routine of fasting.

The other two had ordered with abandon and Mariusz was only too willing to keep the flow coming. The chefs employed by the hotel were on top of their game and the quality was excellent.

'Thought it was to be bacon cobs? What went wrong?'

Mike laughed. 'Couldn't resist it.'

'Me neither,' Samuel agreed. 'Not every day you have the chance of being waited on and a choice of food this good.'

'Besides' – Mike leaned back and gently patted

his stomach – 'by the time we've walked our way round eighteen holes we shall have walked it all down.'

'I'm banking on that,' I said.

'And we may likely have to wait our turn to tee-off.' Samuel poured himself a further cup of coffee.

'The car park is pretty full,' Mike agreed, 'you could be right.'

'Well, nobody's in a hurry. Doesn't matter what time we get back tonight.'

'Talking of tonight,' Mike fished in his pocket, 'I've got tickets for a show at the Southview Park this evening.'

'Sorry . . .' Samuel shook his head. 'Can't do it, Mike. Promised the little woman I'd be home by nine at the latest.'

Mike frowned. 'How will you get back?'

'Oh, I'll get a taxi to the station, catch a train back to Grantham.'

'Oh, OK. Are you up for it, Harry?'

'Why not? I'm a free agent right now. Even Leo's catered for. So, nothing spoiling.'

I didn't say anything about catering for Jake Smith. Mike knew as well as I did I'd loaded up Jake with plenty of provisions. But it wasn't something you mentioned in civilized company. How long the sordid arrangement would last wasn't something I cared to consider. But even as I'd unloaded the box of food at Nathaniel's studio, an idea had occurred to me. It was risky, and a decided nail to be hammered hard into my coffin should the police pick up any hint of my knowing Jake's whereabouts. But it was just possible I could successfully distract the blue boys.

It gave me a decided loosening feeling in my guts thinking about going through with the plan. However, I was fast coming to a crossroads. Something had to be done – and quickly.

Mike teed off, then myself, followed by Samuel, greedily drinking in the keen salt-laden air. We were into the game, walking the damp, springy turf, spikes gripping and grounding. Although the sun had climbed higher, it was a back-end one, pale and without the kick of summer heat.

Mike hit a birdie at the third and was very pleased with himself. Samuel was also giving his best and it was myself who was trailing.

'Know your problem?' Mike said as he dropped his gaze from watching his ball arc up into the pale blue before landing close to the flag on the fifth.

'No, but do tell me.'

He grinned. 'Simple, you need more practice.'

I nodded. 'Can't argue with that little gem.'

Samuel trumpeted his amusement and then delight as his ball also dropped cleanly on to the green only yards from the flag.

'Following on your philosophy, Mike, that suggests both of you need to devote more time to your day jobs.'

Samuel lightly punched my shoulder. 'Well, I blame that bacon rasher you scoffed . . .'

I ignored him and concentrated hard on my stance and swing. And whacked the ball into the rough edging the fifth green. They both sniggered.

149

'See what I mean, Samuel? More practice needed.' Still sniggering, they led the way down the fairway past the public footpath that cuts through the golf course to the north side.

Running from Roman Bank, the footpath crossed the golf course, ending on the beach with the North Sea away to the right. It had been a landmark that had stuck in my memory from when Mike and I had previously stayed overnight.

The last time I'd stood on the narrow path had been at midnight with clouds banking up and obscuring the moon. A black night, in more ways than one. But today, in full daylight, its sombre menace was missing. Today it was simply a public footpath serving the community of Winthorpe.

I stood looking down the half-hidden path. Undergrowth had sprouted unchecked down either side during the growth months over summer, narrowing the path even more.

Overhead, despite the strong winds overnight, the trees growing at the back along the high ridge were still cloaked in heavy foliage that blocked a lot of the skyline. They provided a dark green backdrop to the bright green, short turf of the two fifth greens. One, the nearest to the beach, was reserved for use only on tournaments, whereas the one where Mike and Samuel were even now sizing up the line from where their individual balls had landed was the usual playing green.

Collecting my thoughts and pushing the past back where it belonged, I tugged my trolley over to where my ball seemed to have landed.

The flag was now smartly fluttering. Allowing for the strengthening breeze, Mike swung his iron and, from over twenty feet, holed his ball. His grin spread wide. But Samuel, hard behind him and, from only ten foot away, tapped his in very neatly.

'A two-horse race, obviously,' I said.

'Have you found that ball yet?'

'No.' I shook my head. 'But I'm not giving up; it's not beating me.'

'Unlike ourselves,' Samuel joked. They put their irons back into the trolleys and stood waiting for me.

'Look, you two start walking – you're making me nervous. I'll find it quicker without both of you standing there grinning.'

'As if we are,' Mike said, poker-faced now.

'Want some help?' Samuel offered.

I shook my head. 'This is personal.'

Leaving me to it, they turned and began walking off, heads together, discussing the merits of the irons they'd chosen for their putts.

I'd noted the trajectory of my ball as it had flown up into the air and was now tracking its probable location. Using one of my clubs, I thwacked aside the tussocks of rough grass edging the green. Covering the area methodically, I whacked away knowing the ball couldn't be very far away. I'd be bound to find it soon. And a minute or two later, I did. Caught under what appeared to be dock leaves, the flash of white gave away its hiding place. I gave a grunt of satisfaction and was bending to pick it up when there was a muted crack and a savage swish of air past my bent shoulder. Instead of straightening up, I dropped to the ground and lay still.

151

The bullet, for that's what it was, flew on and ploughed into the public warning sign sited at the back of the tournament green, several yards behind where I'd been standing a split second ago. The wood cracked and splintered but I knew it hadn't the substance to stop the bullet which would have carried on and come out the other side. Where it was now was an unknown. Finally coming down, it would inevitably bury itself in the sand.

And there was a hell of a lot of sand.

Lying cheek down in the grass and without raising my head, I looked sideways across the green. Mike and Samuel were still deep in discussion, still walking away.

They were the only two people.

They were unaware that a sniper had just taken a shot at me.

Whoever had pulled the trigger was no doubt hidden in the trees on the ridge. If they thought the shot had taken me out, there would be no further bullets flying in this direction. I lay still.

Keeping Mike and Samuel in sight, I waited for the moment when they realized I wasn't following them. That needed delicate timing. At the point when I saw them stop and begin to turn around, I needed to come up to at least a kneeling position.

They'd think I was simply bending down, picking up the ball. And I wanted to keep it that way. It was quite obvious I was the target. That meant the other two were safe.

I didn't dwell on the harsh fact that if I hadn't bent at that critical moment, the bullet would have

152

ploughed into my chest – left side. But simply acknowledging how close to death I'd been brought nauseous bile to the back of my throat. OK, race riding was bloody dangerous, nobody denied that. But a bullet through the heart . . .

I continued to lie still.

And Mike and Samuel continued walking. They were approaching the curve of the path leading to the base of the ridge. Wherever the would-be assassin was he'd be making sure of his escape now. Once the two men went round the bend, anyone coming out of the wood above that point was going to be silhouetted against the skyline.

Very reluctantly, I prised myself up from the grass. When I was kneeling, I waited apprehensively for a couple of seconds, the blood roaring in my ears. But no further bullet found me. At this point it seemed utterly ridiculous that somebody had sighted down a gun barrel and actually pulled the trigger.

Who in God's name hated me that much? Nobody, surely. It was a far-fetched flight of fancy on my part.

I turned my head and looked back at the wooden box and the words on it.

Warning. You are going to cross a private golf course.

Keep to the path at all times. Be aware of moving golf balls.

Take responsibility for your own safety.

Ironically, I had, by simply, innocently, bending down.

The box had been intact when the three of us arrived on the fifth green. Now it was in a sorry state. The force of the bullet had slammed into the wood, splintering it and leaving a jagged gap through which daylight clearly showed, proving the bullet had exited by ripping out the rear of the box.

I curled my fingers around the hard, little golf ball and stood up. Thank God for golf balls. Without it, I wouldn't be here now. I felt like I'd been punched in the solar plexus. The whole ganglion of nerves sited there had absorbed the shock and was letting me know about it. I could have thrown up very easily, wasted all that lovely protein I'd allowed myself for breakfast.

If Annabel were here, I knew what she would say. The trauma would have immediately shrunk the thymus gland – it took up to three weeks for it to regain its size – and knocked the endocrine system for six. Annabel was not only a psychotherapist but also a fully qualified spiritual healer. She knew these things. She'd also tell me to counteract the nausea by deep breathing.

Deliberately, I drew in several long, deep breaths to steady myself. Then I strode away, following the other two men who had now disappeared from sight around the curve of the stone path towards the next hole. I had no intention of telling them what had just happened. They would certainly insist on calling off the day's golf, then telling the hotel manager and reporting the incident to the police . . .

I was sailing so close to the wind now by harbouring a criminal, I could already feel the icy blast on the back of my neck. Any further investigations by the police would be disastrous.

There would be hours spent inside the police station, questions asked, a hell of a lot of questions. Statements would have to be taken, SOCOs sent crawling about trying to discover the whereabouts of the bullet.

I shuddered.

Right now, Mike and Samuel were focussed on their golf. I wasn't going to do anything that distracted them. Right now, nobody else knew about it, except the would-be assassin and myself.

No way was I going to come clean. It was going to stay a secret, one strictly between myself . . . and the golf ball.

Nineteen

The other two beat me, predictably by a long way – to be truthful, I was trounced good and proper, Mike marginally holding off Samuel's challenge.

It was several hours later when we trooped back into the hotel. There had been no further incidents. I hadn't expected there to be. At the same time a sense of relief flooded me as we stashed the golf trolleys away in the boot of our car before going up the back steps into the warmth – and safety – of the hotel.

We ordered a meal. Then sat, sipping the strong, scalding coffees poured by the barman that restored spirits and energized bodies. The comfortable armchairs, calm surroundings and civilized atmosphere made a mockery of the earlier attempt on my life.

While we were playing golf out on the course, I hadn't considered who the sniper might be. But now we were relaxing instead of concentrating on playing, I let the question of who hated me that much circle in my mind. It was bad enough with Jake Smith's threat hanging over me; now it seemed he was not alone in the 'hate Harry' stakes.

Guns were generally thought of as men's toys. Not conclusive, of course – there were plenty of splendid shots among the female population. But in this case, I'd put money on the sniper being male. Whoever he was, he must hold a very deep grudge against me. So, it was my turn to think very hard just whom I had come up against before and, following that, who I had bested in whatever way.

Normally, I was pretty easy-going, could get on with most people – some admittedly with more effort than others, but that applied to just about anyone.

What I needed to pinpoint was the person or persons I had had a severe run-in with, leaving them so injured, physically or emotionally, that they felt they needed to get their own back. But even though I scrambled my brains trying to remember, nobody came to mind.

None of my fellow jockeys, even when I'd managed to scoop victories from them in the last seconds of a race, would take it so badly as to try and injure me. It was ludicrous. What they *would* do was wait their chance coming up against me in a future race to even the score that way. A classic case of don't get mad get even – thoroughly acceptable in weighing rooms all over the country. So, no, none of my professional colleagues could remotely be considered.

What did that leave? Friends, acquaintances? Who held a grudge, and for what? Nobody at all that I knew about. Nobody had warned me. Nobody had threatened me. It was a complete dead end. So that only left someone deeply affected by Alice Goode's death or the two men who had died in prison.

The latter could be described as being in prison in the first place because of me. I'd discovered their identities as a direct result of following up information and coming to a conclusion that turned out to be right. They had committed murder, albeit they were on remand, suspected of committing murder, but the police were sure of their facts, had proof, and the two men's guilt was a foregone conclusion.

OK, if I hadn't informed the police of my findings, perhaps the wheels of justice would have taken a damn sight longer turning to bring them in. But the end result would have been the same.

Which left Alice. Or rather, Alice's death. Now had Darren Goode not still been in prison then yes, I could see he was a likely candidate for topping someone in revenge for his wife's death.

But for goodness' sake, I personally had nothing to do with it. Yes, I'd suspected Jake Smith all along, until the last few days. Now, I didn't. So that left whoever *had* murdered Alice. Were they scared I'd find out they were guilty? I was certainly trying to discover who was responsible. Was I perhaps getting closer, even if personally I had no idea who it was? One thing was sure: the more stones I turned over, the more I found out. And if it followed the pattern I'd used in the past, the pieces of information were like a jigsaw. The more bits I found, the more they linked together and the clearer the picture became.

If I could stop turning stones, I'd remove myself from the line of fire – literally! But Annabel and her unborn baby's safety lay squarely in my hands. It was looking even more like a choice between saving Annabel or saving myself. And that choice was most definitely no choice.

Although we no longer lived together as husband and wife, it made no difference to my feelings about her. I was as deeply in love with Annabel as I'd been on the day we married. I'd go on feeling responsible for her until the day I died.

I took a deep breath. That day had so very nearly been today.

'More coffee, Harry?' Samuel's query jerked my thoughts back to the present.

'Oh, yes, yes, thanks, I will.'

'You look like you could use some more caffeine to keep awake. Thought you'd almost nodded off.'

'No, just buried in my thoughts.'

There it was again, a Freudian slip, or more likely, my wrecked nerves replaying the events of the day.

'Don't take it so hard, Harry. Even Rory McIlroy gets beaten sometimes.'

I glanced at Mike, who was attempting to take the mick out of me while innocently sipping his drink.

'Next time out I'll hang you on the clothes line.'

He snorted. 'Oh, yes? Partnering Tiger, are you?'

'Give over, you two,' Samuel said. 'There are more important things to do. Look, here comes dinner.'

And as usual, it was beautifully cooked and presented, the steaks meltingly tender, the vegetables firm and full of taste.

Conversation dwindled away as we applied ourselves to clearing our plates.

It wasn't simply a cliché that a near-death experience made one acutely appreciate being alive and all that implied. It was true. I, personally, savoured each mouthful of the lovely food.

And was bloody grateful to still be alive.

We took our time eating and then repaired to the sumptuous television lounge to relax and digest our meal.

Later, Katie popped her head around the leather room door where we were all sprawling lazily on dimpled leather ottomans watching a football match which had gone into extra time.

'Taxi's here, Mr Simpson.'

'Thank you, m'dear.' He heaved himself to his feet. 'Got to go, fellas. Train to catch.'

'Take care.' Mike flapped a languid hand, eyes still fixed on the match.

'Yes, see you soon,' I added.

The door closed behind him and we returned to giving our fullest attention to the first-rate football being played. It went to penalties, both teams evenly matched.

Mike flicked off the remote and rose, stretching extravagantly and yawning. 'Might as well make tracks.'

'To Southview?'

'Yeah. Give ourselves time to have a drink in the bar before the show starts.'

We took our leave of Katie, promised it wouldn't be long before we'd be returning and crunched our way over the car park. Away to our right, the sea boomed rhythmically under the early stars. The breeze carried a strong, salty tang and Mike sighed deeply with satisfaction as we reached the car.

'Don't know about you, Harry, but I've had a great day.'

'And it's not over yet,' I replied, deliberately not commenting on the day itself.

'It's certainly not.' He unlocked the doors and we climbed in. 'Pity Samuel couldn't join us . . .'

Victor's vehicle was still parked in the same spot on the end of his drive but now a dark blue people carrier was parked upsides. Paula and the kids, no doubt, ministering to the sick. Victor had missed an eventful day. I was glad she'd turned up. He'd just lost a son – commiserations were still needed from me – as well as a daughter. It was no fun being ill, very much worse being ill and alone.

Southview Park Hotel was two or three miles out on the A158 road. It was an impressively big, four-star complex, boasting fishing lakes and golf course with spacious cabins and luxurious caravans, plus the massive hotel itself with its own conference centre, theatre, bars, swimming pool and gymnasium. We'd been once or twice before and thoroughly enjoyed ourselves.

In no time at all we swung off to our right from the Burgh road and dropped to crawling speed past the landscaped grounds with clipped bushes and the wall of steps down which innumerable gallons of water flowed in a spectacular welcome for visitors. Just a short distance from the entrance, the hotel was visible on our left – a long building that stretched away, fronted by a lake. In the centre was a fountain throwing up a high spray of water in a big arc.

Mike drove past and parked the car and we walked over to the separate entertainment centre, the Lakeside Showbar, where the cabaret and shows were held.

'Anyone famous on stage tonight?' I asked as Mike displayed tickets.

'Hmm, that singer we saw once before – does a tribute to Adele.'

'Ha, I see, the one you really quite fancied.'

'Nonsense, I just like her singing, that's all.'

We bought drinks and found ourselves a seat near the front only a few yards back from the stage that was draped in heavy red curtains matching the swirls on the deep pile carpet.

There were already a fair number of people in the auditorium and the atmosphere was light and carefree. It was such a welcome contrast to the tensions inside me that I'd hoped had been hidden from everybody else all day. I was not worried so much about Mike noticing but had had to

161

make a real effort to conceal how I was feeling from Samuel.

Here, of course, the audience was made up of holidaymakers for the most part who had put their everyday troubles to one side and were determined to enjoy themselves. I felt myself pleasantly, effortlessly, unwinding in the safe, happy environment. Good old Mike. Although he didn't know it, and it had been arranged before we even arrived, coming to Southview Park for a laid-back evening of entertainment was exactly what my stressed-out system needed.

Jake Smith's threat against Annabel and the sniper's attempt on my life melted from my consciousness as I followed the rest of the audience's sound example and focussed on the present moment.

The curtains drew back and I continued to unwind as the evening progressed, and by the time the singer was due on stage I was almost back to normal.

After the initial introduction, however, the management had offered an apology for the non-appearance of Mike's lady singer. Apparently she had succumbed to a virus and 'couldn't have sung to save her life', quipped the compère, eyes flicking here and there, trying desperately to conceal his agitation in disappointing the punters.

'We wish her well and hope she makes a full recovery soon,' he said, his voice rising a little now to offset the groans from the disgruntled audience.

'However,' his voice rose a few octaves higher, trying to lift them all, 'we have a fresh new face and talent in the perfect shape of Lizzie. She has been abroad and only just arrived back here in England. And she's here tonight at short notice to help us out to entertain you all. I know you'll give her a rousing welcome. Ladies and gentlemen . . . here she is . . . Lizzie!' He practically yelled out the girl's name. And led the clapping, which satisfyingly rose to a good-natured, welcoming roar as she stepped on to the stage.

I had a quick glance at Lizzie. The singer who'd succumbed to the virus had been a blonde. Lizzie, however, was a brunette. I turned to Mike.

'Tough luck, Mike,' I murmured. Then froze in my seat.

Slowly, I glanced back at the girl in the spotlight on stage.

Today had been bloody strange from the get-go. And now the strangeness was compounded. Although we weren't sitting on the front row, our chairs were just yards away. We had a perfect view. I stared intently.

I'd been staggered when Jake produced the photograph of the girl posing in the stable yard. Now, I was looking straight at her. Lizzie was definitely the girl in the photograph.

She was also one very good singer. One that you only had to listen to once to remark, 'That girl's going places.' She sang all the hits made famous by Adele and each song was received with enthusiastic stamping and catcalls as the crowd revelled in them.

Her last song was 'Rolling in the Deep'.

I was thrown straight back to the last time I'd heard the song played – at Lucinda's wedding. It brought up all kinds of feelings within me. I

163

could see Lucinda there in the centre of the dance floor at North Shore Hotel after the wedding ceremony, wearing her long white wedding dress and twirling around, ecstatically happy.

The memory spoke to me and said, *Remember Lucinda – make the most of each moment*. Well, I was remembering, and I was also remembering the sound of the bullet being fired and the swift passage of wind as it zipped past my left ear.

Lizzie finished singing. The crowd went mad. They were all on their feet now, clapping, shouting, whistling. Lizzie had commandingly swept them away.

I stood and clapped appreciatively with the rest of them. At the side of me, Mike nearly deafened me with his ebullient whistles.

'What a girl!' he enthused.

'You know your trouble, Mike?'

'Eh?' He frowned.

'You're fickle. Not two hours ago you were sold on the blonde girl.'

He laughed out loud. 'But this one is something else, isn't she?'

'Oh, yes,' I said. 'She's certainly something else.'

Twenty

The storm of applause lasted a long time – too long. Before it began to die away, I was looking over my shoulder, trying to see a way through the crowd.

'Hello, gentlemen. Did you enjoy the show?'

Mike and I swung round as one. It was Mark and Gavin, the management boys, who we knew from previous visits.

'Certainly did,' Mike said.

I'd been going to eel through the holidaymakers and intercept Lizzie backstage, but it wasn't going to happen. The crowd was so tightly packed it would take too long to fight my way through to the rear doors.

Lizzie had been the last act on, was no doubt even now changing clothes and leaving before the emptying out of the crush clogged the road. I gave up the idea.

'Where did you find her?' I asked innocently, 'Is she local?'

'More local to you than us,' Mark said, 'Leicester . . . I think. A very much last-minute sub.'

'We were lucky to get her,' Gavin said. 'She certainly saved the day, or rather the evening. Got a good voice, hasn't she?'

We agreed she was a 'find'.

'I shall be booking her again.' Mark nodded enthusiastically.

'You have her telephone number, then?'

He laughed and wagged a finger at me. 'Data protection, Harry. Can't tell you.'

'Perhaps you could tell me her surname.' I raised an eyebrow.

'Oh, yes, don't see why not. It's Hibbertson.'

Disappointment ran through me. I'd been expecting him to say her name was Goode.

'Not very showbiz, is it?' Mike commented.

'Not really.' Gavin smiled. 'But she likes using

just the one name, Lizzie. Says nobody else is using that so she's a one-off.'

'She's certainly that,' I agreed.

As yet, I'd had no chance to tell Mike Lizzie was the girl in the photograph. He was unaware of the importance of seeing her on stage, had merely enjoyed her singing.

There was now a gentle exodus of revellers and we filtered in, heading for the door. We said our goodbyes to Mark and Gavin and walked back to get the car.

Mike drove, branching off the A158 and hitting the A52, the road leading home. Leaving the last of the Lincolnshire villages and bendy roads behind, he put his foot down and made nonsense of the seventy-odd miles.

I lay back in the passenger seat, closed my eyes and let the details of the day spool through my thoughts. I didn't come up with the sniper's name but one thing did become clear: whoever had squeezed that trigger had known we were going to North Shore to play golf. Must have, because they were in place, hidden in the trees on the ridge before we arrived on the fifth green. It gave me a cold feeling down my back to realize we were being watched and our movements monitored. No, that wasn't quite right. *We* weren't, *I* was. The bullet had been meant for me. It was now definitely a case of not only needing to find Alice's killer to save Annabel's life, but also of finding the person stalking me before they made another murderous attempt on *my* life.

The question I needed to answer was did Alice's killer also take a pot at me? Or were there *two* killers on the loose? Debating this unpalatable possibility took care of the rest of the way home and it was with surprise I came out of my reverie to find Mike was swinging into the stable yard at his place.

Flicking off the heater, he rolled his shoulders and ran down the window, letting in the cold night air, taking deep breaths.

'No wonder you fell asleep. Didn't realize how warm it was in here.'

'I wasn't asleep, Mike.'

He chuckled. 'If you say so.'

'I was trying to work out who it was that took a shot at me.'

He stopped chuckling abruptly, hesitated. 'I *think* I heard that . . . but could you repeat what you just said?'

'Hmmm, on the fifth green, when you and Samuel had walked on and I was trying to find the lost golf ball, someone fired a gun at me. Damn nearly took me out too. If I hadn't just bent down at that exact second to pick it up' – I took the golf ball from my jacket pocket where I'd left it – 'I'd be in Skegness morgue right now. Assuming they've got one.'

His mouth was wide open in shocked astonishment. 'Good God!'

'Yes.' I nodded. 'He is . . . otherwise I wouldn't be sitting here telling you.'

With visible difficulty, he closed his mouth.

'I wasn't going to tell you – well, not at the time, especially as Samuel was with us.'

'But for goodness' sake, why not? It needs reporting to the police.'

'Exactly, Mike.'

I watched recognition of the implications spread over his face.

'Oh, bloody hell, I see . . .'

'Last thing I need right now – police investigating.'

He nodded gravely. 'What a bastard of a situation.'

'I'm not going to disagree.'

He blew his cheeks out explosively. 'So, where do we go from here?'

His choice of the word 'we' warmed me more than I could say.

'Personally, Mike, I'm off home to the cottage right now, but tomorrow I'll be following up the whereabouts of a certain lady.'

'Really?' He perked up. 'Do I know her?'

'I think you could say so – her name's Lizzie. She's a singer.'

For the second time, his jaw dropped floorwards. I took pity on him.

'I went to Burton Lazars you know, last night? Had to feed Jake and stock him up so he would last for a couple of days.'

Mike nodded, recovering.

'Last thing I expected to see when I got there was that photograph with the girl posing in the stable yard. I thought Jake had simply looked at it then put it back in Alice's bag. *That's* what he'd told me. Seems he tells lies as well. He also photographed it on his mobile phone. Which, by the way, Leo found under my settee at the cottage. I took it over with me and gave it back.'

'Hmm . . . yes, he turned up at your place when you'd just got out of hospital, didn't he?'

'That's right. We ended up rolling around on the floor when he was giving a very good impression of trying to throttle me.'

'And there we were throwing a party on Wednesday night to try to find this girl . . .'

'And now we know who she is.'

'Yes, a bloody good singer.'

'But we don't know *where* she is.'

He beamed widely. 'I shouldn't worry about that, I've already decided I'm going to ring Mark and ask if I can book her to sing at the party. A good idea or not?'

'Yes . . . a very good idea.'

Sunday morning, sharply cold with a piercing wind that snatched at the car door as I got out in Mike's stable yard. The stable lads were scurrying around mucking out and replenishing water buckets. That had a two-fold result: the horses got looked after and the lads worked up a sweat to offset the weather. They'd had the luxury of a lie-in, it being Sunday – all of an extra hour.

But only fifty per cent of Mike's labour force was required. The other half had disappeared to wherever their respective boltholes were, making the most of their 'weekend' off. All of Saturday afternoon and Sunday – once a fortnight. The lads would be back at work the next morning at six a.m. You had to want this lifestyle or you'd never stay the course.

It was the non-glamorous side of horseracing. The side that most racegoers had no idea about:

169

what hours were worked and the hardships it involved.

For many of the young lads, it was the dream of one day race riding that kept them surviving through the hardships that, on mornings like today, were multiplied by the harsh weather.

I knew what it was like. I'd been there a good many years ago, but I'd been among the tiny number of lucky ones. The ones who began riding winners, then more winners and then started climbing up that slippery ladder to, if not heaven, something close to it – the top jockey's title.

I wrested the door closed and locked the car before going over to let myself in through Mike's kitchen door. The contrast inside was heart-warming as well as physically thawing. Perking coffee filled the kitchen with a tantalizing aroma and Pen, stirring porridge on the Aga, smiled a greeting and waved her wooden spoon.

'His Nibs is on his way. We were pretty late to bed last night.' She poured a mug of coffee out for me and passed me the jar of honey. I laced it with a good spoonful.

'Thanks. Did Mike tell you about the new singer?'

'He's talked of nothing else.' She shook her head. 'Whoever she is, she's made a big impression on him.'

'You could get to meet her. Mike reckons he's going to book her to sing at the party on Wednesday.'

'Hmm . . . I know.' She looked thoughtful.

'Your position's unassailable.'

'You think so?'

'Sure of it.'

Laughing, she resumed porridge stirring. 'Since

170

you've known him from the arc sailing days, I'll take your word for it.'

The door opened and Mike came into the kitchen. Pen passed him a cup of coffee.

'Morning, Harry. Thanks, my sweet.' He dropped heavily on to a chair. 'It was a great day but the late night's found me out.'

'Getting too old for it.'

'Cheeky bugger.'

I grinned.

'What's on your agenda then, Harry?' Pen finished her drink and poured a second.

'Morning stables . . . then . . .' I waved a hand. 'Lunch, whatever.'

'Have Sunday dinner with us. We're having it in the middle of the day for a change.'

'No racing, you see,' Mike said.

'Rare, extremely rare. And I'm making the most of it,' Pen said very firmly.

Mike and I exchanged smiles. It was rare Mike had an opportunity to indulge her. Racing was a hard mistress. I was pleased he was acknowledging his good fortune in having Pen as his partner. She deserved it.

I thought of the emptiness of the cottage on Sundays. For me, definitely the worst day of the week. It was on Sundays when I wasn't racing that I felt Annabel's absence most. The rest of the week was usually busy, very often frantically busy, driving to all ends of the country besides the actual time spent on the racecourses. It went some way to anaesthetizing her absence – not entirely, but it helped. Sundays, however, were different.

171

Before the cost of living with me outweighed the pleasure for her, we'd savoured my race-free Sundays; they didn't happen often. We'd wake, make languorous love, often continuing again under the warm water of the shower, before taking mugs of tea back to bed and lazing our way through the day.

'We'd love you to join us,' Pen pressed, studying my face.

With maximum effort, I dragged my thoughts back to the moment. How much she'd seen from my expression was disturbing. She was a sensitive woman.

'Thanks, Pen, I appreciate the offer but I've already promised Uncle George and Aunt Rachel I'll meet them for lunch at the Dirty Duck at one o'clock.'

'Not to worry.' She smiled. 'Let's take a raincheck on it, hmm . . .?'

'Definitely.'

No racing was scheduled today but, come Monday, White Lace was entered for a race at Nottingham.

I cursed under my breath as I kicked on and brought her upsides Marauder on the gallops. She responded with eager neck-reaching urgency, drawing level with gratifying ease before going on with a fluid ground-eating stride and beating him by three lengths.

The curse was because I, personally, was grounded right now; it wouldn't be me sitting in the saddle tomorrow and, most probably, winning the race.

That honour would be going to Mike's new second jockey, Tim Herring. Tim, who had immediately been nicknamed Kipper by the other lads, was a competent, likeable young man. At twenty-two, he had the time in front to go on and achieve great things. From how White Lace had just performed, it was more than likely she, too, was going places. And right then, I saw the number of years left in front of me as a top jock all too clearly. They were very few. Like footballers, jump jockeys had a short sell-by date. My frustration at the imposed racing ban losing me valuable rides ran high and hot.

I walked the mare back to the stables and untacked. Leaving her rugged up and contentedly pulling hay from the full hay net, I walked over to the tack room, put the saddle over the peg and hung the bridle over the central steel hook hanging from the ceiling. White Lace was the only ride I had this morning.

Calling a goodbye to Mike, I walked away across the yard. It was ten o'clock and I needed to make tracks for home. Thrusting my head into the kitchen, I said a quick goodbye to Pen.

'Offer still stands for dinner if anything goes amiss with your arrangements with Uncle George.'

'Belt and braces, eh?'

'Sure,' she agreed, laughing.

'Thanks. See you tomorrow, OK?'

'OK.'

I nosed the car out of the gateway and headed home.

In the bathroom, stripping off my work clothes, I soaped away under a hot shower. The question

173

mark over my future reared up in my mind. If I reached an age when I couldn't continue race riding, and that was a sad certainty, what else beckoned as a gainful living? It was the ogre living in the dark cave that faced every jump jockey.

It boiled down to the question: what was I good at? Apart from race riding, of course. And at that, my mind stalled. The image that had been thrown up was catching criminals.

I lifted my face to the hot, wet needles and let the soap and the smell of horses and stables rinse away down the plughole. I wouldn't say I was good at catching them, rather, I'd just been lucky in tracking down a couple of murderers. How unlikely was that as a creditable career move? Hardly an inspiring entry to list on my CV.

I scrubbed myself dry and put on a navy shirt and clean jeans. It would take about twenty minutes to drive over to the Dirty Duck at Woolsthorpe. I had time for a quick coffee and a trawl through the *Racing Post*.

Uncle George and Aunt Rachel were already happily ensconced in the pub enjoying the warmth of the open fire when I walked in.

'Harry, son.' Uncle George nodded genially.

'Lovely to see you.' Aunt Rachel patted the chair next to her. 'Bring your drink and come and sit down.'

I did as I was told.

'Now.' Aunt Rachel tilted her head to one side and assessed me closely. 'Tell me, what were you doing with that girl? Who is she?'

Twenty-One

Cheek was one word for it, sheer bloody nosiness were three more.

'We happened to see her, in that red mini.' Uncle George, looking ashamed, softened the bluntness of his wife's questions.

I shrugged. 'We were just having a drink, that's all.'

'But what's her name?' Aunt Rachel persisted. 'Is she a new girlfriend? I mean, there's Annabel and the baby.'

I held down my smouldering annoyance. 'Much as I wish Annabel were still living with me, Aunt Rachel, she isn't. And the baby's nothing to do with me. Sir Jeffrey is the father.' Even as I said it, the words conjured up an unwelcome picture of him in bed with Annabel. I took a savage pull at my drink. 'Just let it drop, please.'

'Annabel is still your wife.'

'Technically, yes.' I gritted my teeth. What was it with her? Her interest in the coming baby was bordering on obsession. OK, Annabel had asked them to be godparents but I wasn't the baby's father. If I had been it would have put a totally different perspective on things, a case then of bloodlines and family.

'Shall we order?' Uncle George was looking acutely uncomfortable and had probably noticed my stormy expression.

'Good idea.' I withdrew from the inquisition by picking up the menu. It wasn't needed. Having eaten here with Georgia on Friday, I knew pretty well what was on offer. 'I'll have the beef, without potatoes.'

'Good choice,' Aunt Rachel said, nodding. 'Got to keep your strength up ready for racing.'

'Er . . . yes, I will.'

She smiled at me and, from the corner of my eye, I saw Uncle George's tension release itself as his body relaxed.

I felt a little prick of conscience on two counts. Firstly, because she had no children of her own and couldn't have any, she was bound to be intensely interested in Annabel's baby.

Secondly, George and Rachel's new-found happiness was fragile. George urgently needed to keep things amicable; the long years of disharmony and misunderstanding had left deep scars beneath the surface. He was desperate to avoid any situation that could threaten their precious togetherness that had been lacking for so long.

I certainly didn't want to upset either of them. They were my only remaining relatives – Uncle George being my father's only surviving brother. Maybe it was because my father was dead that I felt a certain responsibility towards both. They had no son to look out for them. A comfortable, enjoyable shared Sunday lunch wasn't asking much of me.

Aunt Rachel, having rediscovered the joy of married bliss, wasn't to be blamed for wishing everybody else was as happily paired off. Following Uncle George's heart attack, she'd discovered how much she really cared for him. Plus the fact that she'd found out she'd mistakenly blamed him for a very human slip from grace many years before. Now she was trying to salvage as much as she could from the barren waste she'd inflicted upon them both. Yes, her intrusive questions had been unwelcome but I could surely rise above the probing.

'How about a toast?' I suggested, raising my glass. 'To a long and happy life with the people you love.'

'Oh, yes!' Aunt Rachel turned a radiant smile on Uncle George.

'I'll drink to that an' all, son.'

The difficult moment melted away.

The waiter arrived bearing three attractively arranged plates of perfectly cooked roast beef.

'Thank you,' Aunt Rachel said. 'It looks and smells lovely.'

Conversation lapsed for a few minutes as we enjoyed the delicious meal.

'When do you think the doc will let you get back in the saddle?' Uncle George asked as he enthusiastically cut into his beef.

'Don't know exactly. With concussion it can be up to three weeks.'

'At least you didn't break any bones, Harry.'

'Yes, I can do without any major injuries.'

'Are you after the championship, son?'

'I've lost a lot of ground.' I flipped a hand. 'Unavoidable, of course. I mean, this year's been a brute in lots of ways . . .'

'But you've gone through the worst things that could happen and come out on top. Nothing else will go wrong, I'm sure.' Aunt Rachel nodded, emphasizing her words. 'You deserve some happy times now.'

What they would say if they knew I'd found Alice's dead body, knew of the abortive gun attack and the fact I was hiding a criminal . . . I prayed their ignorance of the true situation would continue until I'd sorted out the godawful mess.

'Talking of happy times, Mike's giving a party on Wednesday. Perhaps you'd like to come? I'm quite sure he'd be delighted if you could. Nothing grand, just an informal bash.'

'What do you say, Rachel? Shall we?'

'We've nothing on that evening . . . yes, I'll look forward to it, thank you, Harry.' She dabbed her lips delicately with the serviette.

'Good, glad you're free. I'll tell Mike.'

'It can be a pre-birthday outing.' George patted her hand affectionately.

'Of course, it's your birthday in a couple of weeks, isn't it? What would you like for a present? Give me an idea.'

'I'm not fussed. I'm very lucky – I've got the most important thing.'

I smiled at them. Their pleasure in each other was so at odds with how they'd spent the last twenty-odd years, it was nothing short of a miracle their marriage had managed to endure.

'I'll think of something as a surprise, then.'

'I've already ordered mine.' Uncle George smugly tapped the side of his nose. 'Not telling you what it is.'

She laughed. 'Two surprises, it seems.'

'Mike and I had a surprise last night.'

'Oh, yes?'

'We spent the day at North Shore, golfing—'

'A lovely course,' Uncle George interrupted, nodding.

'Hmm, and afterwards we saw a show at Southview Park. They'd got a new singer, a girl – well, woman, I suppose. And she was good, wowed the crowd. Mike intends to book her to sing at Wednesday's party. You'll get to hear her. Apparently she's just returned to England from Mexico. The singer that was booked caught a bug and this woman stepped in at the last minute.'

'What's her name?' Aunt Rachel inquired.

'Just uses one name, no surname – Lizzie.'

'Surely she must have a surname,' Uncle George said.

'Oh, yes, of course, but she doesn't advertise herself as that. It's Hibbertson.'

'Ah, not the most glamorous. Doesn't roll of the tongue, does it?' Uncle George finished his meal and placed the cutlery neatly together.

Aunt Rachel followed his example and laid down her knife and fork.

'What time does Mike want us to turn up, then?'

'Not rigid, Uncle George. As I say, it's informal but probably seven to seven thirty. OK?'

He nodded. 'We'll be there, won't we, Rachel?' She nodded.

We finished our drinks and I saw them out across the car park. Aunt Rachel was limping. Uncle George saw me looking at her halting progress.

'Going to get a hip replacement. When she gets the call from the hospital,' he explained.

I opened the car door and she slid in with difficulty, her face puckered with pain.

'Take care of each other. See you both on Wednesday.' I waved them off, then collected my own car. Switching on, I sat for a moment. Duty was done as regards my relations. Neither of them, I realized sharply, was young. And I'd not noticed Aunt Rachel's disability before. I was so glad I'd not been petty enough to take offence at her innocent questions.

I suddenly felt weary. It was tempting to head straight for the cottage now and get my head down for a couple of hours. However, there was the slight matter of checking on Jake Smith and his by now depleted food stock. From here I could cut across country and call at Burton Lazars before I went home. It made sense. That way I wouldn't have to set out again later this afternoon. Once I'd checked him out I could go home and spend a quiet evening in peace. Right now, peace seemed to be something in very short supply.

Mercurial as ever, Jake was in a foul mood, his earlier good humour long gone. I pushed open the studio door and he let me have both barrels of vitriolic abuse.

'About fucking time. Where've you been till now?'

'Anybody would think you're my wife,' I said mildly. But his anger was in control and he thrust his face aggressively towards mine.

'Have you found him yet?'

'Who?'

'*Who?*' he shrieked, his spittle flying. 'The fucker who topped Alice.'

180

I shook my head.

'You're taking too long.'

He began pacing up and down like a caged feral animal, unable to contain himself. The burn had obviously begun hours ago and he'd been stoking the fire ever since.

'I'm doing my best—'

'Your *best*,' he spat the words at me, 'ain't fucking good enough. Got it? You've got three days, right? Three days to come up with the bastard's name and get me out of here or you and your woman are dead meat.'

'I can't do it in that time frame.'

'Oh, yes, you bloody well can.'

I was totally unprepared for his assault. His hands snaked out around my neck, both thumbs thrusting hard into my flesh. 'I'm going fucking stir crazy in here.' As he said each word, he slammed my head repeatedly back and forth against the wall. 'Fucking . . . crazy . . . crazy . . . crazy . . .' he ranted and slammed.

I believed him – the strength in the man was phenomenal. I was struggling and wrestling but it was like getting to grips with a bear – no contest. I clawed at his hands, raking and ripping with my nails, scoring deep into his skin and flesh, drawing blood, but he was so far gone it had no effect and I couldn't loosen his grip in the slightest.

Each time my head connected with the unyielding brick wall, pain reverberated through me, shaking every tooth in my jaw . . . bang . . . bang . . . bang. The whole room spun in a crazy red-and-black whirling maelstrom. He'd effectively stopped my airflow and a thunderous roaring filled my ears. My lungs filled with liquid fire, sobbing for oxygen that wasn't there.

His face in front of me melted at the edges, lost form. Blackness began to take me down.

With the last of my strength I drew a knee up sharply and smashed it into his crotch. For a brief second, his hands loosened. I sucked in lifesaving air. Swinging both arms up from low down in front of my chest, I connected with the underside of his wrists and, with a massive heave, flung them violently up and apart. At the same time, I kicked his left shin from under him and bashed my forehead into his face.

The result was gratifying. His hands came away from my throat and he cartwheeled away, hitting the opposite wall with a massive thump. A bottle of linseed oil catapulted off the shelf above his head, arced out and smashed on the floor. It hit the ground before he did. The liquid flowed out into a large puddle and filled the studio with a distinctive, overpowering smell.

Gasping and choking, I saw Jake's eyes roll back in his head. Arms outstretched sideways, he slid down the wall in slow motion before crashing full length on to the floor. I crawled over to where he lay. He was out cold. Pressing my fingers under his jaw, I felt the throb of a pulse. Thank God I hadn't killed him was my instinctive thought, followed by what the hell was I going to do now? Short of tying him up, there was nothing I could do. All I could hope for was that, when he came round, the volcanic eruption of anger would have burnt itself out.

I staggered into the tiny bathroom, ran the cold

water tap and filled a non-too-clean mug. The cold water was purgatory to swallow but it cooled my burning throat. I leaned over the showerhead in the corner, turned it to cold and stuck my head under it. The shock of the icy water had me gasping again but it brought me back to full control. Shaking myself like a sodden Labrador, I staggered back into the main room.

Jake was still in the same position sprawled on the floor, still completely out of it. I'd made a mess of his hands and wrists – they were bleeding into the spilt linseed and enlarging the spreading wet patch.

'*And* they soddin' well hurt.'

My heart gave a quick lurch.

He was still lying flat but his eyes were open. He was watching me watching him. Giving a huge sigh, he rolled over on to his back. 'How many days then?'

'Might find out Wednesday night. Got something lined up that could be key.'

He grunted, all fight now dissipated. 'If I let you live till Wednesday you're going to have to do something for me.'

'And what's that?'

'Can't go messen.'

He was hurting and it broadened his Nottinghamshire accent. It wasn't something that gave me any pleasure, inflicting pain on either animals or humans.

'Where – and to do what?'

'Newark, see how my old man's doing.'

I stared at him. 'I *was* going to Newark tomorrow . . .'

183

'Right, you can call on the old man then, can't you? And I'll let you keep breathing for a bit longer – you and that pregnant bird of yours.'

I didn't rise to it but continued staring at him. We all had our Achilles' heel. It seemed Fred Smith's well-being was Jake's.

'Deal,' I said.

What I didn't say was I'd already decided to go to Newark tomorrow and call at the police station – before they called on me.

Twenty-Two

The weather had out-foxed the council. No frost had been expected overnight so no gritters had sprayed the roads with ball-bearing lookalike chunks of salt. The temperature had dipped suddenly at about dawn and left the pavements and roads covered in a cobweb-thin coating of ice.

I was glad, after spraying and freeing my windscreen, that I'd returned to the cottage and dug out a scarf and a pair of leather gloves. I'd also turned the central heating on again. While it didn't matter for myself – I wasn't going to be here – there happened to be a large ginger tom giving me a baleful one-eyed stare from the depths of his basket. Locking the door, I reflected it wasn't only Annabel who was a sucker for that moggy.

Reaching Newark, I parked down a convenient side street and made my way from there into the centre of the town. Despite the cold walk, disconcertingly on entering the police station, I found I was sweating a little. There was something 'poised ready to spring' about the atmosphere inside a police station, unnerving for even the most innocent member of the public. And I certainly wasn't innocent.

The old cliché of Daniel entering the lions' den came forcibly into my mind. It was fractionally more suited to my situation than, say, the one about angels. I wasn't innocent, neither was I an angel. In fact, thinking back to Jake and myself eating the jacket potatoes together, supping with the Devil was far more apposite.

'Yes, sir? Can I help you?' the officer behind the glass partition inquired.

I swallowed hard and asked to speak to whoever was handling the case of the two men who had died while on remand.

And my name was? One moment please, sir. There was a delay – it didn't help with the sweating – before I was asked to step through into an interview room. A small, bare and totally soulless square contained by four walls, no windows. I sweated some more. It wasn't the same inspector I'd been interviewed by before but the officer seemed well appraised of all the details from my background as a most unwilling amateur detective.

'I was told by Mr Samuel Simpson that you had been to interview him and his daughter, Chloe, regarding the deaths of the two men involved in the Leicester racecourse murder.'

'And what else were you told?'

'Er . . . nothing. But since I was unwillingly

involved, I wondered if you had been trying to contact me? I've been in hospital for a few days, you see, and away from home since.'

'I see, sir. Have you any relevant information that might help?'

I shook my head, regretted it immediately. I was still suffering fall-out from Jake's ill-tempered attack. 'No.'

'Hmmm . . .' He pursed his lips. 'Is there any reason why you thought we wanted to speak with you?'

'I thought it likely you might, because of the circumstances.'

'Is there anything you want to tell *us*? Something you know that we don't?'

'Er . . . no, nothing. I'm sorry the men have . . .' I so nearly dropped myself in the sticky stuff and said 'been murdered' but caught the words back at the very last moment, '. . . have died. It would have been satisfying if they had been brought to court instead.'

'Quite so, sir.' The officer was watching me closely. 'Have you any theories as to why they died?'

I perjured myself. 'None.'

'Very good, sir. Well, thank you for coming in. If we do need to speak to you again, we'll be in touch.' He nodded in dismissal.

'Thank you, Officer . . .' I tried not to break into a trot in my eagerness to get out. I was weak with relief that I wasn't in their sights. Whenever threatened, both animals and humans headed for a place of safety. And, despite the dodgy state of the road surface, I floored it back home.

A black-strength coffee restored my equilibrium and I took it through to my office to check what mail or emails, if any, needed my attention. When my quivering nerves quit quivering, I relaxed into the knowledge that having taken the initiative and gone to see the police, I could confidently draw a red line under the constant anxiety of expecting a call from them. It would negate the power that Jake had wielded over me.

How unpleasant it had been to feel my home had become a possible trap instead of my bolthole from the world. Now everything was back to normal. It was satisfying to take back control. Complacently, I settled down to write my weekly racing column for the newspaper.

It was a full half-hour later I realized the police station in Newark hadn't been the only glee club I'd been going to visit. I'd completely forgotten the second delight – Jake's dad.

Swearing at my stupidity, I closed down my desktop computer and locked up the cottage for the second time.

Shock rocked me backwards. Fred Smith opened the door a full foot. His head poked round the gap like a tortoise peeking out from the shelter of its shell. I'd parked outside. I wasn't bothered about being seen. The residents, it seemed, minded their own business. It was not far from where Alice had lived – and died. Nobody had seen anything. Of course they hadn't. They didn't want to get involved, attract possible trouble.

Fred's face was fleshless, a pasty white skin covering a skull. And he appeared to have shrunk.

187

His eyes were on a level with my sternum. When he saw who it was, he eased open the door another six inches.

'Can I come in?'

An economical nod.

I stepped inside and fought to keep from gagging – the smell was nauseating. From the look of him, he'd stopped washing or shaving a long time ago and most likely was becoming incontinent. The rags he was dressed in hung from bony shoulders like a shroud. The inevitable cigarette dangled from thin lips that chewed constantly, causing the cigarette to jerk and dance, knocking off ash as fast as it formed.

'Jake asked me to come, Fred. He's concerned about you.' By God, if Jake could see the state his father was in he'd go raving mad.

'Ar,' he croaked, 'he's a good son an' all.'

'He wants to know how you are.'

'I'm . . . not so good . . . not so good . . .'

'I can see. When did you last have a meal?'

He shrugged. 'Dunno.'

'Have you any food in the house?'

'Dunno.'

He shuffled very slowly through to the living room and sank into an old armchair covered in cigarette burns. I followed him, repulsed by the state of the place. He took a drag on the cigarette. A big mistake. The smoke made him start coughing. A full three minutes later he was still hacking, coughing up phlegm into a length of toilet paper torn from the conveniently placed roll that adorned the edge of the mantelpiece. The paper had started out white but it was rapidly turning a dirty pink.

'Fred, can I fetch you a drink of water?'

No reply, just a shuddering shake of his head. He was beyond speaking.

'Look, you need to see a doctor.' He made a sharp negative movement with his hand. 'OK, OK . . .' I backed off.

It was obvious he'd been nowhere near a health centre, doctor or even a pharmacy for months, if not years. Which left me in a quandary. It was painfully clear he was a very sick man. Whether he'd gone beyond the point of pulling back was an unknown but I wouldn't put money on it. Eventually the spasm eased and he sank back totally spent, one hand pressed to his chest. Lifting just an index finger, he pointed in the direction of the battered sideboard. One hoarse word issued from his lips.

'Whisky.'

I crossed the threadbare sticky carpet and dug out a bottle of spirits. It was already half-empty – there was no sign of a glass. I offered him the bottle. Fred took it from me with a shaking hand.

'Ta.'

'Does anybody give you a hand? Get you any grub?'

'Who do I have?' he quavered. 'Lost all m'family, ain't I – bar Jake – an' I don't know where *he's* gone.'

I could feel responsibility settling itself on my shoulders.

'Would you see the district nurse if I called her?'

'Can she tek pain off?'

'You got a lot of pain, Fred?'

His lips twisted in a sour grimace. 'Treble it . . .'

I fished in my inner pocket and drew out a

189

packet of painkillers. 'Here you are. I'll get you some water to help get them down. They'll help.'

He reached out with pin-thin fingers and took them from me. Without waiting for the drink, he tore open the packaging and crammed four into his mouth.

'Hey, wait a minute, they're strong . . . Don't take all these in one go . . .'

It was too late. He'd lifted the whisky bottle and taken a swig.

'Don't take them with booze, Fred. You'll be knocked out, or worse.'

He mumbled something that sounded surprisingly like 'good job', closed his eyes and lost any further interest in anything. Within a couple of minutes, he was snoring louder than a foghorn in a sea fog.

I went into the kitchen, expecting to be confronted by a pigsty. It wasn't. The floor was filthy with ingrained dirt but the sink was empty – no pile of dirty mouldering plates and mugs – nothing. Except for one smeary glass with a crusted rim of dried milk. That told the story. I opened the fridge – half a pint of milk, just this side of going off but, apart from that, nothing. Could be Fred was keeping going on just the milk left by the milkman.

I washed out the glass and poured three-quarters of the milk into it. Fred's snores led me back into the living room and I placed the glass of milk next to the whisky bottle. Both were within reach.

Feeling inside my pocket, I debated whether or not to leave any further painkillers. I didn't want to be the one to see him off. Depending on

190

how bad the pain really was, of course, I decided pain was preferable to death. Or maybe not . . .

I compromised and left a couple of pills beside the milk. No doubt Fred would sleep for several hours now his pain was eased. He'd certainly been exhausted by the coughing fit. And the milk plus more painkillers would see him right for a while after that, which gave me breathing space to think what was the best thing to do – considering all the circumstances.

Needing to distance myself from Fred's immediate presence so I could think clearly – not to mention breathe some fresh air – I took the remains of his straggly, matchstick-thin roll-up of a cigarette from between his lips and stubbed it out safely. What the hell he'd put in it was questionable. But I suppose he wasn't able to walk out to the corner shop for a replacement. He ought not to be smoking at all with the state of his lungs.

There being nothing else I could do at that moment, I let myself out and drove the car down the new bypass road, swung left at the Saxondale roundabout and headed for Bingham. The time was now well after one o'clock. I knew of a very good pub, The White Lion, situated on the first crossroads in the village. White lions are rare, so are very good pubs. I parked up and went into the bar. A lot of people had discovered just how reasonably priced and excellent the food available was. The place was almost full.

I bought a drink and glanced down the menu, settling for plaice goujons and salad, light, nourishing. Every day that went past now brought me a day closer to getting back on the racecourse. It was a familiar battle known only too well to jockeys: the need to maintain a fit, strong body without adding weight. An ongoing balancing act. I'd compromise and forego the tasty coating.

While I waited for the food, I sat on a comfortable padded bench seat and mulled over what to do. Telling Jake came first – or did it? What would be his immediate reaction? A thundering stampede to his father's house, almost certainly. And that would blow all of us out of the water. So, should I seek out some medical help? Without Fred's permission, nothing could be done. He'd vetoed using a doctor, albeit had agreed to seeing the district nurse. Question was, how did I go about that?

My seafood lunch arrived. It was beautifully presented and tasted excellent. Conscience pricked as I ate the first delicious mouthful. Here was I enjoying my food while poor old Fred was on the point of starving. Not for long, I subdued the guilt. I'd sort something out this afternoon. Before or after I told Jake? I wasn't sure. Probably before, because if he knew there'd be hell to pay. And there was something else to be attended to – someone else I needed to speak with face-to-face so I could assess their immediate reaction.

Mike had supplied me with enough information to suss out the address I needed to visit. Jim Matthews of Bingham was, apparently, a saddler of sorts. He repaired leather goods, mostly tack restitching, and had a workshop tucked away behind a takeaway down a back street. When I finished eating, I intended to seek him out, follow up on the information Edward Frame had disclosed. I didn't think it would produce any worthwhile leads but there was precious little to go on and even a slim chance was better than none. I ate the last of the succulent fish, thanked Alison behind the bar with compliments to Martin, the excellent chef, and went out to find my car.

Bingham wasn't very large and I tracked down Matthews' workshop without trouble. In the small yard was an old, dark green, much-battered Land Rover of the type usually favoured by farmers. I parked upsides and walked across to the door to the workshop. It was propped open by a breeze-block and a man was sitting at the bench, mending a bridle.

He was a good deal bigger in stature than myself, as I saw when he noticed me and stood up. At least six foot four and probably two hundred pounds – not someone you'd care to antagonize.

And I sure as hell was going to antagonize him with my out-of-order questions. Perhaps he enjoyed an equable temperament.

I sincerely hoped so.

Twenty-Three

'Hi, can I help?'

'Could I ask if you're Jim Matthews?'

'Yes, that's me.'

'Got the right man, then.' I sought for the best words to use without provoking him. He was waiting, arms loosely by his side, puzzlement now spreading across his face.

'I, er, I went to see a Mr Edward Frame a few days ago.'

'He's a friend of mine, out Wilsford way.'

'That's right. I went to his house. It's a bit delicate what I need to ask you . . . Edward told me you knew a lady friend of his, Alice Goode.'

'Knew? That's hardly the word. Alice was a prostitute.'

'I know.'

We eyed each other, neither sure where this conversation was heading.

'Edward used to invite Alice for the weekend, he told me.'

'So?'

'They were a bit closer than the usual, er . . . client and—'

'Look, what is it you want to say?'

'When was the last time you visited Alice, because you did visit her, didn't you?'

'You cheeky sod!'

I spread my hands to placate him. 'I'm trying to piece together what happened, that's all. You did visit her, didn't you?'

'Why the bloody hell should I tell you?'

'Because I *know* you were a client. Right now, the Newark police don't.'

'Are you trying some sort of blackmail here?' His face had reddened with anger.

'No. But if I don't track down Alice's killer, you, along with all the other punters, will be under suspicion. Do you fancy that?'

'No,' he said sullenly.

194

'So if you level with me, it gives me half a chance of finding out who did murder her.'

'Are you a private 'tec?'

'Well . . .' I didn't finish the sentence but let it drift.

He hesitated. 'Yes, OK, yes, I did visit Alice. She wasn't your usual sort of prossie.'

'I know. Alice was a caring person, very respectful and discreet with her clients.'

'You were one of hers as well, then?'

'No. Not in the way you mean. She helped me out with some information.'

'Really?' he sneered. 'How likely is that? Did *you* kill her, you bastard?'

'Me! Good God, man, I'm trying my damnedest to find out who did. Alice didn't deserve what she got.'

'You expect me to believe you? I know Alice was alive the day I spoke to her. She wasn't taking clients that morning. Said she'd been working all night, needed some rest.'

My pulse went into overdrive. Alice had been talking about the night spent with Jake. He'd been telling the truth, it seemed, and Alice had been alive when he left her.

'I didn't kill her, right? OK, yes, the first time I was a bit narked – you would be, driving over to Newark, expecting a good roll . . . But don't try hanging her death on me.'

He grabbed my shoulders, bringing his face unpleasantly close to mine. I had an unwelcome, crystal-clear view of his nasal hairs. Breathing hard, he shook me roughly.

'I spoke to Alice on the doorstep. I never went

195

into the kitchen. Wasn't me that killed her, d'you hear? I'm in the clear.'

I pursed my lips and nodded. 'Do you want to take your hands off me?'

Realization that he'd crossed the line and could be done for assault made him instantly drop me like a grenade with the pin pulled.

'Thank you.'

'I was just *emphasizing* my point, that's all.'

I wasn't bothered. His action had left me on the high ground and I could ask for an answer and get it. As it stood, I could drop him in it with the police as one of Alice's punters and also threaten him with court action. Neither of which I had any intention of doing, but Jim didn't know that. At the moment, he was sweating. Ideal for me to get more information if, of course, he knew anything more.

'Run it past me again, right from when you drove up to Alice's.'

He sighed heavily. 'Come inside the workshop. I don't want anybody earwigging.'

He closed the door behind us and indicated a chair near the bench. Warily, I moved it into the corner. The wall was now an effective bodyguard on two sides. At least I wouldn't get an unexpected bash over the back of my head. There were plenty of hefty tools lying around that would have easily seen me off if wielded in anger.

Jim went over to a kettle sitting on a narrow shelf and dug out two mugs.

'Tea?'

'Why not?'

While the kettle was boiling, he began talking.

'I drove up about three houses short of where Alice lived. A vehicle was already parked outside.'

'Just a sec, what type, can you describe it?'

'A Range Rover, white one.'

I immediately thought of Victor; he'd got one of those. Probably a high percentage of drivers favoured that motor, too.

'I cut my engine,' he went on, 'and sat there waiting.' The kettle sang and he made tea and handed me a mug. 'I'd only been there two or three minutes when the door opened and this well-to-do chap came out. He was still talking to Alice on the doorstep. I saw her wave to him as he walked off towards his car.'

'Then?'

'I let him drive away and went and knocked. Alice answered it. She didn't ask me in, said she'd been working all night and needed some sleep.'

'And what did you say?'

'Like I said, I felt a bit narked, but women call the shots.' He shrugged. 'Unless you want to face a charge of rape. I wasn't *that* desperate.'

'Go on.'

'Went back home. All I could do. I did say could I come back later and she said yes, after lunch.'

'Right. When you spoke to me to start with you said you were narked the first time. What happened the second time?'

'Haven't finished telling you yet, have I?' he growled. 'As I was driving off, I got to the corner and looked in my rear view. Couldn't believe it, and I don't know where he'd popped up from, but there was another bloke, an older one again, a bit rough looking, walking up to Alice's door.

I wasn't bothered, I knew she'd turn him back, but that was three of us in less than half an hour. Popular woman or what?'

'Did you go back, then, after lunch?'

'What do you think? 'Course I did.'

'And?'

He screwed his mouth up, swallowed hard at the recollection. 'I saw her. She was lying on the kitchen floor – dead. Blood everywhere. God, it was awful, the sight of her – and that smell.'

'What sort of smell?' I immediately thought of Fred Smith's place but the overriding stench there had been one of stale – and recent! – urine.

'I dunno how you'd describe it, sort of like . . . on a farm, silage maybe, burning or rotting straw . . . And the smell of blood, of course.' He gave a convulsive shudder. 'I can't get it out of my mind; it's keeping me awake at nights. Giving me nightmares. Bloody terrible, it was.'

I knew it was. I'd seen her dead body myself.

He gulped his tea, trying to steady himself.

'Do you think the smell was caused by body odour . . . cigarette smoke . . . by loss of bowel control?'

He shook his head. 'No.' He said the word emphatically. 'No, nothing like that. It was something else.'

I let it go. There was no sense in pushing him – he didn't know. I'd not smelled anything other than the result of a bloodletting. But that had been a day or two later. Whatever the smell was, it had dissipated by the time I walked in. Whether it was important or not was an unknown.

Jim was watching me closely. 'I know you.

198

Thought you looked familiar.' His eyes narrowed. 'You're that jockey, aren't you? Harry Radcliffe?'

'Yes.'

He took another gulp of tea, his eyes never leaving my face. 'You get your name in the papers as a bloke who solves racecourse murders.' It wasn't a question, more a statement. 'Reckon you'll find Alice's murderer?'

'I'm hoping the police will.'

It was a prudent answer, not the one he was hoping for. The police demanded all information relevant to a case be handed over to them; otherwise you'd find yourself up on a charge. I didn't fancy either option.

'But you don't think they will, do you?'

'Why say that?'

'Because here you arc bothering me, asking questions . . . If you thought they'd get their man you wouldn't be here.'

'Alice needs justice to be done. Bottom line.'

'Hmm . . . well, I can't help you. I don't know who killed her – or why, but it wasn't me. And I'm not bullshitting.'

I believed him and mentally crossed him off the list. I stood up and walked to the door. 'Thanks anyway for the information and the tea.'

He nodded. 'Hope you get the swine.'

I raised a hand in acknowledgement as I carried on walking out across the yard. It narrowed the suspects but it hadn't helped me with any further leads.

Heading home, I reviewed the scraps of information he'd given me. One thing was clear. Jake was not the killer – unless, of course, he'd gone back later that morning. But I didn't see it. What would make him do that? If he'd wanted to kill Alice he'd have done the job when he was there that night. And anyway, like I'd felt instinctively about Jim Matthews, Jake had been telling the truth.

So, where did that leave me? Despondent, as regards catching the killer, still grounded from racing plus the additional responsibility now regarding Jake's dad. Definitely have to do something about him.

The rumbustious welcome I received from Leo when I entered the cottage was a spirit-lifter. For the nth time, I was grateful Annabel had left him behind when she'd gone away. He took the raw edge off coming home to an empty house.

Maybe it was reviewing Fred's house or Jim's descriptive powers of Alice's place or, possibly, both that was playing havoc with my olfactory nerves, but I found myself sniffing. There was the faintest tinge in the air of . . . what?

Leo, ignoring my twitching nose, had taken up his usual perch on my shoulder. It prompted my memory. Yes, of course, that's what I could detect – a whiff of pilchards – undoubtedly left over from a couple of nights ago, he hadn't been indulged since. But just where was it coming from? Not the cat himself – he was busy kneading my shoulder with half-sheathed claws, but he wasn't a sadist and knew just how far to dig in without hurting me. He was headbutting my cheek gently. And he certainly didn't smell. I knew all the last vestiges of pilchards would have been fastidiously washed off. And Leo's dishes were washed out daily after his meal. So, that left . . . where? Only one place remained – his basket.

I walked over, bent and sniffed at it. The cat dug claws in deeper as he sought to retain his balance. Yes, the basket was definitely a bit on the smelly side.

'Let's get your blanket washed, eh, Leo? Can't have you sleeping in a dirty bed.'

I drew out the cover, holding it aloft. It had an offending stain near the middle. It also let slip from the folds a small, scrunched-up envelope, much chewed on one corner.

Leo jumped down from my shoulder and began rubbing his jaw along the paper where it lay on the floor near my feet.

'A love letter from one of your lady cats?' I bent and retrieved it. Leo stood on his hind legs and batted a paw tipped with grappling irons, trying to reach the ball of paper.

'Uh-huh . . . Let's see what it is first; you can have it back afterwards.'

I smoothed the envelope and slid out the half-sheet of paper it contained. The message written on it was very short.

You're not after the Cheltenham Gold Cup, Harry. Give up the chase. Let the past undisclosed folly remain just that. I have warned you.

I hooked a foot around the leg of the kitchen chair and sat down heavily. When threats reached the homestead they were getting too close. I didn't need to question who had sent it – it was obviously the same person who had spoken similar words to Alice. It was the same flowery

201

style, the usage of the word folly. This was one of the mice. Not Mousey Brown but the other unknown one. And I had no idea who he was. But conversely he definitely knew me – knew I was trying to track him down. Which left him holding the aces and me at a disadvantage.

Leo jumped up on to my knee and rubbed the edge of his chin against the paper in a display of delight. It couldn't be simply for the paper itself. I lifted it up and sniffed it delicately. There was a smell but it was very faint, almost like the sweetish smell of watermelon. What it was I'd no idea. I checked the postmark; it had come from Grantham. The location was no help. Neither was the smell – I couldn't identify it. I crumpled the envelope into a ball again and flicked it to the far side of the kitchen. Leo was on it in a flash. But his interest was transient. It was the inner piece of paper that he was keen on.

'No, you're not having this.'

I held it up to the light and could see that there was something like a dried, faint watermark across one corner, punctured where Leo's teeth had mauled it. That corner had either been dropped in something or something had dripped on to it. Obviously, the envelope had been delivered by the postman when I'd been out and Leo had found it first, deeming it sufficiently tantalizing to take to bed with him. How long it had been in his basket was unknown. Not long, though. I'd shaken his blanket out on Friday morning, prior to pilchard guzzling that evening.

There was no information as to who had written it. The only clue, if you could call it that, was

202

the smell. And as to what that *was*, I didn't have a clue. But I knew a man who did, or rather, a woman. Annabel might know. If it were something Leo found tempting, she'd be bound to know. And it was a 'girlie' sort of smell. Yes, Annabel was easily my best bet.

Twenty-Four

'You're in luck, Harry,' Annabel said in answer to my query. 'My four o'clock appointment has rung and cancelled so I could shut shop early and call on my way home.'

'Great. Are you in any hurry to get back later?'

'No, not at all. Jeffrey isn't home at the moment.'

He never bloody was; what did the man think he was playing at? Did he not realize what a treasure he'd got, and just how he was neglecting her? I deliberately relaxed the physical tension in my jaw and unclenched my teeth. What an almighty wicked waste of womanhood.

'What about a bite of supper then? Nothing grand, I'm afraid. Omelette, maybe?'

'Yes, love to. About half an hour, then. Bye, Harry.'

I felt my usual rush of satisfaction at the thought of Annabel coming for an hour or two. Crumbs from the table, Harry, I told myself – from Sir Jeffrey's table. But it wasn't enough to take away my pleasure at the thought of seeing her again. I placed the half-sheet of paper on the mantelpiece out of Leo's way and anchored it under the stone carving of a cat. If Annabel could tell what the smell on the paper was, maybe I could follow it up. There was precious little else.

Another thought struck me: she might know what to do about getting a district nurse for Fred. I sincerely hoped so. It was a situation that could only get worse unless I took some action. It was still a knife-edge decision whether to tell Jake or try to help the old man first. I'd shelve it until I'd spoken with Annabel.

Leo heard the engine first. From deepest sleep to instant awareness, he sprang up to the side window, burrowed behind the curtain and set up his pneumatic drill of a purr. He might be a domesticated cat but he still retained all the jungle cunning of his larger relations.

'Your radar's still in good working order.' I scratched behind his ear on my way past to let her in at the back door. But he beat me to it and was, gleefully, scooped up and cradled against her breast almost before she'd locked the Jaguar's door. Jammy sod! It was one thing being jealous of Sir Jeffrey, yet another to be green-eyed about the cat.

'Come in. Lovely to see you – how're things?' I closed the door firmly behind her, symbolically staking my sole claim to her, even if it was for only a little while.

She grinned smugly. 'Baby-wise?'

I spread my arms wide, a stupid grin plastered across my face. 'Every-wise.'

She laughed, reached up and kissed my cheek. 'Everything's good.'

'Cup of tea?'

'What a stupid question.'

We took mugs and ginger-nuts – Annabel was very partial to them – through to the lounge. She subsided gently on to the settee, slid a cushion behind her back and sighed contentedly.

'I know I'm not living here any more, Harry, but I have to say, it still feels like home.'

As if agreeing with her, Leo took a dive off the arm of the settee and laid himself across both our laps.

'He remembers,' I said, smiling at her.

'Yes, animals don't forget good things.'

Heartened by her words, I let my arm creep along the back of the upholstery and rest gently on her shoulders. She relaxed against me, head cradled against my shoulder. I closed my eyes, drank in every second. Whether spoken or thought, arguably the saddest words were *if only, if only, if only* . . . I think Annabel had her eyes closed too – she certainly had when I risked a peep at her dear face. And even as I looked down, her breathing slowed, deepened and the weight of her body sagged against mine. All three of us became a blob – four, if you also counted the unborn baby – the world and its problems non-existent in the ever-present now, a wonderful experience, a total letting go.

Twenty minutes later, tea gone cold, ginger-nuts not dunked and my right arm as dead as Queen Victoria, Annabel stirred, nuzzled Leo and yawned magnificently.

'That was some powernap.'

'Wasn't it? I don't know when I've felt so at peace.'

205

My heart threatened to cut off my airways as it swelled with love for her. 'Annabel . . .' I said thickly, rescuing my arm and drawing her close to me. I didn't know what I was asking her but just my saying her name had rung a warning chime. She wriggled free and patted my cheek.

'Let's keep these precious moments, Harry, because they are precious. Don't spoil them by asking for more. You know I can't.'

'Yes, I know you can't, not now.'

She took my hand and placed it over the rise of her belly. 'He's changed things forever.'

I nodded. 'I know, and I do accept that.'

'How about you make us some fresh tea, hmm? Both these mugs are stone cold.'

'Coming up.'

We sipped the fresh scalding tea and then Annabel, now invigorated, insisted on being busy in the kitchen. She chopped onions, mush-rooms and an orange pepper, then fried them in a smidgen of olive oil. I added my input of four beaten eggs and she combined the raw ingredients with a generous sprinkle of oregano and produced a masterpiece with a smell and taste good enough to bring sailors back from the sea. We tucked in.

'Hmm . . .' she closed her eyes briefly in appreciation, '. . . that was *very* nice.'

'That, my love, was sublime.'

She laughed and patted my arm. 'It's because you're not used to being cooked for.'

'Not any more, that's true.'

'Harry! I'm sorry . . . I didn't mean to—'

'Rub it in? I know you didn't. At least we can

still be civilized and enjoy good food and each other's company.'

'Long may we be able to.'

'Amen.' I said it with feeling.

The awkward moment passed and I insisted on clearing the dishes while she put her feet up on the settee.

'And while you're doing that, take a good sniff at this piece of paper. Tell me if you can place what smell it is.' I retrieved the slip from the mantelpiece, folded the paper over so the words were hidden inside and handed it to her.

When I returned from the kitchen a few minutes later bearing hot coffee, I found she had taken me literally, kicked off her shoes and was snuggled up comfortably against the squishy cushions on the settee with Leo luxuriating beside her.

'The smell is very faint but I think I've discovered what it is.'

'Knew you would.'

'Such confidence,' she said and shook her head.

'Is it something Leo likes?'

'Hmm, yes, I recall he used to come over all roly-poly when I used it.'

I stared at her. 'Come on, woman, tell me.'

'It's aloe vera. I used it to soothe skin irritations.'

'Why on earth should Leo go into ecstasies over that? I mean, it's not like, say, cat-mint.'

'I don't know the answer to that. Cats have some strange foibles. They like the oddest things. I've heard the smell of leather is one some cats can't resist.'

'And Leo's got a thing about aloe vera?'

'Yes, seems like it.'

'Odd.'

'You can't get away with one word. Tell me what it's all about. I know you, Harry, it's important, isn't it?'

'Not sure. But it could be.' I took the paper from her hand and unfolded it. 'Whoever sent it meant me to take it seriously, as a warning.'

'A *what*?'

'Read it.'

She did, frowning. 'You're so right. But why are you being warned?'

'A long story, Annabel. But I think it's time I told you how things stand.'

Her eyes grew wider as I filled in all the unsavoury details from the very beginning.

'That man Jake's a maniac.' She spat the words out. 'To threaten an unborn baby, my God, he's not only a maniac, he's a monster.' She was breathing heavily, spots of red staining her cheeks.

'Annabel, it goes without saying, what I'm most concerned about is your safety and the baby's.' I reached for her hands, cradling them between mine. 'He's got to get past me first. But I wanted you to be aware of the situation. That way it's less likely you'll be caught unprepared.'

'And what do you suggest I do to be a "card-carrying" Boy Scout?'

It was so unlike her to be sarcastic. That alone told me just how very concerned she was about the whole situation.

'I wish I knew which way Jake will jump, but I don't. Of course, the safest thing would be for you to pack a bag and take off for a bit.'

'I can't do that. What about my business?'

208

'You could cancel your appointments for the next week.'

'Harry?' She leaned forward, staring into my face. 'What are you planning to do?'

'Things are going to be hotting up – I can feel it happening. I've been here before. I can't explain it logically but the strands are drawing together. This party on Wednesday at Mike's, I'm hoping it will provide a breakthrough, a definite lead. And there's certainly a crisis right now as regards Jake's father. It could tip the balance with Jake's reactions.'

'Whoa. Just what is this crisis?'

'Fred, Jake's father, is very ill. Refuses to see a doctor. Maybe would agree to the district nurse. I was going to ask you about how to arrange a visit.'

'You can't,' she said flatly. 'It needs a doctor's clearance first.'

I sighed. 'That's gone west then.'

'How bad is he?'

'Very.'

'Right, only one thing to do then: he has to be admitted to hospital.'

I shook my head. 'He'll oppose it.'

'Square one, then.'

'Yes.'

'Does Jake know?'

'I was waiting to speak to you before I decided which came first: telling Jake or obtaining help for Fred.'

'Jake's likely to blow a fuse when you tell him.'

'Bound to.'

'He's next of kin.'

'He can hardly announce it. On the run from the police . . .'

'And you can't be seen to be helping, Harry. You're already in deep trouble, hiding a criminal.'

I ran a hand through my hair. 'You don't need to remind me.'

'But it's not only the problem of Jake. There's also the person who sent you this warning.'

'True enough.'

She slumped back on the settee. 'God, what a mess.'

'Hmm.'

Taking a ragged breath, she said, 'So it really kicked off after you'd left our house at Melton, after you and I had both been signed off from the hospital and been told to take things very easy?'

'Yes.'

'And Jeffrey had jokingly said having survived hunting down two lots of murderers, he hoped there wouldn't be a third time.'

'There you are.' I inclined my head. 'It's all Sir Jeffrey's fault.'

'I don't know how you can be so flippant. I mean, when you were driving home from our house you detoured and called in at Alice's at Newark – and found her dead, murdered.'

'I'm not being flippant about Alice. I care a great deal about seeing her murderer being put away.'

'That note Jake gave you, with the strange message about mice and cheese that Alice had let slip, have you any idea who the other man might be? Could he be the killer?'

'That's what I'm hoping I'll find out on

Wednesday night. The key to his identity is Lizzie, of course, who will be singing at the party.'

'Ah, yes, her unknown father.' We were both silent for a moment. 'You're up against it, Harry.'

'Yes.'

'What happens if you don't get a lead?'

'I push, until something does give.'

'You've already been pushing, that's why you've been shot at and warned off. I think what you need is a big helping of luck.'

'I'm sure you're right. But in the last two murder cases, that's exactly what happened. OK, without my continued digging, it probably wouldn't have come about. But the outcome was the killer slipped up and I was lucky enough to spot his mistake.'

Into the silence that followed my words, a loud *rat-a-tat-tat* sounded on the kitchen door. The door-knocker was a defunct racing plate welded to a cast-iron frame I'd screwed to the wood. It made enough noise to be heard throughout all the rooms in the cottage.

I got up off the settee.

'Are you expecting anyone?' Annabel's eyes reflected her inner anxiety.

'No.'

Praying it wasn't the police, I walked through to the kitchen and opened the door. It was Mrs Oldershaw, one of the village residents who ran the local greengrocery shop.

'Hello, Mr Radcliffe.'

'Hello. Do come in.'

I felt rather than saw Annabel come up behind me. I silently applauded her courage in backing

211

me up when it could have been someone unpleasant standing on the doorstep.

'Oh, hello, Mrs Radcliffe. Nice to see you again.'

'And you, Mrs Oldershaw.'

'Well, I don't know if Mr Radcliffe will be saying that in a minute.'

'Oh?'

The woman bent down and lifted up a cardboard box from beside her feet. She stepped inside and carefully placed the box on the kitchen table.

'What have you got there?' I queried.

'I'm afraid you will have to accept them. I've managed to place the other three but now I'm stuck.'

She opened the box and Annabel and I found ourselves looking down at two ginger kittens that stared back at us with wide blue eyes.

'Oh, the little darlings,' Annabel murmured and scooped them up into her arms.

A satisfied smile spread across Mrs Oldershaw's face as she looked at me. 'They're Leo's,' she declared. And, indeed, I couldn't argue with that. He was the only entire ginger tom in the village. 'I've exhausted my opportunities to rehome these last two little mites and I can't keep them, so here they are. They're fully weaned and trained to use a litter tray.'

We eyed each other and her smile broadened as we listened to Annabel getting broody with Leo's two little problems. We both knew the mission to dump them on me had been simplified one hundred per cent by Annabel's presence.

'Well, I won't keep you . . .' Mrs Oldershaw

went to the door. 'No doubt I'll see you in the shop sometime, Mr Radcliffe.'

'Oh, no doubt you will.'

'Goodnight then,' she said. 'And just so this situation won't happen again, I'm taking Matilda to the vet tomorrow.' She took her leave and the door closed behind her.

'Talk about lightening the atmosphere . . .' Annabel, her tension released for the moment, grinned at me.

'It's all right for you – what am I supposed to do with these two by-blows?'

'Leo has cast his bread upon the waters, and I'm afraid,' she was laughing openly now as she added, 'it has multiplied and returned.'

Twenty-Five

'Hi there, Uncle George. It's Harry.'

Annabel had departed, leaving me now the grand owner of three cats. But not wishing to have two more lives dependent upon me, especially in my present tricky situation, desperation had thrown up an idea. I'd been searching around for what birthday present I could buy for Aunt Rachel. If I could get Uncle George to agree, one of the new kittens might have just fallen on its paws. I supposed it was asking too much for him to accept both kittens. Still, I could ask.

'Ah, Harry . . .'

I hesitated. There was something wrong. But

he was waiting so I ploughed on. 'I wonder if I might pop over to yours tonight? Bring a birthday present for Aunt Rachel, if you're agreeable.'

'Harry, son . . . I was going to ring you . . . to explain.'

'Oh?'

'We can't come to the party at Mike's.'

'What's wrong? Is there anything I can help with?'

'Suppose it might help if you just turn up like, so she's not expecting you. See if she'll tell you what's biting her. I don't know what to do, Harry.'

'Would now be a good time?'

'Aye, it would – she's gone to the hairdressers. Wasn't going to go but I persuaded her. If you're here when she gets back . . .'

'No problem, I can come straight over. Just hope I can help with whatever she needs doing.'

'Good on you, Harry.' There was a definite lift of relief in his voice. But I felt somewhat of a Judas as I replaced the lid of the cardboard box firmly and carried it out to the car.

Aunt Rachel hadn't arrived back home by the time I'd driven over the county boundary into Leicestershire and swung in through the open gates on to the tarmac drive. Uncle George, who had been peering through the lounge window as I drove up, opened the door.

'Come in. Make yourself at home. The kettle's boiling.'

'Great. Love some tea.'

I waited while he poured us a mug each. With conscience pricking and knowing there was only

214

a short time before Aunt Rachel returned, I dived straight in and asked him.

'Now say no if you really don't think she'd be pleased, but I've brought a birthday present.'

'I'm sure whatever it is will be fine.'

'Wait until you see . . . them.'

'Them?'

I lifted the lid of the box and he stared inside. Two fluffy ginger kittens stared back.

'Good grief!'

Remorse filled me. 'I can take them back. Stupid of me to bring them really.'

'No, no, wait a minute, Harry. It might not be a bad idea, y'know. Something to take care of, fill her day. Yes, I reckon she'd like one for her birthday present.'

The remorse melted away, supplanted by relief. The idea had paid off. Well, in part – he had said *one*.

'If you're sure, she can choose which one she likes. The slightly larger one is a tom and the other female.'

'Why don't you ask her?' he chuckled. 'She's walking up the path now.'

It must be a common trait in women. Annabel had loved them on sight and Aunt Rachel followed suit.

'For me, for my birthday, Harry? Thank you so very much – they're gorgeous. I remember you did say my present would be a surprise – well, I think you did, at the pub that lunchtime.'

I hadn't the heart to come clean and tell her they'd been even more of a surprise to me.

'Which do you want?' Uncle George put his arm around her waist as she bent over the box.

'This one.' She picked up the male.

'You're quite sure about this? I can just as easily get you another present if you'd rather.'

'I'm going to call him Toddy. He's the same colour as a fox.'

Unnoticed, Uncle George and I raised eyebrows and shared a little nod. One down, one to go, I thought.

'Rachel, I hate to break up the loving going on here, but we have some bad news for Harry. You remember? You said you couldn't possibly go to the party on Wednesday. Have you perhaps changed your mind?'

Aunt Rachel's face changed instantly from relaxed pure pleasure to tense apprehension. It was impossible not to notice. Both Uncle George and I were unprepared and disturbed by the sudden change of emotion.

'No. I . . . I can't.' She shook her head emphatically. 'I'm sorry, Harry.'

'But you were quite keen.'

'That was before—' She stopped abruptly.

'Before what, Rachel?'

'Don't ask me to explain, George, please, please don't.' Her eyes were full of tears. 'I've got you back, thank God. It would kill me to lose you.'

'Now, now, old girl. You're not going to lose me—'

'Oh, yes, if I go to the party, I will. Don't ask me to say why. I can't. That would be as bad as going there.'

'No one's pushing you to go to the party, Aunt

Rachel. If you don't feel you can, well, OK, that's fine. Your decision.'

'Bless you, Harry.' She dug in her pocket for a tissue, dabbed her eyes and nodded. 'Much safer all round if I don't go.'

Uncle George and I exchanged a swift glance. His concern over the phone earlier was, I could see, fully justified. But if she didn't want to expand on the reason behind her decision then we had to accept it. I placed my empty cup on the side table and stood up.

'Better make tracks, get this kitten back.'

'To its new home?' Aunt Rachel queried. Her self-control was returning. Danger past, I thought, the upsurge of confident relief.

'Well, no, not exactly. I meant back to my place.'

'Harry, am I right thinking this one's waiting for a new home too?'

I pulled a rueful face. 'Yes, it does need a new home. They're Leo's kittens, so I'm involved in placing them.'

'George?' Aunt Rachel tilted her head to one side and gave him a penetrating look.

He smiled at her and nodded. 'Yes.'

'I'm going to be greedy, Harry – can I have both? I mean, if Leo's the father, well, they are family too, aren't they?'

I spread my hands. 'I feel I've put you on the spot.'

'Nonsense. I think two babies together would be company for each other; play together if I'm out.'

'I can't argue that point.'

'Sorted then,' Uncle George said. 'We'll have both kittens.'

I pondered on what Aunt Rachel had said all the way back to Harlequin Cottage. Uncle George had clutched the kittens almost gratefully. He knew they would be good therapy in a difficult situation. Looking after the kittens' demands would certainly take Aunt Rachel's time and attention away from whatever the problem was. And I had to acknowledge, his grateful acceptance had mitigated the guilt I'd felt on foisting them on him. But as I thought over my aunt's words, I also gave some brainpower to what she *hadn't* said.

She had accepted the invite readily to begin with. So what had happened since to give her such disquiet? I ticked off what going to the party entailed: travelling, eating, drinking, meeting friends, meeting strangers, listening to music . . . The last item pressed a button in my brain. It was only afterwards that Mike had had the guest appearance of Lizzie confirmed. There was nothing else.

So assuming it was that, what connection could there be between Aunt Rachel and Lizzie? Absolutely none I could think of. The girl had only just arrived back in this country from Mexico. And why should it jeopardize George and Rachel's marriage? It was obvious from the level of anxiety Aunt Rachel had displayed that she considered attending the party and maybe meeting someone there, possibly Lizzie, a very definite threat to their new-found happiness.

I allowed that, given their past history of

married life, to have survived that and come through to the happiness they now shared, it would undoubtedly have made her ultra-sensitive to anything that threatened to destroy the utopia they now enjoyed.

'That was before . . .' Aunt Rachel had said. Before she had found out what, about Lizzie? With a jolt, I realized it was *me* who had innocently rabbited on about the girl singing at the party *after* they'd happily agreed to attend. So, assuming it was the girl who was the problem, why should Lizzie pose a threat?

But Aunt Rachel had gone on to add, if she were to explain, '. . . *it would be as bad as going to the party*'. With that in mind, maybe it wasn't the actual *meeting* but what would be disclosed. And if so, that meant she and Lizzie must share some history and it was the rattling of old skeletons and exposing secrets that had spooked Aunt Rachel.

By the time I'd arrived at that conclusion, I'd also arrived home. But instead of getting out of the car, I sat and thought about something else that Aunt Rachel had said. It was quite enlightening and entirely consistent with her main motivation. And was an unexpected lead I could follow up.

I concentrated on the scenario inside the Dirty Duck. Uncle George had not altered his demeanour at all, finishing his food, placing his knife and fork down on the empty plate with satisfaction. But Aunt Rachel had gone very quiet, followed his example, placing the cutlery down – but leaving the rest of her food uneaten. She'd hardly spoken again. And I'd noticed as we'd left the pub and gone outside she'd seemed to age as she made a difficult job of limping across the car park and climbing into their car. It was obvious now, having seen and spoken to her this afternoon, the news about Lizzie's appearance at the party had been the cause of her distress and had had a very depressing effect.

I locked the car and went into the cottage. I knew I had to speak to Uncle George, tell him I'd discovered the reason. Maybe, knowing the source of her distress, he could winkle out the back history.

Sticking the kettle on, I considered my immediate priorities. I'd certainly have to go out and get a takeaway of some sort and zip it over to Jake. Not something to look forward to, but necessary. It was going to prove increasingly difficult to see him grubstaked when I resumed racing. The thought of returning to ride sent a frisson of pleasure running through me. It had been quite a time since I'd left hospital, more than enough time for recovery, surely.

I poured scalding water on to the waiting teabag and counted the healing days. Even allowing for Jake's rough treatment, I reckoned there were enough. OK, I'd taken more punishment to my head than I should have since the racing fall that ended with my concussion and receiving a red entry from the racecourse medical officer. But even so, the nausea, the affected vision and the headaches were all long gone. I felt good. It was odds-on, when I presented myself for assessment, he was going to pass me fit to ride.

I reached for my mobile and called Mike. 'How about a ride on one of Wednesday's declared runners?'

'Sure?'

'Well, depends on the medical officer's decision, but yes, I reckon I'll pass. Got no lingering problems.'

He mused for a moment. 'Penny Black at Leicester suit?'

'Fine.'

'Coming in tomorrow morning? Doesn't really matter because Kip can fill in.'

I felt a twinge of disquiet at the ease with which he had fallen in with the rest of the stable lads' lingo and was calling Tim Herring by his nickname – the short one as well, not even Kipper. Not only that, I was acutely aware that Tim was the shadow standing by my elbow, ready to take over when my time for race riding was up. I knew I needed to bridge my reins and get a grip.

'Not sure, Mike, I've a lot on. Got a big problem with Jake's dad, Fred. He's in a pretty poor way and there's no one else in the frame to look out for him . . .'

'Don't tell me you're feeling responsible, last man standing and all that, right?'

'Right.'

'Just watch yourself, Harry. You're in damn deep now – stop digging. If this Fred drops into the gutter somebody is bound to pick him up.'

'Point taken, but try explaining that to Jake.'

'Oh.' He drew in a sharp breath. 'I see, yes, difficult since you're first in the firing line.'

'Exactly.'

'You've always got my back-up, you know that.'

'And I'm eternally grateful for it, Mike. I might certainly need you when we get to the hairy bit . . .'

'Just holla, I'll come – safety catch off.'

'Thanks, and the same goes for me too. If you're up against it, just bellow.'

He chuckled. 'When have I ever been up against it, eh? Bye, Harry.' He disconnected.

I checked the time; coming up to six o'clock. It was early to be going over to take Jake's food. However, I also wanted to check on Fred's state before it got too late in the evening. I downed a very strong black coffee, filled Leo's bowl with dry food and headed out for the hot food outlets in Bingham. Jake could have fish and chips tonight. For myself, my plaice goujons would have to do; Wednesday I was, with a bit of luck, back in the saddle.

I ordered cod and double chips, double wrapped, and motored swiftly over to Burton Lazars. We had maybe ten days or so before Nathaniel was due home. I had to come up with answers before he got back and reclaimed his studio. The time factor was just one more piece of pressure but I couldn't afford to ignore it. The last thing I was going to allow was to let Jake move back into Harlequin Cottage. He'd successfully disrupted my life for too long already. And my energy was needed now to bring home winners, not criminals.

Curbing my speed, I entered the village; my vehicle was one among the scores of cars transporting home weary workers. They had my sympathy. Thankfully, I didn't have to spend precious hours every day cooped up in an

222

overpoweringly centrally heated office. I drove sedately, watching for a gap in the commuters that would allow me to turn off into Nathaniel's secluded driveway unnoticed. It was certainly not the best time to be here. Any one of the people heading home could suddenly remember that Nathaniel was away and my presence was highly suspect.

Pulling in beside the kerb at a deserted bus stop, I let the stream of back traffic overtake me. I was banking on tiredness and hunger motivating the drivers to hurry on home. A gap presented and, taking advantage, I drove the last fifty yards unobserved and thankfully swung off the main road and parked between the comforting, discreetly obscuring holly hedges.

Jake was his usual charming self. He flung open the door and barely let me get through before snatching the aromatic parcel from my hand.

'Christ! I'm starving.' He dropped down on to the old couch and began stuffing vinegary chips into his mouth. 'Pass us the knife an' fork, Harry boy.' He pointed a greasy finger at the drawer containing the cutlery.

No word of thanks for the food; just an assumption I'd do as he commanded had raised my hackles but there was no sense in antagonizing him. I'd already, on the way here, decided I'd have to tell him about Fred's condition. And that bit of news was enough on its own to antagonize the hell out of him.

I didn't have a choice really. My scheme of calling in a district nurse to help Fred hadn't even made the first furlong marker. And since I was no doctor, the only thing left was to do as Annabel had stated: take him to A&E.

Letting the beast feed first, I braced myself for the nuclear explosion to come.

While Jake munched, I made a couple of builders' mugs using the milk from a big plastic bottle I'd also brought. Holding one out, he took it gracelessly.

I bit back my resentment and thought of the very few days left now, hopefully, until I discovered the name of Alice's killer and could be rid of the man. I leaned against the wall and looked out over the dark garden. It was amazing we had avoided the police getting even a sniff of what we were up to. But that luck couldn't last. And now, because of Fred, the odds were stacked against us. The chance of the police's continuing innocence was becoming more and more slender as each day passed.

The sound of a well-aimed ball of paper hitting the waste bin alerted me to Jake's hunger being appeased. I turned to face him, saw he was watching me.

'So?'

I shrugged. 'What?'

'The old man. How's he doing? You *did* bloody go, didn't you?'

'Yes. I went.'

'Aaand?' He had risen slowly to his feet, eyes narrowed.

'I'm not pulling wool. He's bad. Isn't eating by the look of it. He's smoking which makes him cough. But when he does, he's coughing up some blood—'

224

'Fucking hell! And you just left him like that? You shitbag . . .'

His fist smashed into my face, knocking me backwards. I went sprawling, cannoning into the wall.

'Get up, you arsehole!' he screamed. 'What y'waitin' for? Start the fucking car.'

I levered myself upright, rubbing blood away from where it was trickling from a cut under my eye. 'Where're we going?'

'Where do y'bloody think? We're going to Newark.'

'And if the police are staking out your dad's house, what then?'

'I don't give a fuck. I'll take the bastards out before I let them get me.'

He seized hold of my right wrist, wrenched my arm up agonizingly behind my back and frog-marched me out of the door into the black night.

Putting his lips near my ear, he hissed, 'And the first one to die will be you, Radcliffe.'

Twenty-Six

Not a word was spoken on the entire journey. The cut on my face had stopped bleeding and was merely a sore reminder of Jake's temper. I'd got away lightly and I knew it. His lashing out was because he felt impotent to help his father and I just happened to be the nearest person on which to vent his frustration. But that was before he actually saw Fred. Depending on how the old man was, things could get very ugly.

I drove slowly up the street and past Fred's house, pulling in and parking beside the kerb at the midway point between two street lamps. The second one along had a dodgy bulb and wasn't lit. It left my car in a smudge of darkness. From any distance, it would be very difficult to read the number plate. The inhabitants of the houses on both sides were totally invisible behind drawn curtains. The street itself was empty.

Jake and I exchanged a mutually conspiratorial glance and each of us reached for a door handle. In seconds, we'd legged it back to Fred's house and slid inside unobstructed by any lock.

'Fucking hell! What a stink.' Jake pulled a face.

And it was: best described as an overused urinal at a stag do, but worse – much worse. The odour rolled over us like an unwelcome wave, filling nostrils, curdling stomachs.

Was this the smell inside Alice's house? Matthews had emphasized how bad it was. But no, I'd asked if it could have been caused by loss of bodily control and he'd said definitely not. Something else entirely, something, possibly, like rotting or burning straw? That made no sense. But he'd been unable to account for what was causing the offending smell. It might not be the same as the one in Fred's house but this was certainly offending.

'Dad! Dad, where are you?' Jake projected the words in a loud, hoarse whisper. There had been no signs of any police around but both of us were extremely twitchy.

226

'Dad!' he rasped urgently.

'Last time I was here, Fred was in his chair in the lounge.'

Jake cast a swift glance at me and led the way.

Fred was still in the same position as when I'd left him. The glass of milk was untouched beside him as well as the rest of the brandy. The two further painkillers I'd given him were on the side table, still in their wrapper.

'Dad, o'my God, Dad . . .'

Jake flung himself across the room and slid to his knees on the floor beside Fred. He seized his father's hand, shook him a little.

'Dad, come on, Dad, it's me, Jake. Wake up.'

There was no reaction whatsoever. I noted the slight rise and fall of the skeletal-thin chest and breathed a sigh of relief. He was alive.

Then I noticed the trickle of blood oozing from the corner of his mouth, tracking its way between the growth of stubble and staining his shirt collar.

Jake shook him again, more roughly now.

'Wake up, Dad. Come on, try. I've come to see you. It's Jake.'

I was about to intervene, knowing I'd get blasted but was concerned for the old man, when Fred's eyes opened.

'Aaargh . . . Jake . . . y've come.'

''Course I have, Dad, 'course I have. Wouldn't leave you now, would I, not when you need me?'

A faint, beatific smile came across Fred's face. He sighed. 'You're . . . a good son . . . knew y'd come . . .' His voice tailed away and his eyes closed again.

'Oh my God!' Jake looked wildly across at me. 'He's croaked!'

I leaned forward and placed my forefinger under the old man's jawbone.

'No.' I shook my head. 'He's still with us.'

'We've got to do something.' Jake heaved himself to his feet. 'Get a doctor or something.'

I shook my head. 'He refuses to see one.'

'Well, what the fucking hell are we going to do then? We can't just leave him.'

'No,' I agreed. And whatever the outcome might be, I knew I'd have to drive Fred to hospital. It was more than odds-on Jake and I would both be arrested but, as he'd said, we couldn't leave Fred to die. And right now it was a toss-up if he'd pull through.

'Get your dad into the car. I'll drive to A&E, take it from there. Grab a blanket to wrap around him while I drive the car up as close as I can to the front door, OK?'

Jake nodded, eyes dilated with fear for his father.

With the car in place, back door standing wide open, we carried Fred, wrapped up in a blanket like a rolled-up rug, and laid him down safely on the back seat. He was no heavier than a young child. Jake met my eyes as we closed the car door. We didn't need to say anything.

I pulled the house door closed behind me and put the keys in my pocket. If the police came sniffing around and tried the door it might reassure them to find it locked.

It wasn't far to the nearest hospital. I reversed the car and parked so that the boot was square

228

on to the kerb outside the A&E admission doors. Not knowing what reception would make of my unorthodox entry, I decided to play it dumb and distraught.

Walking up to the desk, I ran an anguished hand through my hair. 'I say,' I cleared my throat loudly, 'I say . . .' I let my voice rise a few octaves higher. 'I've an emergency outside in my car. This old man, his name's Fred Smith from Newark. He's dying . . . and he's bleeding from his mouth.'

Heads turned in my direction. The magic word – bleeding – had activated the swift response button.

'You'd better show me where he is.' A burly male nurse took charge. 'Are you a member of his family?'

I raced on in front and mumbled a reply I knew he wouldn't be able to hear. We reached my car and I opened the back door. Fred was totally out of it but with his head now laid flat on the back seat, the blood had found an easier passage down his chin and his shirt front was now a scarlet splash. The nurse took one look and set the machinery in motion. In a few seconds it seemed, Fred had been transferred from the back of my car to a trolley and been hastily wheeled into the hospital.

I waited until the outer doors had swung to behind the nurses then dived into my car and drove away smartly. There would be flak flying tomorrow when I called to see how he was, but right now I had to collect Jake from where he was lying low, in a deserted bus shelter on the edge of town.

I cruised along and, with no other vehicle in sight, slowed to a crawl as I drew level with the shelter. He was watching for me and shot out like a greyhound after the hare. Still running, he grabbed the door handle, wrenched open the door and threw himself inside the car without me stopping. I floored it.

'Did they take him in?' he asked urgently. His hand gripped my left elbow like a vice. 'What happened?'

'Let's just get away from here.' I shook his hand off. 'Yes, he's safe inside now. I didn't stop to find out anything else. I'll call tomorrow, make sure he's being attended to.'

Jake flopped back against his seat. 'A bloody nightmare, that's what it is.'

'And I'm damn sure I'm not arguing with you.'

Our return was a replay of our outward journey. Neither of us spoke until I swung in between Nathanial's holly hedges and cut the engine. Now it was my turn to slump in my seat and exhale a long, exhausted sigh. Jake, his face bleak, grabbed the studio keys off me and opened up. He flung himself down on to the couch and covered his face with his hands.

'Got any hard stuff in your car?'

'Stuff?' I was feeling punch-drunk from the nerve-stretching stress of avoiding the police for the last couple of hours.

He dropped his hands briefly. 'Fucking hell, I mean liquor, o'course. Any booze, whisky . . .?'

'No.'

I left him growling away to himself and made two strong coffees.

'I'll phone in the morning, see how your dad is. Get the number of the ward he's on.'

'Huh, you'll be bloody lucky.'

'Why?'

'It'll be family only. The bastards won't tell you.'

'Well, I'll just have to lie then.'

He glowered at me. 'And say bloody what?'

'That I'm his son.'

'*Thanks*,' he sneered. 'That's sure to alert the fuzz, ain't it?'

'You've any better ideas?' I was losing patience fast. 'Look, you want to know how he is, don't you?'

Grudgingly, he gave a single nod.

'Right. It's me in the firing line, don't forget. I'm the one who took him into the hospital. Several nurses saw my face. If they inform the police about me . . .'

'Yeah, yeah, we'll both share a cell.'

And suddenly I saw only too clearly that it was not only a possibility but rapidly becoming likely that I'd get sent down. Despite the scalding black coffee, a shiver of acute apprehension ran through me. The only way out of this damn mess was to find the killer, present him – and even more essential, the necessary proof – to the police and bow out. Whether even that would be enough to save my skin, I didn't know.

As I saw it, my main chance, maybe my *only* chance to find out who it was, was to pray for a breakthrough at Mike's party. I had to find out the name of the second man. He was a man involved in horseracing, probably late middle age, possibly older. And he'd used Alice's services for years. Anything else about him was an unknown. I groaned aloud. It looked like an impossibility.

Annabel had told me I needed luck and I'd agreed with her. But right now, any luck I might have had seemed to have packed a bag and flown off. Even as I thought about it, I remembered what Edward had told me when I'd been round to his house. It was a phrase Alice had used. One of her clients, she'd said, and she was referring to a horseracing contact, '. . . *was a dab hand at strokes even if his horses never ran.*' I'd known even as Edward repeated the words that Alice had been referring to Nathaniel and his horseracing paintings.

Could *he* be the second mouse? It was a preposterous thought, but by now I was more than desperate for a result and ready to accuse any man in racing.

I pulled myself up short. I needed to get out of here, away from Jake's malignant presence and back to the cottage, release the load of tension I'd built up tonight and start thinking straight. I downed the last of the coffee, went to the sink and rinsed my mug out.

'I'm off.'

'What about me?'

'You stay put. I'll contact you as soon as I get any further information. If they won't tell me how Fred is tomorrow I'll have to call in at the hospital and find out. OK?'

He grunted. 'No fucking choice, have I?'

I looked squarely at him. 'No.'

He glared venomously. 'Don't forget, Radcliffe, I trusted you to see my old man was all right.'

'I've taken him to hospital. What more do you want?'

He stood up, tense with aggression. 'If anything happens to him, you'll pay.' He jabbed a rigid finger hard into the side of my neck. 'Your precious lady friend's first for the chop – then it's your turn. And I'll make fucking sure both of you die slow – real slow.'

Twenty-Seven

Back at home, I tossed off a double slug of whisky and felt no guilt. At the moment Jake had asked for a stiff drink, he'd warranted one, needed one – but he hadn't received one. OK, seeing Fred in that dreadful state was bound to have been a hell of a shock. But following his last words, he wasn't the only one in shock. Nor was he a man who delivered idle threats. His track record bore that out. I poured another drink.

The entire journey back to my cottage hadn't registered – I'd driven on automatic. There was small chance of Fred coming out of hospital alive. Jake knew that, I knew that. So where did that leave me? Ordering a coffin, if Jake was to be believed – and I believed him.

I put the glass down on my side table. It rattled alarmingly, was a fair assessment of how rattled my nerves were. The threat wasn't simply against me; despite the fact he was fully aware she was pregnant, Jake had said it would be Annabel he'd

233

murder first. Dear God! She was right, the man was inhuman.

I reached for the glass and swallowed the rest of the whisky. I wasn't going anywhere tonight except bed so I could get as drunk as I wanted. It would certainly lower the level in the bottle and no doubt give me a sore head, but I knew it wouldn't give me the solution nor make the slightest bit of difference to the situation.

I picked up my mobile and switched it on. While we were on manoeuvres dealing with operation Fred I'd made sure it was switched off. Now, I tapped in Annabel's number. She needed to know.

A sleepy voice answered. 'Who is it?'

'Me. Did I wake you?'

'No, not really, Harry. Just one of those days when I'm feeling a bit worn and weary.'

'But you're feeling all right otherwise?'

'Oh, yes, it's been a really busy day so I thought I'd get an early bed.'

'Sorry to intrude, Annabel, but are you on your own or is Sir Jeffery home?'

'He's right here, beside me.'

I felt the familiar and unwelcome jealousy rise. 'Good!' I said the word with a very strange mixture of strong feeling. I was relieved and pleased that for once he was at home taking care of her instead of down in London, yet at the same time I was sour at the thought of all the favours he was entitled to as Annabel's partner.

'Harry? Why, good?'

'I'm glad you're not on your own.'

'What you're actually saying is I might need a bodyguard.'

Before I had time to reply, I could hear a muffled interruption followed by Annabel's soothing assurance that everything was all right.

'Look, Annabel, if Jeffrey's home that's fine, you're safe. Nothing to worry about.'

'Hmmm, yes, that's what I've just told him.'

'I'll give you a ring tomorrow, fill you in. OK?'

'Yes, sure,' she said brightly. 'Good night.'

I reciprocated, wished her good night and switched off the mobile. I knew she'd deliberately played it down for his benefit. Sir Jeffery was a mild soul – extreme physical violence never touched his world. And Annabel now lived in that same world. I hope to God it remained untouched. Levelling with her would have to wait until I could speak to her privately.

I looked at the whisky bottle. It wasn't going to solve anything. I left it sitting on the sideboard, followed Annabel's example and went to bed.

Early the next morning, I telephoned the hospital. With luck the nurses who had been on duty yesterday would have gone off shift.

'I'm enquiring about a Mr Fred Smith who was admitted last night . . .'

And who was I, a relative? My perjury stakes were already high – I lifted them further.

'Yes, I'm his son, Jake.'

The outright lie opened doors. Fred's condition was critical. Could I bring his things, pyjamas, toiletries in asap, please? Today if I didn't mind. I did mind, very much. There was nowhere in the entire universe I wanted to go less.

235

'Of course,' I reassured the female on the phone. 'I'll come straight away.'

Swearing into my breakfast cereal, I wondered how the devil I was going to avoid being found out as an impostor. No point yet in informing Jake his father's condition was critical – it would only inflame his temper even more. What he didn't know would keep Annabel safe for at least a little while longer.

Checking I still had Fred's keys in my pocket, I locked the cottage and headed over to Newark. It was busy, the tail end of the rush hour, and took me nearly twice as long as it should have done before I pulled up outside Fred's house.

If the house was under scrutiny it was too damn bad. It was just one more risk I had to take. The old man had to have his stuff and there was only myself who could collect it. Even so, I glanced both ways and picked up the bottle of milk waiting on the doorstep before sliding the key into the lock and gaining entry. The house already had an empty, unoccupied air about it. I put the milk in the fridge. It seemed very doubtful whether Fred would ever drink it.

Opening a drawer in the kitchen, I pulled out a plastic shopping bag. I cast a glance around the downstairs rooms but they seemed undisturbed and just the same as I remembered from yesterday.

There was a pair of worn, down-at-heel checked slippers beside Fred's chair. As I bent down, the strong ammonia smell of urine was breathtaking – the chair appeared to be saturated. Gagging, I pushed the slippers into the bottom of the bag and added his spectacles in their case from where they lay on the sideboard. Also on the sideboard was an open tobacco tin practically empty but with just a few shreds of cigarette filling in the bottom. I left it there.

Climbing the staircase, I went into the bathroom. It was a sight I'd rather not have seen. Filthy was a massive understatement. Biting back a feeling of revulsion at the squalor, I looked in the wall cabinet and found an ancient toothbrush and a three-quarters empty tube of toothpaste together with his razor and some soap. I added a comb that had far more gaps than teeth and was clogged with greasy hairs. Lifting the lid from a round plastic pot, I grimaced as Fred's false teeth smiled up at me. They joined the rest of his stuff in the plastic bag.

Backing thankfully out of the bathroom, I went in search of his bedroom and some pyjamas. The overpowering smell of urine in the house was something I'd braced myself to deal with but, if anything, it was slightly less noticeable upstairs, so I was totally unprepared for the smell that hit me when I opened the next door along the landing. Then, before I'd identified the cause, I knew this must have been what Jim Matthews was having trouble trying to describe. He said it was like rotting straw. Stepping carefully into the tiny bedroom, I could see the source of damp. There was a huge damp area on the ceiling near the one wall with a window. On top of the lino covering the floor was an old single mattress that had obviously been absorbing the rainwater coming through the ceiling from a defect in the outside roof. It was covered in mildew and mouse droppings.

At one end, the mattress cover had been ripped away, exposing the interior contents. Lying on the lino by the side of the mattress was an open empty tobacco tin. Empty, except for an old, used, dried-up tea bag. That, too, was ripped and the dried leaf scattered in the bottom of the tin.

How a human being could sink to this stage of degradation was beyond shocking. I stood and shook my head in disbelief. Just looking at it answered one of my questions as to how Fred had managed to smoke roll-ups if he had been unable to get to the shops for either food or tobacco.

The mattress wasn't made of flock or padding with springs like a modern conventional mattress. It was an ancient palliasse. I'd heard of them but never seen one. Basically, it was a mattress made out of compressed straw. And underneath the portion where the outer cover had been ripped away was a gaping hole disgorging mouldy straw.

This was Fred's source of material for filling his home-made paper roll-ups.

I left the little room of horrors, located Fred's bedroom, snatched up some pyjamas and hastily exited the house, locking it behind me with thankfulness.

I'd never have to go in there again. I didn't envy the people who would have to clean it all out. The whole place was rampant with germs and would need sterilizing.

I double knotted the plastic bag and put it in the boot. Whether the contents would be of any use to Fred was debatable. The next thing would be to drop the bag off at the hospital. Undoubtedly, I'd have to lie again, and resentment rose in me. Being over a barrel forced me to do things I never usually did and rankled strongly. I retraced my journey of the previous night and turned off the main road on to the approach road to the hospital. I never got there.

Up front, turning into the car park of the hospital were two police cars, blue lights flashing. They swung round and stopped in front of the main entrance. I didn't stay to count the number of officers hastily exiting the cars and entering the hospital. I took a sharp right-hand turn down a side street and kept going. Obviously, an incident was taking place inside – most likely an assault on the poor overworked nurses to warrant that amount of manpower. Whatever was happening, there would now be one less spectator – me. Running into the arms of the police at this moment was a no-no. Even as I drove away fast, I was thinking at least Jake would agree that hightailing before the police spotted me was the only thing to do.

I drove home. I wanted to talk to Annabel but although I tried her number twice it went to answerphone and invited me to phone back to make an appointment. She was clearly busy with clients. I gave up and decided to leave it until she was back home this evening.

I booted up my computer and attempted to bury myself in producing some copy, with a rapidly approaching deadline, for my regular newspaper column. For once, the prose flowed and with satisfaction I saved it to read through later before sending to the editor of the paper.

Stretching and yawning, I ambled through to the kitchen and fixed a coffee. There was no sign of Leo. I hoped he hadn't staked out another lady friend. Any more ginger kittens being dumped on the table I could do without. Taking a gulp of coffee, I wondered vaguely just what his score was right now. Cats have upwards of around six in a litter twice a year. The number could conceivably run into the hundreds – conceivably was the right word! My musing was interrupted by my mobile stridently playing *The Great Escape*.

'Yes?'

'Harry?'

'Yes. Who is it?'

There was a breathy little sigh of relief at the other end. 'I'm so glad to get through; I've been trying for ages. You're either switched off or engaged.'

'Would that be Georgia?'

'Oh, sorry, yes, it's me.'

'How are you?'

'Good, thanks. But I need to speak to you, see you, because it's too difficult over a phone.'

'Right.'

I'd initially thought she'd rung simply to re-establish contact but it clearly wasn't just to further our possible friendship.

'Could we make it soon, Harry? How about if we met up for lunch, say, Wednesday? It's my day off from the shop.'

'Sorry, no, can't make Wednesday. I'm hoping to be passed as fit and racing at Leicester. You could come to the racecourse and watch the racing if you'd like.'

'I'd love to, Harry, but, really, I need to see you, speak privately. It's a bit, difficult . . .'

I had a quick think. 'Look, I'm free around lunchtime today. How about we meet up, say in a pub?'

'Well, there's a decent café only a couple of doors away from the shop. I could lock up for half an hour and be there at twelve thirty.'

'Fine, yes, let's do that. What's the name of this café?'

'The Whistling Kettle.'

'See you there then. Bye.'

Georgia said goodbye and disconnected. She'd seemed flustered but I didn't see what could be so important. We'd only met the once. As far as I knew there were no loose ends demanding tying. I'd intended to head back to the hospital and check on Fred when the police presence had disappeared but it was already well gone eleven. It was not viable now. I had to be in Grantham at lunchtime.

Instead, I went upstairs and had a very hot and protracted cleansing shower – the second today – followed by dumping my clothes in the washer. I didn't want any vestige of eau de Fred lingering on my person, especially when I was lunching with an attractive female.

The Whistling Kettle café was about half-full when I arrived but there was no sign of Georgia. The colour scheme was a fresh-looking yellow and white and the interior was ultra-clean. I slid into one of two seats at a corner table and ordered a pot of tea for two. By the time it arrived, Georgia

241

was just hurrying through the door. She cast a quick glance around. I raised a discreet hand an inch or two off the table and her face brightened. She came over.

'Would madam like some tea?'

She grinned and nodded. 'Madam certainly would, it's been so busy in the shop this morning. Mustn't complain . . . business and all that.'

Slipping off her jacket, she hung it over the back of the chair. We sipped hot tea appreciatively for a few moments.

'Do you want anything to eat?'

'Hmm, yes, a cheese toastie would be lovely.'

I went up to the counter and ordered two. No telling where I'd be later, or even if I'd have chance to grab any food. Since I'd been unable to go over to the hospital this morning, it looked like the only chance I'd have to take Fred's possessions would be much later tonight, after I'd placated Jake with some hot food.

'Now,' I sat back at the table and finished off my tea, 'what is it you have to tell me? You said it was a bit tricky.'

'And it is.' She nodded. 'I know I told you I couldn't disclose that name of the person who bought the dozen white roses . . .'

'But?' I prompted, my interest sparking.

'I've done nothing but wonder ever since if I ought to . . . I'm aware of data protection but it seems important, apart from the flowers, that you should be aware who the person is.'

We were interrupted by the waitress, who brought two crispy-looking toasties with side salad. I thanked and complimented her on the tempting look of them. Then switched my attention back to what Georgia was saying.

'This is getting intriguing.'

'Not for me.' She gulped, fixed her attention on cutting off a small piece of her toastie and putting it in her mouth. I realized she'd done it deliberately to give herself thinking time, so I also made a start on my own lunch.

'You know when we were in the car park at the Dirty Duck . . . after we'd had our meal?' I nodded and chewed.

'Did you wonder why I zipped off so quickly out of the car park?'

I stopped chewing. 'Yes, I did, actually. Unless you were just relieved to be rid of me.'

She smiled briefly. 'Don't be silly, we had a lovely evening. No, when we were saying cheerio, I was put in a difficult position. I couldn't drive away immediately because there was another vehicle coming in through the entrance. Do you remember?'

'Yes.' I did remember. It had been Uncle George and Aunt Rachel. I'd waved to them.

'I had to wait,' Georgia went on, 'and I saw you put your hand up to them. You knew those people.'

I nodded and waited.

'The lady in that car – *she* was the person who bought the white roses.'

'*What?*' The shock went right through me. 'Are you *sure*, Georgia?'

'Hmmm.' She sat opposite me, nodding. 'I'm quite sure.'

'But . . . it couldn't have been. Honestly, Georgia, it couldn't.'

243

'It was, Harry. I don't know her name; I'm guessing the one she gave was false. I'm sorry if it's a shock but it was definitely her.'

I was speechless. Knowing the family background and Aunt Rachel's opinion of my mother, it was unbelievable.

Twenty-Eight

'It's not possible.' I said aloud the words that were emphatically echoing around in my brain.

Georgia shook her head gently. 'You'd better believe it, Harry, it *was* that woman.'

It seemed a standoff. And there was only one way to resolve it – I had to ask Aunt Rachel if she'd bought those white roses. But assuming she had, what prompted her to do so? And even more disturbing was the reason for writing those words on the card.

'I'm sorry it's upset you, Harry, but did I do right telling you?'

'Hmm?' I brought my attention back, 'Oh, yes.' I nodded. 'Just a pity you didn't tell me before. I went over to visit both of them yesterday. I could have asked her then.'

'You haven't told me who we're talking about.'

'No, sorry, I haven't. It's my Uncle George and Aunt Rachel.'

'Oh, dear.' She looked stricken. 'They're your relatives . . .'

I smiled ruefully. 'My *only* relatives.'

'Could I ask why it's so important, because the effect it's had on you is . . . awful?' She shook her head. 'You can't see your face, but it's as white as this plate.'

Her words drew our attention to the food that was rapidly cooling.

'I suggest we eat. Be a shame to spoil the cook's efforts.'

She took heed of my suggestion and made a determined assault on her toastie and salad. I followed her example but it could have been anything I was eating. Georgia was right about the outcome of her revelation – and revelation *was* the correct word. I felt shocked through to my core. The words on the card accompanying the flowers had read . . .

> *Forgive me, Elizabeth. I should have had the courage to ask you long ago. Too late for us now – my loss. May you and Silvie comfort each other.*
> *My sincere love to you both.*

Initially, I'd assumed it to be written by a man. Subsequently, on reading the order-book entry, I'd been forced to agree that a woman had bought them. That fact had caused enough shock, but now . . . if Georgia was correct and it was my own aunt . . . what in God's name was it all about?

Just what was it my mother hadn't been asked? I didn't have a clue but I sure as hell was going to ask Aunt Rachel for an answer.

After escorting Georgia back to her shop, I drove from Grantham to Mike's Leicestershire stables. I found him laid out in his favourite leather armchair making the most of the after lunch dead part of the racing day. There were no runners today. It was all kicking off tomorrow at Leicester racecourse.

'Hi, Mike.' I flung myself down in a comfortable winged armchair.

'All OK?'

'Yes, thanks – well, as OK as this crazy world gets.'

'Any developments in any direction?'

'Huh,' I snorted. 'Where do you want me to begin?'

'That crazy, eh?'

I nodded and leaned back against the softly accommodating chair.

Pen popped her head round the door. 'Harry.' She smiled. 'Like coffee, both?' We nodded in unison and she withdrew back to the kitchen.

'Give, then.' Mike settled himself more comfortably. 'With the look of your face, you need to unload.'

He listened without interrupting while I unloaded.

Pen came in when I was about halfway through, left two steaming mugs and took herself quietly off again.

'Phew,' Mike whistled softly when I'd finished and shook his head. 'It gathers momentum.'

'Yes.'

'And poor old Fred sounds like he's on the way out.'

'Yes, I'm afraid so.'

We each reached for our drinks.

246

'It's coming to a showdown, Mike. I'm seeing bits of jigsaw that are starting to interlock.'

'If you say so, Harry. Myself, well, I can't see where any of this is leading, except the whole situation's getting bloody dangerous.'

'I need to set up a back-up plan. You still OK for riding shotgun?'

'Yep, pardner, I sure am.'

We looked at each other and grinned.

'Thanks for listening and for standing in the firing line.'

He flipped a dismissive hand. 'So, tell me, have you worked out a plan?'

'I'm working on it but until anything erupts I don't know which way it will go. However, Barbara's involved somewhere; Lizzie was photographed in her stable yard. I'm going to do some more digging before tomorrow's party and then buttonhole her. You remember; she helped out the last time it came to the crunch.'

'She certainly played her part.'

'I've a feeling she might know something crucial and be needed this time, too.'

'So if I get an urgent call from her, it means saddle up and bring my loaded shotgun?'

I nodded. 'Very likely. You see, Jake knows we're mates but he doesn't know Barbara's a feisty lady. He's a slippery bastard. And I might need an ally he knows nothing about. I had thought I might have to call on her help at Southwell Races that Tuesday. I didn't in the end, but I knew I could rely on Barbara to help.'

We sat and finished our coffee and I felt a great deal better than when I'd arrived.

'Changing the conversation, Mike – racing, tomorrow. I'm on Penny Black, then?'

'I'm sure your being OK'd to ride is a formality, Harry. Like you say, you're feeling well. And Chloe also wants you to ride White Lace for her.'

I nodded. 'Just get cleared and we're in business.'

The grandfather clock in the hall struck three thirty.

Mike stretched and pushed up reluctantly from the comfortable seat. I knew he'd got evening stables to attend to. Had thought maybe I'd give him a hand, but since Georgia's bombshell I was determined to drive over and confront Aunt Rachel.

'See you late morning tomorrow, then, Mike. I'll take my own car to Leicester. I'm not sure where I'll be going after racing.'

'Fine by me. See you then, Harry. And for God's sake, take care.'

I grinned as I took my leave. 'You bet. Nothing's going to stop me getting back in the saddle tomorrow.'

Back at the cottage, I opened up the boot and took out the plastic bag containing Fred's things. No point leaving them in the car now – there'd be no time today to get them over to the hospital. And I didn't want them perfuming the car if I left them inside any longer. I fully intended to deliver them to the hospital but it wasn't as if the bag contained any necessary drugs and, when push came to shove, my own problem had to be sorted first. Right now, my problem was Aunt Rachel.

I opted for the main road route instead of the scenic one and pulled up on the drive behind their car. I got out and pushed the doorbell. Uncle George answered, exclaiming with pleasure at seeing me again.

'Come in, Harry. There's tea in the pot. Reckon you must have smelt it brewing.'

'Thanks.' I waited until we were seated in the lounge before I explained why I was back so quickly. 'I really wanted to speak to Aunt Rachel.'

'Oh, that's a shame. She's gone to see a film with her sister, Lucy.'

My irritation rose a notch. 'When do you expect her home?'

'I'm sorry, not until after dinner tonight. Can I help?'

Even before he'd offered, I knew I couldn't grill him about the flowers. They were a very personal offering from Aunt Rachel to my mother. I doubted if he would know about them either.

'Don't think so, Uncle George. I'll have to catch her some other time.'

'She's really taken up by the kittens. It was a darn good idea of yours to give her them for her birthday.'

'Just as long as she's happy, that's OK. I didn't intend to dump them on you.'

'No, no, to be honest, Harry, I'm very grateful. At the moment they're flat out asleep in their basket. But there's something worrying Rachel – well, you saw her reaction yourself – and having Toddy and Trixie is helping to take her mind off whatever it is.'

'Good. She certainly reacted badly. But actually,

Uncle George, it's not the reason I'm here but I seem to have found out the cause of her distress.'

'You have?' He sat bolt upright. 'You must tell me. Especially as she's not here at the moment so she won't find out. I need to know, Harry.'

'OK, calm down, it's to do with Mike's party.'

'Yes, I know that.'

'Well, not the party as such but the fact that woman, Lizzie, is to be there as guest singer.'

He leaned forward, his gaze never leaving my face. 'Go on.'

'I think there's some history between them. How, I don't know. But Aunt Rachel's worried that it will all come out in public. I'm hoping to find out a great deal more myself tomorrow night and other things as well.'

'You in the middle of another one of your sleuthing jobs?'

'Unfortunately, yes, I am.'

'Hmmm . . .' He tapped his chin with a fore-finger. 'Why am I getting the feeling that Rachel could be deeply involved?' His gaze sharpened. 'She is, isn't she, Harry?'

'Don't really know, Uncle George. But I'm expecting to wrap it up in the next couple of days. If I don't, it's not going to happen.'

'And you'll tell me, when you find out?'

'Yes.'

He sighed and sat back. 'We'll leave it there for now. But you'll be calling to see Rachel herself, will you?'

'Have to, I'm afraid. Anyway, won't keep you. I'm glad the kittens are helping.'

'So am I. They were a complete surprise.'

250

'What was it you bought for her birthday? You said that was a surprise as well.'

'Haaa, yes, I picked it up last Saturday. I went over to collect it from Victor. Lives at Skegness, you know.'

'Hmm, yes, lovely place.'

'Oh, it is. Saddler's Rest is a beautiful big house facing the sea. Well, I'd already placed an order with him some time ago and he rang and said it was ready if I'd like to collect it. He took me down the garden – stretches right down to the beach, you know. He's got a workshop built at the bottom, windows looking right out over the beach and sea. Smashing place to work, if you can drag your eyes away from the view.' He chuckled. 'And the walking stick's a real beauty, with a handle all carved in the shape of a Labrador dog's head. We had one, you know, years ago – a yellow bitch called Honey.'

'I can tell she's going to love your surprise too, Uncle George.'

'I hope so, son, I hope so. I want to make up for all she's lost.'

I stood up. 'Have to push off now, Uncle George, things to do.'

'Yes, of course.'

He walked out with me to my car. 'Come again any time.'

'I will, bye, Uncle George.'

I may not have got the answer I'd been hoping for from Aunt Rachel but Uncle George had unknowingly given me a gem of information and I drove home in a state of suppressed elation. The information was a vital piece of jigsaw on

251

its own, but not only that, it also connected up to a great many other pieces.

The picture was emerging. I couldn't wait to see the whole thing.

Twenty-Nine

The Midlands had escaped a frost last night, just. It was still damnably raw and cold with spits of sleet in the wind this morning. However, thankfully, there was no threat to racing at Leicester later today. But, conversely, as I parked in a space at the far end of the hospital car park, my hands were slick with sweat.

An opening night performance couldn't have caused more butterflies to flutter. In a way this was similar; I had to put on an act and convince the staff I was Jake. It only needed a suspicious nurse and my number would be called.

I lifted Fred's bag from the boot, locked the car and put the keys into my pocket beside my mobile.

Queuing at the reception desk, I sought the right words that would gain me admission to Fred's bedside. Abject grovelling, I decided, was the way forward.

'I'm so sorry – I was prevented from coming yesterday with my father's belongings.'

'And your father would be?'

'Fred Smith, he came in the night before.'

She consulted the computer. 'Ward Three, straight

down the corridor, turn left at the end then second right.'

I found Ward Three, door firmly closed to repel boarders, notices stuck up everywhere exhorting everybody to squirt alcohol cleanser on to their hands to prevent the spread of germs. Obediently, the instructions carried out, I pressed the button and waited . . . and waited . . . and the door was, eventually, opened by a nurse.

I got my apologies in first. 'I'm so very sorry, I know it's not visiting hours but I have my father's belongings here.' I raised the noxious plastic bag. 'I was hoping I could just see him for a few minutes. It was impossible for me to get here yesterday during visiting hours . . .' I ran out of entreaties.

The young nurse opened the door wider. I slipped through before she could change her mind. She pointed to a corridor further down with individual doors leading off.

'Visiting isn't restricted.'

'Oh.'

She didn't have to say anything else, nor that the rooms were set aside for end-of-life patients.

'He is lucid just at the moment but it won't last, I'm afraid.'

I thanked her, walked down the corridor and opened the door with Fred's name on it. Guardrails, firmly locked into place, were raised on both sides of the bed for safety. Fred lay, lost in the middle, eyes closed, packed around with loads of pillows. A tiny frail form waiting to be released from his woes. At least, thank God, he was no longer in pain and could slip

253

away peacefully. My conscience took heart from that. I stuck the plastic bag inside his locker and straightened up to see his eyes following my movements.

'Hello, Fred. Just brought your bits and pieces, specs, slippers, et cetera.'

He gave a low, acknowledging grunt. Followed by the hoarsely spoken words, 'I'm . . . dying.'

'I'm very sorry . . .' I shook my head. 'And I'm sorry I had no choice but to bring you into hospital. Jake wanted me to.' Well, it was true, I suppose.

'Good boy . . . Jake . . .' It took a very great effort for him to get the words out.

'Yes,' I agreed. 'But don't try to speak – save your strength.'

His fingers convulsively clutched at the hem of the sheet.

'Can't die . . . must . . . must tell you . . . wasn't Jake.'

'What are you trying to tell me?'

'Need to . . . confess.' His voice was weak and wavering.

With a sickening jolt to my solar plexus, I knew what he was about to say. Had suspected it, hoped to heaven I was wrong. But knew hopes were useless. And when Jake found out, my chances – and Annabel's – of continuing to draw breath were nil.

However, a man was dying here; this was his last chance to make peace with his conscience – and his Maker. If he didn't tell me, there was no one else to listen.

'Wait a bit, Fred.' I took my mobile from my

pocket. 'Nobody will believe just my word – there's got to be proof.'

I switched the phone on and hoped the mobile would be able to pick up his words.

'What is it you're confessing to, Fred?'

'Mur . . . der . . . I did it.'

'You're confessing to a murder, Fred, is that what you want to do?'

'Yes.'

'OK. Now just tell me the person's name.'

I waited to hear what I'd already worked out.

'Alice,' he whispered.

'Do you mean Alice Goode?'

'Yes.'

'Why, Fred? Simply confessing isn't enough. The police need proof.'

'Jo-Jo . . . my daughter.'

I nodded. 'Because Alice introduced Jo-Jo to Louis Frame; she was in his car when it crashed. And they were killed. Is that why? If she hadn't met him she wouldn't have died?'

'Yes . . . yes.'

'But it was a while ago. Why now?'

'Jake . . . slept with her . . . saw him leave.' His eyes closed in exhaustion.

I could barely make out his words but I put them into a coherent sentence.

'You're confessing to murdering Alice Goode because she introduced Jo-Jo to Louis Frame and then Jake slept with Alice. Is that why?'

His fingers clutched at the sheet. 'Yes . . . yes.'

'Fred, I don't like to pester you but I need something more. Do you understand? The police want concrete proof.'

255

I could see he was all but spent but I knew he wanted the same result I did. If I didn't get it now there wouldn't be a second chance.

'The fag . . .' he began.

Slowly, cruelly laboriously, speaking one word every few seconds, he gave me the proof – concrete proof. It blew me away. And I recorded every word he said.

Life had improved immeasurably by the afternoon. Not wishing to face any more exploding bombs, I'd temporarily shelved going over to see Aunt Rachel. I'd have to face her before tonight's party but that was OK. I needed all my concentration right now for my racing.

The weather had given the raw start to the day the elbow, sleet was now a memory and a weak yet cheering sun had broken through the clouds, lighting up the race meeting at Leicester. And having been given a clearance and fit to ride decision, I was now changing into white breeches inside the jockeys' changing room. The valet held out my body protector. I slipped into it and fastened the front zip before putting on my silks.

'Good to see you, Harry.'

'Thanks. You're not half as glad as I am.'

'Hmm, no rides, no pay.'

'True.'

'Say, did you hear about Dunston, the box driver?'

'I knew his son was on remand and was found dead.'

'Yeah, we all reckon that must have been what did it.'

'What're you going on about?'

The other jockeys in the three o'clock were all beginning to troop out. I picked up my helmet and whip.

'Only topped hissen, didn't he.'

'Get away!' My head jerked round. 'How?'

'Chucked hissen off Flamborough Head. He lives up near Bridlington, well . . . he did.'

'No,' I said slowly. 'I didn't know. Are you sure it wasn't an accident?'

'No, reckon he meant to do it. Left a note. Said something to the effect that all the people he cared about were on the other side and he was going to jump off and join 'em.'

And I'd thought the day had improved. Just showed how gullible I was. The valet's words had shaken me but I needed to push the gruesome scenario out of my mind and concentrate on riding my half-a-ton of horseflesh. Half my mind elsewhere wasn't going to cut it.

Lord Edgware was standing with Mike and Darren, the stable lad, in the middle of the parade ring. I walked across and joined them. I touched the edge of my cap briefly. He beamed at me from all of his six-foot-four advantage.

'Sound in wind and limb . . . and head?' he chuckled.

'Yes, thank you, sir – fully fit.'

'So what are the chances for Penny Black?'

'He should come in the frame.'

'And you've put blinkers on him.' Lord Edgware turned to Mike.

'Well, it certainly sharpens him up for the race; can't get distracted so easily.'

The familiar words 'Jockeys please mount' were called and Mike flipped me up into the saddle. I found the irons and shortened up the reins.

'Bring the old devil back safely, Harry, and yourself. Winning comes second to that.'

'Yes, Your Lordship. Do my best.'

And as the starter's tape flew high, the joy thrilled through me as we jumped away. I knew the horse was as excited and keen to run and win as I was. But very often, safety and winning didn't come together in harmony. The intrusive thought crept into my mind that I'd heard of one pending death, one death that had already occurred and I didn't need a third to complete the hat-trick.

Penny Black, however, was a skilful jumper, needing little prompting on approaching fences. With ears pricked, snorting his pleasure loudly through wide, flared nostrils, the blinkers kept him focussed on the fence immediately in front and not sidetracked by horses to his side. We kept a steady, fluid pace four back from the leader and flew the fences as they came at us. With three left to jump, I took him into third place and he cleared the next two beautifully. It was now or not, and both of us were keen to go for it. I kicked him on at the last brushwood fence and he sailed over, gaining two lengths and landing smoothly, passing the second horse and chasing the leader. With hands and heels, I pushed him along and he responded, reaching forward with his head and neck. As the post flashed by we were a short head in front.

Joy flooded through me. What a way to earn

a living. I wouldn't swap it for any other job on earth.

Back in the winners' enclosure, Lord Edgware's face was one big smile.

'A wonderful race, Harry, well done.' He patted Penny Black's hot, sweaty neck. 'Well done, well done.'

Mike and I exchanged wide, satisfied grins. Keep the owners happy. Keep our jobs.

I unbuckled the saddle, pulling it away from the horse's steaming body, the smell of hot horse-flesh filling my nostrils as I folded the girths over my arm and headed for the weighing room. A first ride and a winner – life was very sweet.

And it continued to be sweet. I rode White Lace in the three thirty and she showed the rest of the horses how to do it over hurdles. Chloe was ecstatic when we walked into the winners' enclosure and went into the first spot.

'That was wonderful, Harry.' She laughed up at me as I took my boots out of the irons and dismounted. The rest of the cheerful crowd agreed with her and clapped enthusiastically.

'Great to have you back riding, Harry,' one man shouted.

I'd no idea who he was but raised a hand in acknowledgement of the goodwill.

'If tonight's party goes as well, you'll have everything sewn up by tomorrow,' Mike said, beaming.

I flashed him a glance as I unsaddled. 'You reckon?' He didn't know what I knew.

'Oh, yes,' he said expansively, 'every faith in you.'

I went to weigh in. A few minutes later, now dressed in my normal clothes, I had to disappoint Chloe.

'Sorry, but no, I can't stop for a drink. I've got things to do before the party, best crack on.'

'What a shame,' she pouted.

'Have a drink with me when I get to Mike's tonight.'

She perked up. 'Yes, I will. I'll hold you to it.'

I left her with Mike and drove away from the racecourse.

Without ringing in advance, I went to see Aunt Rachel. This time she was in.

'Harry, oh, do come in. Have you come to see the kittens?'

Without waiting for my reply, she opened the door to the lounge and both ginger bundles tumbled out. Their comical gambles brought a smile to my face. It had been a long time since Leo had acted like that.

'Keeping you busy, Aunt Rachel?'

'Oh, yes.'

I bent and scooped them up but their fluffy, innocent persona lasted about three seconds flat before their tiny claws were unsheathed and they were struggling and kicking to be put down.

'Ouch!' I said, laughing. 'They're tigers in disguise.'

'Here,' Aunt Rachel said, 'put some of this on your scratches, Harry.'

I reached for the tube she was holding out.

'It's aloe vera. Very good at healing skin irritations. It's the only product that promotes cell growth.'

'Thanks.' I rubbed a little on to my hands. The smell was exactly the same as that on the warning letter. Annabel had been right.

'What else can you use it for?'

'Oh, George uses it for his feet, says it soothes them.'

I rubbed the gel thoroughly into my sore skin. 'I really wanted to ask you a potentially difficult question, Aunt Rachel. It's very personal but I really do need an answer.'

Her shoulders stiffened and her face became instantly shuttered. 'I may not wish to *give* you an answer.'

'Is Uncle George around?'

'He's just gone down to see to the greenhouse skylights. He'll be back in a minute or two.'

'Then I'll ask you straight away, before he comes in. You might find it easier if it's just ourselves.'

'You'd better ask then.' She turned away and leaned her hands on the edge of the sink for support.

'You bought a dozen white roses for my mother's grave . . .' I didn't say any more.

Aunt Rachel spun round to face me. 'It was that girl, wasn't it? The one I saw you with in the Dirty Duck. She *told* you. I knew she would.'

'Not immediately. Why did you buy them and write that card? What did you mean?'

Aunt Rachel's shoulders slumped and she sat down suddenly on a kitchen chair. 'Harry,' she said in a low voice, 'I've been a cruel, heartless woman.' She lifted a hand as she saw me about to counter her words. 'No, don't say anything. I blamed George and your mother, as you know,

261

for having what I thought was an affair. I set myself up as judge and jury when I had absolutely no moral right to do so. If I'd had the courage to ask your mother straight away, I'd have found out the truth. But I didn't. I blamed them both for years. And do you know why, Harry?'

I shook my head.

'Jealousy, green-eyed jealousy.'

I didn't know what to say. She finished what she needed to tell me.

'Elizabeth, your mother, had what I wanted most – children. She had you and she had a little daughter, Silvie – I had none.'

I left Aunt Rachel in the kitchen, went out and got into my car. I drove home in a sombre mood.

The pieces of the jigsaw were falling into place. I was joining them together fast. The picture, becoming clearer, wasn't a happy one. It showed the heartache of a lot of people but, like a festering boil, it needed to burst and open up; only then would the people involved be free of the hidden poison in their lives.

And I seemed to have got the sticky end once again. There was only me who could do it.

There was a message waiting for me on my landline. Nathaniel had rung. *Just to let you know, Harry. My family over here in Switzerland are down with flu. I'm in the way right now. So, I'll be back home tomorrow night. Can you get rid of the lodger?*

Today had already been a roller-coaster of ups and downs.

And today wasn't over yet.

262

Thirty

I'd just poured myself a whisky when a loud
click sounded from the kitchen – Leo was back.
He slid sinuously round the lounge door and
bellowed a greeting.

'Good to see you too, Leo.'

He stopped, one paw lifted before cautiously
putting it out in front with exaggerated care.
Pacing slowly up to me, ears flattened, he delicately sniffed my trouser leg, whiskers trembling.
Then, instead of leaping up to my shoulder as
normal, he turned his back on me, shook a disap-
proving back leg and walked to the door. Giving
me a dirty look over his shoulder, he headed for
the kitchen.

'Ha, I see,' I said. 'Kittens.'

Taking the hint, I took myself – and the whisky
– upstairs, stripped off my clothes and dropped
them in the linen basket. Then I ran a deep, very
hot bath and climbed in. The water eddied,
dispersed itself around me and settled. Lifting
my whisky glass, I sipped and soaked, eyes
closed, and let myself relax.

Running the events of the last few days slowly
through my mind, I connected the pieces I knew
fitted and allowed myself to drift, giving my
subconscious every chance to join a few more
for me. It was a method I'd tried with success
in the past. It was a process rather like ceasing

struggling to remember a name and finding a short while later the elusive word popping up of its own volition.

I ran the tape of memory back to the start and fed every fact into my conscious mind, looking closely at each one before going on to the next. It took some time to consider all that had happened. Then I deliberately let go of the whole puzzle. I finished my drink, sank lower in the bath and closed my eyes. And having done so, I unwound even more in the soothing hot water and adopted a confident expectation that the answers would come.

A lot of famous people had discovered the amazing medium of water to come up with solutions. Agatha Christie had reportedly washed dishes and discovered unexpected results. The great man himself, Dick Francis, had apparently waded out waist-deep into the sea and found help with his plots.

I drifted, dozing . . . allowed my mind to empty . . . and waited. It was enough to know it worked.

At seven o'clock, dried, dressed in a navy suit, white shirt and dark red tie, I locked the cottage and pointed the Mazda towards Burton Lazars. I did a slight detour on the way and went into a fish-and-chip shop in Bingham. Taking a hot meal for the beast might deflect his undoubted anger at what I had to say. The aromatic parcel safely stowed, I drove on to the tiger's cage.

Predictably, his temper went through the roof.

'What are you fucking saying?' he spat the words out at me while stuffing hot chips into his mouth.

264

The effect wasn't pleasant. I should have let him eat first.

'Nothing I can do, Jake. Nathaniel's had to pull out and he's heading home tomorrow. You can't stay here.'

His jaws masticated rapidly. 'So just where *do* I stay then, arsehole?'

I shook my head.

'Bloody fucking great.' He returned his attention to the rest of the food and it disappeared quickly, his anger fuelling his intake.

'If you don't come up with somewhere, I'm at yours.'

'Oh, no.' I waved my forefinger from side to side. 'We've done that bit. No more.'

'I'm not bloody sleeping rough.'

'Look, stay here tonight. It's OK for tonight. Then tomorrow, in the morning, I'll come over. Try to think of somewhere to hole up – I'll drive you there.'

'I can stay tonight?'

'Yes.'

He calmed down, grunted, 'And you'll be back in the morning?'

'Yes, but I can't stay any more just now. I've to be somewhere at eight o'clock.'

He ignored me and began making a mug of tea. 'How's me dad?'

'I took his bits and pieces to the hospital today. He was what the nurse called lucid. I stayed a little while. He was talking to me.'

'So he's OK, then?'

I avoided the bomb going off. 'Yeah.'

'Hope they'll let him smoke. Can't get by without his smokes.'

What did the man think the nurses were going to do? Offer Fred a light?

'I'm off. Bye.' I opened the studio door and escaped thankfully into the cold night air.

The party had begun and was revving up when I reached Mike's stables. Cars were parked up all around the tarmac area to the side of the main house. I added the Mazda.

Pen welcomed me in to an ear-filling burst of music and laughter. She took me over to the temporarily installed bar and poured me a drink.

'Did you know your aunt and uncle are here?' she whispered.

I actually felt my eyebrows rise in incredulous surprise and took a gulp of the champagne.

'No, I didn't. I thought they'd made it clear Aunt Rachel had pulled the plug on coming.'

'Something must have made her change her mind.'

Pen shepherded me across to the buffet table, sagging dangerously under all the delicious, lovely eatables.

'Now don't say you can't, Harry. I purposely had you in mind when I was preparing the food. Lots you can indulge yourself with.'

She waved a hand. I followed her direction and agreed I could certainly spoil myself. Tasty bites with low calories abounded: little gem lettuce leaves topped with cottage cheese and chives, thin-cut ham, tuna and cucumber, thinly sliced chicken, prawns, stuffed olives, vegetable croutons – the choice was vast. Annabel wasn't the only thoughtful, caring woman around.

266

'Looks lovely, Pen.' And I meant it. 'Mike's a very lucky guy.'

She blushed.

The doorbell sounded and she excused herself to let in more party people. I walked over to speak to Samuel and Chloe. 'Hello, both.'

Samuel smiled and nodded, mouth full of sausage roll. Chloe, dressed to kill in a deliciously tight-fitting dress in midnight blue, reached up and kissed me lingeringly on the cheek.

'I'm so grateful to you winning on White Lace today.' Her eyes sparkled.

Over her shoulder, I caught Samuel's sardonic look. He didn't need to say anything – I could read his thoughts. Daddy's little girl was no longer a little girl. And she was also no longer involved in a divorce case, which meant she was free to do exactly what she wanted. I didn't need Samuel to tell me Chloe wanted me. The available sign was clear enough to read for myself. Suddenly I seemed to be surrounded by extremely eligible females and opportunities. Maybe when I'd put this case to bed I could begin to put my own life back into decent order.

Mike came up, bringing with him two old acquaintances of mine. Both trainers – I'd ridden for each.

'Hello, Tally. Nice to see you.'

'I keep seeing *you* in the papers – not just the *Racing Post*, either.' She laughed. 'Very Philip Marlow. Are you thinking of it as a new career when you stop riding?'

'God forbid.' I turned to the man beside her. 'Good to see you, Jim.'

He nodded. 'Don't know why you should say that, Harry. From what I've read in the news as well, you're outgunning the police in catching baddies.

Jim Crack – the endless leg pulls about his name were legion – was a very successful trainer. When his own riding days had ended after a fall, he'd taken on a similar role as private detective, albeit not for long. He'd discovered horses were his life and set up stables not far from Tally.

Tally was a nickname derived from the one on her birth certificate, Albertine. Raised by her father, the late Jack Hunter, she had taken up the training reins after his death. Barbara Maguire had done the same after her husband, Sean, died. There were certainly some spunky women around.

'I think it's what's called "helping the police with their inquiries", Jim.'

'No, no, Harry.' Tally giggled. 'That's what they say before they slap the handcuffs on.'

'Think she's right there, Harry,' Mike said.

'What's your next case, then?' Jim took a gulp of his lager and waited expectantly.

'I don't go out looking for "cases", as you put it,' I protested. 'They just seem to find me.'

'Ah, do I detect you have one ongoing at the moment?'

'Well, yes, sort of. It started out as one but it seems to have morphed into two somehow.'

'And have you solved it yet?' Tally leaned conspiratorially into me.

'Yes, the original one, not the offshoot from it.'

'And what case would that be, Harry?'

I spun round and saw it was Victor Maudsley. There was a cautious watchfulness in his eyes. 'Hello, Victor. Just talking about my new in-famous doings, that's all. But I did want to have a word.'

'Leave you to chat. See you later.' Tally caught Jim's elbow and tugged him away. Relieved, I watched them amble away through the crush. What I needed to say to Victor – and ask him – was for his ears alone. However, at that moment, Mike appeared on the tiny, hastily erected stage at the far end of the room.

'Ladies and gentlemen, your attention, please.' The volume of chat and chuckles diminished. 'We have a special treat in that Miss Lizzie Hibbertson has come over to England from Mexico for a visit. She has happily agreed to sing a selection of songs for us tonight made famous by Adele. Do please give her a warm welcome. Thank you. Ladies and gentlemen . . . Lizzie.'

I switched my gaze across the room and spotted Uncle George and Aunt Rachel. Her hand had flown to her mouth, eyes wide with alarm . . . and what?

I could be very wrong but my self-indulgent time lazing in the bath had borne fruit. The look on her face at this moment verified what I'd conjured up from my subconscious during my bath. Absurd and wildly unlikely, I'd thought it, but now it actually looked like I'd struck the bullseye.

Up on stage, Lizzie firstly, with a smile, thanked Mike for booking her and then extended the thanks to everybody present. She proceeded to give her all in each of the three songs. The thunderous applause that followed was truly appreciative of a wonderful performance. She blew kisses from the stage and promised to sing again later. I'd been as riveted as the rest of the guests and it took an effort to bring myself back to business.

I turned to Victor. 'Perhaps we should talk somewhere private.'

He dragged his eyes away from Lizzie. 'Yes . . . yes, might be favourite.'

The conservatory at the back of the house was empty of guests.

'Do you mind?' He produced a packet of cigarettes from his pocket.

I shook my head.

'OK, what do you want a word about?'

'Oh, I think you know exactly what needs airing.'

'I suggest you tell me what you know and we'll take it from there.' He took a deep drag of the cigarette. I noticed his hand had a slight shake.

'Fair enough. I suggest we take a seat.'

I didn't want him doing a sudden runner if I touched a nerve. And I knew what I had to say to him would definitely hit the spot. If, indeed, what I'd worked out was the truth. I forced down my quiver of uncertainty. There was no way I could be one hundred per cent certain without confronting him.

We parked ourselves in the comfortable, bamboo-framed, well-upholstered chairs. Taking a lungful of smoke, he blew it out sideways and looked at me. I met his gaze steadily.

'Alice,' I said.

'Carry on.'

'You visited her on the day she died.'

Panic crossed his face. 'Oh no, you've got that wrong. I didn't kill her, poor woman . . .'

'I know you didn't.'

He gaped. 'How . . . did you know I was even there?'

'You were seen, Victor, I don't mess about clutching smoke. I like facts – solid facts,' I bluffed, straight-faced, and mentally crossed my fingers.

'So, what do you want?'

'The truth would be good, save a lot of time and then we can get back to the fun and games – and the singing.'

He stared at the floor.

'Come on, Victor, admit it. You were the person who sent that note to Alice asking her to keep quiet.'

'And what *exactly* did I say?'

'Word for word? OK. *I hope you're not going to reveal the follies of youth. Not after playing cat and mouse all these years.*'

He shook his head. 'You're wrong, Harry. You missed out the word callow: *the follies of callow youth.*'

He knew the game was up and we both knew I hadn't made a mistake. He'd given me the word I'd deliberately missed out.

'So, who is the second mouse – and who is the cheese?'

'I'm surprised you haven't worked that out as well.'

'I've sussed out that one mouse is certainly well-named. It's Mousey Brown, the trainer, isn't it?'

'Eh?'

His look of surprise wasn't put on. My shored up yet still-shaky confidence dipped.

'Barking up the wrong one there, Harry. Oh, I'll give you old Mousey was one of Alice's long-standing regulars. And you and I both know the reason for that, I don't doubt.'

I nodded.

'But he wasn't the second.'

'So who was?'

He pulled a wry face. 'Sean Maguire.'

'*What?* Barbara's husband?'

'That's right.'

'How the hell do you know that?'

'Because I'm the first mouse. And I was there, that night. It was just us two young chaps – and the two girls.'

'One being Alice . . .'

'Yes.'

'Are you going to level with me and tell me who the other woman – the cheese – was?'

He shrugged in despondent resignation. 'It's all going to come out in any case; nothing I can do now to stop it.'

'And you did try, didn't you, Victor? Because you knew I'd keep on digging until I found out the truth.'

He nodded.

'It was you who fired the shot at me on the fifth green at North Shore golf course.'

'Yes, it was me,' he said in a low voice.

'It was so important to you to keep the secret that you were prepared to try and kill me.'

'It was to protect someone . . .'

'So,' I tried him with the million dollar question, 'why didn't you shoot again and finish the job?'

'I couldn't. I didn't intend to kill you, Harry. I'm not a cold-blooded murderer. I fired to frighten you off, not kill.'

'You came bloody close to it!'

'I know, that's why I ran. I wanted to frighten you and ended by frightening myself because the bullet nearly hit you. I never intended to kill you. It was only to stop you from finding out.'

'You certainly scared me.'

'I'm sorry. It shook me up. I wasn't aiming for you but I damn nearly took you out. That was never my intention.'

'Right.' I took a deep breath. 'Now, you're going to tell me the other woman's name. Or shall I tell you?'

Thirty-One

'Harry, *please* . . .' His face screwed up in genuine anguish. 'Don't make me do this.'

'Do you think it gives me a kick?'

He looked into my face searchingly. 'No, I don't, you're a good man. But the fallout could be goddamn awful.'

'Help me out here, Victor. Let's wrap it up.'

He shook his head. 'I still don't know how you knew it was me.'

'A little matter of a warning note, sent to me. The note had become splashed with some aloe vera. And the fact that you get gout, like Uncle George, and most likely put aloe vera on your feet, like he does, to soothe it. But you hadn't got gout the day I was playing golf, had you?'

'No. How did you know . . .?'

'Because Uncle George called at your place and you walked all the way down your garden to the workshop with him. He'd come to collect the walking stick he'd ordered.'

'And all this mess . . . All these years later, it's come about from that one night things got out of hand . . . Sean and I, we kept plying the girls with drink . . .'

'Tell it straight. You're talking about a foursome – an orgy?'

'Licentious revels, yes, I can't deny it.'

'And what was the outcome?'

His voice dropped very low. 'Both girls ended up pregnant.'

'And you didn't know who the father was for either of them?'

'That's right.'

'Finish the story, Victor.'

'Alice, well, she had an abortion.'

'And the other girl?'

'You know, don't you?'

'My Aunt Rachel.'

'Yes. Her family was shocked but wouldn't hear of an abortion. They sent her to relatives in Mexico. The baby was born over there and . . . they adopted it.'

'Their surname was Hibbertson, wasn't it? And the baby was named Lizzie?'

'Yes.'

'Did Aunt Rachel ever see the baby again?'

'No. Alice was paid to infer it was her baby and her name given as a contact should it ever be needed. It was hushed up and kept secret. The tragedy was that Rachel had a bad time giving birth, couldn't have any more children.' He buried his face in his hands. 'God forgive me, she was a little innocent, a virgin . . .'

'It explains her obsession with the family bloodline. It even extends to Leo and his kittens. And I can understand now how bad things were when my mother had Silvie. Like rubbing salt in the wound. Poor Aunt Rachel. Now she's terrified Uncle George will find out and leave her.'

'Maybe she isn't. She's here at the party and so is Lizzie. When I saw them both tonight I realized it was over, it was all going to come out. I was trying to protect Rachel. I knew what a bastard I'd been – as had Sean. Alice knew, of course. She'd had a letter from Lizzie. Told the girl Barbara was a distant relative.'

'Why didn't Alice tell her about yourself? Surely that would have been better.'

He spread his hands helplessly. 'We didn't know who the father was – none of us did. What sort of news would that be to present the girl with when she arrived?'

'Devastating, I should think.'

'Exactly.'

'You could,' I said tentatively, 'have a paternity test done, you know. DNA . . .'

'Harry, I don't want to know. I couldn't handle it. Paula's my daughter, my only daughter.'

'I never offered my condolences on your son's death . . .'

'Then don't!' he snapped. 'He was no son of mine.'

'I can understand how you must feel.'

'No, you bloody can't.' He thrust his jaw forward. 'What you heard me say, Harry, was the truth. He wasn't my son.'

I didn't believe it. 'Now, come on, Victor . . .'

'You don't believe me. OK, I'll let you into another little sordid secret, Harry. But you're going to have to swear to me on Elizabeth's grave you won't disclose it.'

I swallowed, thought about it. 'Victor, if it's needed in a court of law, I shan't lie for you.'

He brushed the idea away impatiently. 'Nothing like that. He was Elspeth's son, right?'

I nodded, wondering just where the hell this was going to go.

'She had an affair with Nathaniel Willoughby. Did you know that?'

I was stuck – the proverbial rock and a hard place. However I answered the question I was in a mess. I had known about it but kept quiet. Now it left me without an answer. However, he didn't wait for me to speak.

'The child was his. And that's why we had a divorce. Not the other way round, OK? It was *me* who divorced Elspeth. I agreed it was the other way round to save her good name. Got it?'

'Yes.'

He stubbed out his first cigarette, reached for another and inhaled like a man desperate for air.

The door to the conservatory opened and Barbara came in. 'Thought this is where I'd find you two chaps.'

She accepted the offered cigarette from Victor and flopped down in a chair, crossing her shapely legs. They extended a long way from beneath her short, scarlet skirt.

'You dishing the dirt, Harry?'

'More like shovelling it on to the muck heap.'

She laughed throatily. 'So, we've got little Lizzie back with us. Seems her adoptive mother died a long time ago – breast cancer, she told me. But a couple of months ago the poor girl lost her dad over in Mexico.'

I tossed a glance at Victor. He flipped a dismissive hand.

'Barbara's the only person alive who knows about Lizzie.'

'Well, I knew about Sean's little . . . "dalliance" – or, possibly, paternity. It was before we were married.' She laughed huskily. 'The old sod left it late. Told me as he left to go out on his stag night. Said if I wasn't in church the next day, he'd understand. But he knew I was dotty about him, knew I wouldn't leave him standing there alone at the altar.'

Victor stood up. 'I need a drink, a double. Have we finished, Harry?'

'I guess so.'

He walked to the door, hesitated and turned back. 'We still on for playing golf at some point?' he said, smiling crookedly.

'Anytime you like, Victor. But I'd watch out for the fifth green if I were you.'

His smiled relaxed. 'Don't you mean we *both* need to play it safe on the fifth?'

'Do you know, you're dead right.'

He winced, still smiling. 'Don't use that word, Harry.'

'Not applicable now, is it?'

'No. Never was.' He closed the door behind him.

'What was all that about?' Barbara took a sip of her gin and tonic.

'Something and nothing.'

'Do you know the full SP about Lizzie?'

'Yes. The bits I didn't figure out Victor just filled in.'

She nodded. 'Good, saves me explaining.'

'There is something I need to ask you, Barbara.'

'Go on then.' She smiled roguishly. 'Your place or mine?'

'What, with your canine killers as minders?'

We both laughed.

'Seriously, though, Barbara, there's a situation brewing – a dangerous one.'

'Oh, yes?'

'Hmm, afraid so.'

'Similar to the last time?'

'Very much so. At the moment, Jake Smith considers you a possible threat – certainly your tame wolves.'

'Give me the backstory.'

I levelled with her about our nocturnal visit to her stables.

'Bugger me!' She stubbed out her cigarette.

278

'So he's not going to suspect you as an ally.'

'What do you want me to do?'

'Don't know, that's the devil of it. We have to play it moment by moment right now. What will tip the fat into the fire, of course, will be when Fred Smith dies.'

'Is he likely to?'

'Oh, yes, afraid he is and it's imminent. But as soon as I tell Jake . . .'

'He'll go off like an IED?'

'Yes.'

'OK,' she said slowly. 'So after he dies, if you tell me *before* you tell Jake, I'll hold myself ready to do . . . what?'

'Call up Mike as reinforcement.'

She nodded soberly. 'Like last time.'

'Yes. Mike's my main man – in at the kill.'

'Right, and does Mike know, or expect to receive a "go get him, boy" call from me?'

'He does.'

She nodded. 'Count on me, Harry. We can't leave you without help when you need it. I mean, you're helping other folks now with this new, shall I say, job? We need you to keep cleaning up our mean racecourses.'

'It's supposed to be mean streets, I think, Barbara.'

'Could well be.'

'Think we should get ourselves back to the party, don't you? We're missing the fun.'

'I'm with you. Don't want to miss Lizzie's encore.'

'She's good, isn't she? Did an overseas agent book her for Southview?'

'Yes, but I can see her being snapped up by an English agent before long.'

'Might mean she stays in England.'

She nodded. 'Yes. When the dust settles, and it will, it would be lovely for Rachel.'

'Do you reckon Uncle George will be OK about it all? I'd hate to think it was me who split them up.'

'You know, Harry, I think when he gets over the shock he'll be tickled pink to have a beautiful, talented step-daughter.'

I grinned. 'Be great, wouldn't it? Reckon you could be right.'

'Come on then, I'll introduce you to Lizzie.'

We rejoined the party.

Mike was running around Lizzie like a happy dog who'd found a bone. There was an aura of deeply relaxed contentment radiating from her. She herself kept casting unbelieving, wide smiles at Aunt Rachel and Uncle George. And they, in turn, were returning the smiles. I looked across at all of them and realized for the first time it wasn't just my aunt and uncle who had suddenly acquired a relative. I had a new cousin. A staggering thought.

Aunt Rachel spotted me. She rushed up and threw her arms around me.

'Thank you, Harry. What a wonderful birthday present! The best in the world.'

'Count me in on the thanks, Harry, son.' Uncle George was shaking his head in wonder at what had just occurred. 'It's been the biggest shock of my life but I couldn't be more pleased, and especially so for Rachel. She deserves to be happy. It's amazing. She always wanted children and now . . .' His eyes wet with unshed tears,

280

the words dried up. Rachel reached up and kissed him.

Unnoticed, Lizzie had come up behind me. 'Hello, Harry. Can I thank you, too?'

'No need.' I grinned. 'I'm very happy for you, Lizzie, and for my aunt and uncle.'

'Oh, yes, you and I are cousins, aren't we?'

'Looks like it.'

'I can't believe it. I came over to England without any family and now here you all are, ready-made for me.' She threw her arms out wide and laughed with sheer happiness.

'Don't thank us,' I said, 'just sing.'

And she did.

And the last one she sang exquisitely, previously released by Eva Cassidy, was 'Songbird'. It couldn't have been more appropriate.

Thirty-Two

It had been a marvellous bash. Even Barbara, who was, justifiably, known to throw amazing parties, rated it the best she'd ever been to. I eventually arrived back at the cottage at two o'clock and crashed out ten minutes later.

My mobile, sitting on the bedside table, sang out *The Great Escape* at a quarter past three. Groaning heavily, I reached out a searching hand and answered. It was a replay of a couple or more calls I'd received from various hospitals before at this unholy hour. Basically, the hospital needed me there, like, hours ago. They didn't say so, of course. What they said gave the impression that if I gunned my car at top revs, it might not be too late to say goodbye to Fred. The reality was Fred had almost certainly already shed the burden of pain and departed.

'I'll be right with you,' I said, and forced leaden legs out of bed.

'I'm so sorry, Mr Smith,' the staff nurse on night duty told me. 'Your father died a short time ago.'

I nodded, looked at the floor, suitably knocked over by the news.

She led the way down the familiar corridor and left me in Fred's room to grieve in solitary respect.

'You may want to take his possessions, but if so, you'll have to sign for them.' I nodded, still looking at the fascinating floor.

I'd taken a big risk in doubling for Jake as Fred's son but, seeing Fred's serene face, I didn't regret it. He had departed as he'd wanted, with a clear conscience. And I'd given him that. Even now, if I got a kick-back from authority, it would still have been worth it. They couldn't alter his confession.

'Bye, Fred,' I said as I stood at the foot of his bed. 'You did the right thing and confessed. I'll let Jake know and I'll pass on your things to him.'

There was no response or reply but, wherever he was, I hoped he'd heard me.

I looked at the time – just five past four. Too early to do anything else but get back home. So

I did. And dropped thankfully into my still vaguely warm bed. I slept until 6.30 a.m., when the alarm stridently woke me.

Groaning again as realization of the old man's death penetrated my sleep-deprived brain, I took myself off to the bathroom and turned the shower on full bore: hot, then cold. It certainly woke me up if nothing else. Coffee, strong, black and a bowl of cereal would energize the system – with luck.

With blood sugar on the rise, I tapped in Mike's mobile number. By now, he was most likely getting ready to go out on the gallops, but as I'd told him last night, keep the mobile switched on – we'd reached the last furlong and he could expect a call at any minute of the next probable twenty-four hours.

'Hello, Harry. Take it the post's in sight?'

'Not quite yet, Mike. But the inevitable has happened.'

'Right. Does the next of kin know?'

'Will do soon, but you're first, Barbara next, then I must warn Annabel.'

The jolt, that now the death had occurred the danger to her was suddenly very real, brought sweat out on my forehead.

'Take care of yourself as well, Harry. Well, if you *can.*'

'Trouble is, Mike, I don't know what form his reaction will take. He's a man of impulse.'

'Hmm, violent impulse. Keep me in the frame. My car's full of juice and ready to roll.'

'Thanks, Mike. I'll ring off now and tell Barbara to stand by.'

'Do that. See you soon, mate.'

I rang her mobile and she answered immediately.

'Hello, Harry. Have the pearly gates swung open?'

'Indeed they have.'

'So, it's all systems . . .'

'Will be, when he's told the news.'

'I'm on red alert. I've got the back-up muscle of all my lads if you need it, Harry.'

'Appreciate it, Barbara, thanks. But I don't know which way it'll swing. Got to take what comes and run with it.'

'Does Mike know?'

'Yes, I've just filled him in.'

'And Annabel, what about Annabel, does she know yet?'

'I'll ring her next.'

'Get her away, Harry. The little person's in the firing line as well.'

'You don't need to remind me . . . it's a devil of a situation.'

'Do it now – give her chance to think where to go. She could come here, of course, but it might not be the safest.'

'Good of you to offer, Barbara, but, like you say, may not be such a good idea. Don't sweat, I'll keep her safe. Must ring her now.'

'Of course, bye, Harry. My phone's on all the time, good luck.'

'Thanks.'

I disconnected and checked the time: seven forty. Annabel would be awake now. I hoped I didn't get Sir Jeffrey – it would be the devil's own trying to explain to him. I rang her mobile. It took several rings before she answered it.

284

'Annabel, you on your own?'

'Hello, Harry. Jeffrey's downstairs fixing drinks. It's very early – what's the matter?'

'Yes, sorry, but I need to speak to you urgently.'

'Are you in trouble?'

'No, yes . . . listen, Annabel. I want you to pack a few necessary things and go away for two or three days, now, straight away.'

'I can't, Harry, I'm not well. I don't want to go. I shall be OK at home.'

'No, darling, you won't. But what's wrong? Have you caught a bug or something?'

'No, nothing like that. I just feel ill, my back hurts and I feel sick all the time.'

'I'm sorry. I wish I didn't have to pressure you but it's imperative you go. You remember we talked about this at the cottage? Fred Smith has just died in hospital. I've got to tell Jake.' I heard the gasp as she caught her breath.

'So that's the reason?'

'Yes. You *do* have to go, there's no other option. Think of the baby, Annabel. Please don't fight me on this.'

'Jeffrey's going back to London in a couple of hours. He's buying a flat down there. I suppose I could just go with him. He wants me to see it.'

'Yes. Do that, darling, it's absolutely the safest thing to do. There's no need to tell him why, just go. Promise me you will?'

'I just wish I felt a bit better. I really do feel very ropey.'

'Can you lie down and rest when you get there?'

'I expect so, yes.'

'If necessary, book in at a hotel.'

'Don't worry about me, Harry, I'll be all right. But I know you're in for a bad time with that Jake. Promise *me* you'll take care of yourself.'

'Now I know you're going to be safe, and the baby, I can concentrate on what I have to do.'

'That's right. I'll see you when I come back.'

'Look forward to it, darling. Bye.'

'Bye, Harry.'

With Fred's bag of possessions stashed in the boot, I started the car and drove to Burton Lazars. I had to get Jake out from the studio before Nathaniel came back and discovered him. It wasn't something I wanted to dwell on. It only needed him to see Jake and he would then become an accessory to harbouring a criminal. And that would definitely be my fault.

I shivered. Nathaniel's safety looked like being in my hands. If Jake thought there was a chance Nathaniel would go to the police, I really didn't give much for his chances. I had to play this very carefully. There was an awful lot at stake.

The car covered the miles and I swung into the drive and parked. Taking the bag from the boot, I walked down the garden path to the studio. Opening the door, I went in. The studio was empty. What few belongings Jake had had were missing. I called his name in case he was in the toilet. But even before I opened the bathroom door and discovered that empty too, I knew Jake had jumped ship.

Thirty-Three

What now?

I sat down on the settee to think it out. My first feeling was massive relief. If he had truly gone, and it looked a certainty because he'd taken all his things, then I was immediately off the hook. I didn't have a clue where he was now and I could not be accused of harbouring nor assisting.

I rested my head back against the upholstery and felt the accumulated tension drain from me. Thank God, the danger was past at last.

Maybe I shouldn't have insisted on Annabel travelling down to London when she wasn't well and hadn't wanted to go. Too late, she'd agreed to do what I demanded but at least Sir Jeffrey was on hand. He would look after her.

I got to my feet and began the business of transferring all the items I'd brought over from my cottage back into my car. All the kitchen equipment: kettle, toaster, saucepan, etc., and dismantled the bedding from off the settee that Jake had slept on. The least I could do was leave the studio clean and tidy, as it had been when Nathaniel flew off to Switzerland.

I ran the hoover over the threadbare carpet, wiped down the surfaces and cleaned up the bathroom. It might not have been thorough enough to remove DNA evidence of Jake's occupancy but at least it looked much more wholesome. If the police had no idea that Jake had ever been here, there would be no systematic search for evidence.

I toyed with the idea of posting the studio keys through the letterbox in the bungalow's front door but decided as Nathaniel had delivered them into my hands before he left I should hand them back to him.

Taking a final look around, I locked the door, pocketed the keys and drove home.

My mind drifting along pleasurably on the lines of maybe asking Chloe out this evening, I opened the kitchen door and stepped inside.

A hand shot past my face and immediately slammed it shut behind me. Jake Smith detached himself from the wall. He'd been flattened against it, unseen, awaiting my arrival. My heart rate hammered itself up into the stratosphere until I could scarcely breathe.

'You on your own, Harry boy?'

Unable to speak because my tongue seemed to have glued itself to the roof of my mouth, I managed a nod. He had successfully jumped the surprise on me. I'd no idea that he might be here, waiting for me, it rendered me instantly wrong-footed. The shock left my legs feeling as soggy and weak as wet cotton wool.

I groped for the kitchen chair and slumped on to it.

'What are you doing here?' I croaked through stiff lips.

'You wanted me out of the other place, so, here I am.'

I shook my head from side to side very slowly,

trying to gain time to think. No way could I tell him about Fred's death while he was here at the cottage. He would trash the place – after he'd trashed me. I'd got to get him out.

'You can't stay here.'

He hitched a leg on the corner of the table. 'Go on, then, tell me where we're going? You said you'd drive me.'

'I . . . I don't know of anywhere . . .'

He lunged across the table and grabbed the front of my shirt collar, twisting it, trapping my flesh painfully against the unyielding button.

'Try.'

I was beginning to choke but he abruptly released me. 'And while you're *trying*, you can make me a mug of tea.'

It ended with me making two mugs, one each. It was bizarre, seated either side of the table, drinking tea in a civilized fashion, knowing his flashpoint of anger might ignite at any moment and he could kill me. But the sharp awareness of this all too likely scenario had my mind jinking in terror like a fish taken from the water.

'Haven't you got any other friends who are away from their pads right now?'

I stared at him. It was a brilliant question. Of course, that was how we'd fallen lucky in the first place with the studio. Just that one question gave me the answer. I considered it briefly; there was no time to drive around aimlessly looking for an empty gaff. Not when I knew where there was one for the taking.

Draining my mug, I stood up. 'Get your things. We're off.'

'You thought of somewhere?'

I nodded.

'Safe?'

I shrugged, feeling my self-confidence coming back now I seemed to be the one in charge. 'Safe as the next.'

The journey into Leicestershire didn't take long. I turned off the main road down a narrow side road then turned left into the entrance to a long drive. We passed a sign board that read Unicorn Stables.

Jake flashed a glance at me as I drove on. 'You sure you know what you're doing?'

'Yep.'

'If you're trying to trap me . . .' He didn't finish the threat, the aggression in his tone said it for him.

I ignored him and swung left in an arc when we came to the house, followed the drive around to the back where it ended in the stable yard. I cut the engine and we both sat silently scanning the runs of closed stable doors, the total absence of stable lads. There was an unmistakable deserted air hanging over the whole place.

He grunted. 'Looks OK.'

'Come on.'

I got out of the car and went across to the feed room. He followed me. The room housed the stock of horse-nuts, oats, etc. Additives like linseed oil and molasses were stacked tidily on shelves. The hay bales were stored separately in an open-ended barn. The air smelt dry, not musty.

'This do?'

He grinned wolfishly, 'You know, Harry boy, I think you and me should go into partnership.'

I repressed the shudder of disgust that ran down my spine. His comment was doubly bitter since I'd stupidly thought him out of my hair only to find I was still as trapped as ever.

'Let's get your stuff moved in here out of the car.'

He'd brought the one bag containing his own things, but there was all the equipment I'd thought destined for the cottage to shift.

He returned to the car, collected his bag and took it inside the feed room before following me round to the back of the car. I opened up the boot – and froze.

He came right up behind me. 'What's up?'

He looked into the boot and saw what I'd seen: the distinctive bag from the hospital containing his late father's possessions. He took a deep breath, clenched his fists and pressed them to his mouth.

'He's . . . dead . . . yes?' But there was an agonized pleading in his voice, wanting me to contradict him.

'Yes, early this morning. I'm very sorry.'

'Oh, you will be, by Christ, you will be.'

He caught my right arm, twisting it up my back to breaking point.

'Walk.'

He kicked my left leg behind the kneecap. I staggered forward and he kept up the momentum by frog-marching me into the feed room.

'Where is she?'

I knew who he meant but played dumb. 'Who?'

'Your pregnant bitch.'

He accompanied the words with a vicious, sharply jerked knee into my coccyx. Pain, like a bolt of red-hot electricity, shot up my spinal column into the base of my skull.

'She's out of your reach.'

They were the last words I was going to say to him about Annabel. Thank God I'd made her go with Jeffrey to London. I couldn't tell him where she was, even if he tortured me, because I didn't know where. London was a very big place.

If Jake intended to kill me, there was nothing I could do about it; I wouldn't be able to stop him. He was several inches taller than I was and a good deal broader and heavier. He was also stronger.

I didn't kid myself. If it came to a fight he would undoubtedly win. But if he didn't know where she was, he couldn't hurt Annabel.

It was some consolation.

'I have got something I need to tell you.'

'What?'

'Fred confessed. In the hospital, when I took his things. He told me he murdered Alice.'

It stopped him dead. I let the grim fact sink in. His fingers dug deeper into the flesh of my arm.

'And . . . *did* he kill Alice?'

'Yes.'

'That's me stuffed then. I can't tell the fuzz it was my dad . . .'

'No.' I could see only too clearly he couldn't besmirch his own father's posthumous reputation. I wasn't going to tell him that Fred had confirmed it by admitting he'd stubbed out his cigarette in Alice's ear, singeing her hair and setting it alight. The burning smell hadn't been cigarette smoke – Matthews was right. It had been hair. The police alone knew that salient fact. I'd tell them, play back the confession, give them the concrete proof. They'd prove it from DNA.

'So,' Jake snarled, 'I've nothing to lose now he's dead, no family left . . . nothing to lose.'

Thirty-Four

He laughed, an evil, high-pitched snorting sound, his eyes wild and merciless, still holding my arm in a steely grip.

'You will tell me, Radcliffe. When I get through, you'll be begging to tell me.'

'I can't. I don't know where she is.'

'Then I'll have to see if I can jog your memory.'

'Whatever you do to me, it won't help because I don't know where she is. That's the truth.'

He reached down swiftly to the side of his right, laced-up boot. Then straightened up, a knife in his hand. I immediately thought about that Tuesday at Southwell Races. Unseen by any of the punters, he'd slid a knife up inside my shirt and drawn blood. I'd thought my number up then but he'd merely used it as a gentle persuader to ensure I followed him out to the car park and into his car. It was probably the same knife. If so, I could vouch for the fact it was razor sharp.

'I'm gonna ask you once, only once, then you get a slash, OK?'

I didn't bother to answer him, but fear brought a reflux of hot burning acid into the back of my throat. He'd got a grip on me that was unbreakable. I could try wrestling but all I'd achieve would probably be a dislocated shoulder.

'Where . . . is . . . your . . . whore?' The words were spaced and filled with intent.

I swallowed down the hot acid. 'I don't know. If I did I wouldn't tell you.'

Then I closed my eyes and knew a fraction of a second in advance where and when the knife would go in. I felt the wind brush my right cheek, braced myself against the savage pain on the way and jerked my head to the left. I wasn't wrong. He'd swung the knife in an arc that, thankfully, missed my eye but sliced down my cheek, the sharpness of the knife splitting the skin and sending blood pouring down.

'You gonna tell me? Or do you want some more?'

I certainly didn't want more but I knew then that he wasn't going to risk killing me. He wanted to exact the maximum revenge, and to do that he was saving killing me until he'd killed Annabel. As I realized that, a plan began to form in my mind. It would depend on just how much punishment he was going to inflict. It would also depend even more on how much pain I could take. But unless the savagery had reached a really impossible pain level, he wasn't going to believe what I was going to tell him.

'Where is she?' he yelled at me.

Blood was running into my mouth. I tossed my head, sent a spray of scarlet drops over my right shoulder, knew some had landed on him when he let out a bellow of rage. With luck the drops would soak into his shirt. They could prove very useful as evidence of his guilt.

'You fucking bastard, tell me!'

'I don't know,' I said sullenly.

He jerked me unexpectedly backwards. I saw a movement of his arm reaching for something on one of the benches, but with my eyes now looking up at the ceiling, I couldn't make out what he was doing.

I soon found out. He'd picked up a heavy metal measuring scoop. The next second he slammed it down with all his strength on the top of my head. The grip on my arm slackened and, with knees buckling, I fell to the floor.

The world reeled around me and the lights went out.

How long I'd been out of it was an unknown, but consciousness reluctantly took its time returning. The blackness slowly turned to grey, pain sending stabs of sharp bright lights through my head. My befuddled brain struggled to make sense of where I was, what had happened. My immediate reaction was I'd come off a horse. I could handle that. It was the norm. I'd been here many times before – on average, falls happen every dozen rides, give or take. Only this time I wasn't lying down on either muddy grass or a clean bed.

My arms were in a stiff position at right angles to my body. I couldn't move them, tried wriggling my

295

toes – they worked, thankfully. Gingerly lifted my knees one at a time – they too obeyed instructions. Not too bad then. No spinal injuries.

The analytical, assessing part of my brain ran through the usual checks I did after a racing fall. I tried opening my eyes. The reason I couldn't move my arms was because they were lashed to the arms of a chair – a chair I recognized. It was the one used by Bert Merriman, head lad at Elspeth's stables. No, my rapidly functioning brain informed me, former head lad. Elspeth was no longer in business. Maybe she wasn't but this was definitely Bert's chair that he'd used when cleaning his tack.

It was sited directly underneath the metal rod hanging down from the ceiling, ending in several huge hooks used for hanging bridles that were waiting to be cleaned.

And at that point, I remembered where I was – in the feed room at Unicorn Stables. Close but not correct. This wasn't the feed room; it was the tack room next door, although Bert's chair wasn't in its usual place. The soreness down the right side of my face told me it wasn't imagination wrought by a bang on my head. The reason why I was here was because of Jake Smith.

Although my arms were pinned, my legs seemed free of the chair itself but still somehow restricted. I tried bending forward to look and couldn't. A length of rope encircled both the back of the chair and my chest. OK, if I couldn't bend to see what the situation was regarding my legs, I could move them to find out.

I tried bringing them both out in front away

from the two front legs of the chair and found I could lift my lower legs all the way up, bringing them parallel to my thighs.

Around my ankles there was a hobble doing its job. Basically, hobbles were used, often by gypsies, to prevent horses wandering away too far. A short length of rope was attached to each of my ankles with a further piece of rope, maybe a foot or so in length, stretched between them. The reason they were used on horses was because they worked. This hobble would work on me if I tried escaping. A slow shuffle at best could be achieved. Anything faster and I'd topple over and fall flat on my face.

Escape at this point was impossible. I'd have to wait for Jake Smith to release me. A cheering thought. He wasn't intending to release me, though. I was trussed up helplessly because he intended to extract the details of where Annabel was. The body's parasympathetic nervous system was physically impossible to control, and the thought that brought the dampness of sweat to the palms of my hands was just what form of persuasion was he going to use?

The door opened. Jake Smith came into the tack room. He was carrying a rope, a shallow metal tray of the sort that was used to collect drops of oil from under car engines and a heavy plastic bag filled with some white substance. He came up in front of me, noted I'd come round and sneered. Dropping the items, he went out again. Obviously he was going to use all these disparate objects for my delight.

When he returned a few minutes later carrying

an old-style Alligator saw, the sweat began to drip from my hands. He stood with the saw held across his upper thighs. He smiled chillingly at the tension and acute apprehension I had no doubt he could see on my face.

'Ask yourself, arsehole, is she worth it?'

I played an ace.

'She said you were a monster.'

His eyes glittered with hate. '*Where is she?*'

I shook my head and deliberately upped the aggro. 'No dice.'

He dropped the saw, picked up the rope and tied a loop in one end. Coming round behind me, he dropped the loop around my neck and I felt it tighten as he strung it up around the bridle hooks.

'Going in for the overkill?' I challenged him.

'You just fucking wait. You'll be crying like a baby soon.'

I hoped not but, knowing the savagery he could deal out, I wouldn't have bet on it. I needed to judge the next few minutes to the exact second before I actually did cave in. Having secured the hanging rope, he came round in front of me and, to my utter amazement, undid the ropes that secured my arms. Then undid the rope around the chair that encircled my chest. I eyed him without moving.

'Stand up,' he ordered.

I did so. If I'd been amazed a moment ago, I was even more so now.

'OK. Drop 'em.'

I gaped.

'Come on, for fuck's sake.'

'What?'

'Get 'em off!'

My heart rate, already as high as I thought it could get, found another gear. I undid my waistband. The trousers concertinaed down my legs to the floor, leaving me sporting my boxer shorts.

'Kick 'em away.'

I obeyed. Where this was going I didn't want to speculate. It had suddenly turned into a horror movie.

He jerked on the rope and the noose around my neck forced me to sit back on to the chair. He proceeded to clip a leading rein to the front of the noose around my throat and then tied the other end to the leg of a solid bench by the side wall. I was going nowhere, not up, down or sideways.

Plugging in the electric saw, he brought it round but the flex was too short to reach me. Tossing it to the floor in anger, he slammed out of the door. I was shivering. I'd like to have thought it because of the cold blowing around my naked thighs but knew cravenly that I'd got to admit to myself – I was bloody terrified. But this situation had to reach the final stage. I couldn't afford to fail now.

Jake returned with an extension cable. Attaching the plug for the saw, he gave it an experimental firing up. The high-pitched sound hit the walls and reverberated. Jake switched it off and the silence was stark.

'You can stand pain, can't you, you're a jockey – used to it. Think you can stand this?'

He waved the blade around in front of me. It

was a fearsome thing with deep serrated teeth. I thought it was probably the saw Elspeth had instructed the gardener to use to cut up logs for the wood burner. I also thought it about time I acted.

'So, you going to tell me or do I use this?'

'No.'

He pounced on the word. 'That says you *do* know . . .' He laughed viciously. 'I knew you fucking did . . .'

And switched on the electric saw. The very size of it was respect-making when it wasn't on, but in full action . . . The noise it made within the confined space of the tack room was deafening. The thought that it would probably hide the sound of my own screams occurred to me only a split second before I found out.

He drew the high-pitched howling blades sideways across both my kneecaps. The teeth shredded the skin like tissue paper, cut through the underlying flesh and gronched into both patellas, the blades stuttering and juddering as they met real solid bone opposition.

The pain was purely out of hell itself. I screamed out loud, jerking in agony, but the leather leading rein held me down and the noose around my throat threatened to choke me.

Jake put the saw down and slid forward the tray he'd brought in.

I screwed my eyes up and endured the sharp agony now screaming silently through my entire nervous system. Now, I'd tell him now, when he asked.

But he didn't ask.

Instead, he emptied the plastic bag of white stuff into the tray and slid it along the floor until it was just in front of the chair. Judging the length of the rope, he kicked the chair away from under me.

I fell forward on to my lacerated knees, and discovered the depths of depravity his mind could conceive. The pain was acid sharp, ongoing and ghastly.

The bastard had filled the tray with salt.

Thirty-Five

Salt! Burning like fire, filling the open bleeding wounds in my knees. Hurting like hell itself. A monster, Annabel had called him. What I was calling him couldn't be voiced. All energy was needed now to hold myself together.

I writhed in agony, almost strangling myself.

He thrust his face within inches of mine. 'Where is she?'

It was time to tell him. If I'd caved in earlier I doubt he would have fallen for it. But in the state I was in now, and it wasn't in any way put on, he would think he'd won.

Gasping for breath, I forced the words out with an effort that was for real.

'Barbara . . . she knows. I don't.'

'That trainer . . . where we went that night . . .?'

'Hmm.'

'She there, then? Your bird's at this Barbara's?'

301

'N . . . o . . .'

'But she knows where your bird is, that right?'

'Hmm.'

'You don't know where?'

'Get Barbara . . . to . . . take you . . . to the place . . . where Lizzie's father . . . used to work.'

'And your bird's at this Lizzie's dad's old works?'

'Yes.'

'How come you don't know, eh?'

'Case . . . you got . . . me.'

He laughed. 'Yeah, I can take that. You're dead scared of me, ain't you, Radcliffe?'

'Hmm.' I agreed. And prayed he'd believe me. If he did, he was going to go for it.

'Right. I'm off to get her. And when I do, Radcliffe, I'm gonna bring her back here for a seeing to. She's first, and you can watch.' He laughed mirthlessly. 'Then it'll be your turn. Don't throttle yourself before I get back.'

He went out of the tack-room door, still sniggering at his own sick joke.

The pain didn't diminish, and I was still hog-tied, but I felt better. The pervasive evil atmosphere that surrounded Jake had left with him.

I bit the inside of my cheek to offset the pain raging in my knees and considered what I could do, if anything. There had to be something. I looked at the positives of my situation. Number one, which he seemed to have overlooked in his perverse pursuing of the whereabouts of Annabel, was the fact my hands were free.

I tentatively tried the heavy clip fastened in the front of the noose around my neck. If Jake had managed to press it far enough into my flesh to engage and fasten then I should be able to reverse the procedure. My first attempt only achieved a gagging for breath. Frightening on its own, with the noose supported from the hooks waiting to tighten each time, there was an infinitesimal easing of pressure that could strangle me so easily it was off-putting to try again.

Fighting down the thought of a slow death by my own efforts to escape, I turned my attention to my legs. The wounds had bled quite a lot. I wasn't concerned about infection from the dirty, oily tray. There was enough salt in there to cure a cow and certainly enough to defeat an army of germs.

However, what I did see was where the blood had pooled beneath my kneecaps, the salt had started melting. I knelt there, the pain a constant, and considered how I could use the knowledge for my benefit.

To the right-hand side of me, only a couple of feet away, was the saw where Jake had tossed it on to the floor. And attached to its plug was the extension cable snaking back to the far end where it was plugged into the socket on the wall. It was still switched on.

If my knees bled some more then it would certainly melt the salt, deepening the level inside the tray. But how long would it take for enough blood to leave my body to do that? Far too long. I was mindful of the horrendous possibility that Jake might smell a rat and return. My chances then would be zero.

What was needed was more liquid to add to the blood.

What could I use to do the job? Of course, it was obvious.

It helped that I now had no trousers on. I adjusted the leg of my boxers and relieved myself into the tray. The hot urine mingled instantly with the salt and the blood and turned the tray into a floating asset.

Very cautiously, I lifted my left knee a fraction and pressed down with my right. It was tricky; every movement, even the smallest, tended to put strain on both the leading rein holding me down towards the floor and also the noose rising up to the large vicious hooks above my head. The crafty bastard had known there was no way I could get loose by myself. But I was determined not to let him get away with it. I would have to risk one or other of my tethers.

I put up my left hand and dug my index finger inside the noose, holding it down and, at the same time, lifting the pressure again from my left kneecap. Then, using my right hand, I brought the heel of my hand down sharply on the edge of the tray. With the amount of liquid now swilling about unsteadily instead of dry material, the tray tipped up.

The salty liquid sloshed out, spread across the concrete floor and flooded the junction where the saw plug was connected to the extension cable.

The result was gratifying. There was a textbook flash and a bang and, over in the main house, I heard the alarm system go off, loudly and persistently. I knew Elspeth's system was connected to the local constabulary. It was a very sweet moment to know that England's finest would soon be hot-rubbering over to find out the cause.

The thought that my rescuers could be here in a few minutes and I would be released from the hateful bonds brought an enormous relief. I knew even now, one slip either way and the noose would do the business. A staying absolutely still job was required and, if the pain in my kneecaps was bad, which it certainly was, and made worse by having to remain kneeling and putting my full weight on my knees, I would carry on bearing it until help arrived.

If Jake didn't return first.

He would be at Barbara's by now. I had a qualm that I'd put her in a dangerous situation. But she was a plucky, capable woman. She would know, if he passed the message on word for word, and I thought it very likely, exactly where I was holed up. And if she passed on the message to Mike, I could expect reinforcements to arrive from that direction too. A beautiful belt-and-braces job. How she would actually handle Jake was the big question mark. But forewarned and all that, as she'd said, she could recruit a lot of available muscle from her staff if she needed it.

And the great thing overall was that Annabel was safely down in London with Sir Jeffrey looking after her.

To take my attention away from the pain, I kept my thoughts entirely focussed on her, remembering all the exquisite, beautiful times we had shared. It worked – to a certain extent – but the following twenty minutes were some of the longest of my life.

And then I heard it: the most wonderful sound I could have wished for. Barrelling along, with the blues and twos belting it out, the police cars charged up the drive and swept into the stable yard.

Thirty-Six

Laughing out loud at the memory, Barbara leaned her forearm on the cage that was taking the weight of bedclothes off my bandaged knees. Despite being in a hospital bed, I, too, found myself smiling – the painkillers were doing a magnificent job.

Happily, my X-rays had shown no deep damage to either patella, the teeth of the saw having bounced off rather than grinding into the bone. I'd been grounded while the soft tissue healed but there was no lasting damage – a massive relief. When I told Mike and Barbara the good news it had relieved their tension and they were now in high spirits.

Still laughing, Barbara recounted what had happened at her stables when Jake arrived.

'But he did have the knife,' Mike said. 'Weren't you scared even a little bit?'

'What I was scared of,' she replied, 'was if he hurt one of the dear dogs.'

I caught Mike's eye and we both smirked. Dear dogs – dear heavens – they were guard dogs of the first rank.

'So what happened?' I prompted.

'Well, he repeated what you'd told him. I knew straight away that you were being held at Unicorn

Stables. Then he demanded I take him there, laughable really, seeing he'd just come straight from the stables. Well, of course, I needed to let Mike know. I asked to use the toilet first, was going to ring him. But Jake wasn't playing ball. So I whistled up the dogs. That's when he produced a knife and waved it about. But Maxi, the German shepherd, saw that as a threat to me, leapt up, grabbed Jake's wrist and knocked him flat. Jake dropped the knife and I snatched it.' She laughed again. 'The dogs penned Jake in the corner; they wouldn't let him get up. They stood on guard in front of him, growling and showing their teeth. He was scared pants-less.'

We were all laughing now at the picture she'd painted.

'After that, I just called in three of the lads to guard him while I went to fetch Mike and help you. I'll never forget the look on Jake's face when the three lads walked into the lounge, shoulder to shoulder and each holding out a pitchfork.'

She'd then, apparently, telephoned the police, who had already been alerted by the alarm system going off at Elspeth's stables.

'And where is Jake now?' I asked.

'In police custody.'

'Thank God for that,' Mike said. And I heartily agreed with him.

A nurse was walking purposefully down the ward with the blood pressure equipment trolley.

'We'll push off now, let you get some rest and recover,' Mike said.

Barbara nodded. 'I brought your car back, by the way. It's at the cottage when you want it.'

'Thanks, both of you. You're the best.'

'Aw, shucks.' She rolled her eyes.

'Don't forget, you're a vested interest, Harry,' Mike said.

The nurse had almost reached my bed and they stood up to leave.

Mike hesitated, then bent over the bed. 'Not long to March. Just over a couple of months to the Cheltenham Festival, Harry. Reckon you'll be fit to race?' There was a trace of anxiety in his voice.

Barbara shook her head sadly at his naivety.

I glanced across, caught her eye and we shared a complicit, knowing grin.

'Well?' Mike demanded, frowning at us. 'What do you think? *Will* you be riding?'

'Do horses have hooves?' I said.